INSPIRATION DRIVE

ISBN 978-0-9861037-6-6

www.gilsoltz.com

Cover art by Sonja Bajic

Teg Down Publishing, 23 rue Boyer, 75020 Paris

POR **ZVI LEO SOLTZ,** ז״ל

INSPIRATION DRIVE

GIL SOLTZ

PROLOGUE

After laboring for years to develop work in my own notebooks I discovered these alphabetically arranged pages by Mordechai Campbell, the great historian of the Ꙩꟷꟷ family, with many unattributed verse, and this was the epigraph that I followed.

> The author has something to say which he perceives to be true and useful, or helpfully beautiful. So far as he knows, no one has yet said it; so far as he knows, no one else can say it. He is bound to say it, clearly and melodiously if he may; clearly at all events. In the sun of his life, he finds this to be the thing, or the group of things manifest to him; — this, the piece of true knowledge, or sight, which his share of sunshine and earth has permitted him to seize. He would fain set it down for ever, engrave it on a rock if he could saying "This is the best of me; for the rest, I ate and drank, and slept, loved, and hated, like another; my life was as the vapour, and is not; but this I saw and knew: this, if anything of mine is worth your memory." That is 'writing'; it is, in his small human way, and with whatever degree of true inspiration is in him, his inscription or scripture. That is a 'Book.'[1]

The work that you are holding in your hands is a promonostory: a point of literary form that juts out over a large body of fluid content, or raw matter. Mordchai Campbell's work and mine go well together, if you like letters and numbers. Someday I may share the alpha as well as the numeric chapters. Together they account for legacy of Ꙩꟷꟷ. I used to suck on his earlobes and scrape out his dry scalp, and in the autumn of his life, while he was being cut down from the inside — all his intellect, wit, professional know-how, all the stories along with him — this is what happens.

PART ONE

January 2011

1

The sign hanging from a tree out in front of my dad's mountain home says *Yefé Nof*. When it was a small cabin his bedroom used to be where the entry is now. Dad and I are in the living room just to the right of the entry. He's talking about his days as a paratrooper in the Israeli military and what paratroopers say before they jump out of planes: "*She he patach*. May it open. The chute." He's told me before how he didn't like the military, how I wouldn't like taking orders from stupid people. That was when I was close to enlisting. Dad is a skinny-legged, handsomely greying bearded man, with pouty lips and sparkly brown eyes. He is most comfortable in jeans and never wears a tie. I tell myself that I judge a person stupid or smart like I judge success. The institutional learning facilities and professional practices and credentials don't mean much to me anymore. Information doesn't make a difference to me. It's all in how the cat uses its lives to make kittens. That is a somewhat failed metaphor if you are literal like me. And what I'm telling myself is also something of a lie.

Thursday in the mountains it is cold and clear outside. The leaves are off the trees so that in the suck between gusts all sound disappears except for the chimes going madly, pinging and clanging out a dream to match the blue sky. A hint of wind draws down the chimney and the heart lifts at the feel of fresh air. My head is up to the sun and I am more aware that this roof is sturdy overhead and that all ambition is a waste of time. The ticking clock is throttling away.

3

Dad says once his glasses broke on the top of a mountain in the middle of the night and the battalion commander and second in command had to take him down the mountain. He says that the second in command, Segal Petro, died a couple of years later pursuing a terrorist. A Bedouin woman came out when they reached a cave and they thought it must be safe so they went in and were opened fire upon. Another time the chute didn't open so Dad threw the reserve and then the chute opened and the reserve was all in his face so he was falling blindly and in the confusion lost his glasses on the desert floor. I ask him what would happen if he lost his glasses in war. He says he would die. He couldn't see.

I'm working on a novella about a girl who rehearses her family allegiances by spying on her mom and stepdad. I want to finish it so I can see how close I really am to what I want to say. I don't even know what I want to say. I ask myself what's the real story, but it's a lot of stories about me. Some is my story about the first year I went to the prom. I can't remember a damn thing about the prom, but what I do remember is crossing the lines in a motel room. So I guess I already know what I've got to do. I just don't want to keep going backwards.

Most of the work I do is a compilation of short stories about the town in the valley below where I grew up. I write about what goes on behind closed doors there. The idea comes from my childhood fascination with statistics, the same sort of confounding interest that I take through my life reconciling the concepts of God and death. I like to imagine myself and my former classmates as part of a grand American social experiment, which, in my opinion, succeeded.

It takes a long time to see something succeed and then you have to measure in what ways it succeeds, which requires you to define success. I won't wait to get to the end of this story to see what I have.

The day after I arrive in the Inland Empire, my sister, Toots, flies down from San Francisco for a visit. We look alike but she is far more fashionable, very thin and occasionally functions in a hypoglycemic state. She spends a lot more time and money doing the little things to revisit her life with gold touches. We still talk about our parents' divorce—it's been thirty years—and my mom's second ex-husband because we want to give our formative years back to our Dad. For us having a stepdad was like housesitting a beloved worm. My sister says she's surprised I didn't kill him. Everyone takes this concept of ending a life lightly, but that's because we're freaked out about the scenario of what we'd have to do if it was us or them. Anyway, I killed him in my head. Dad says a lot about his character disorder that helps me to improve my novella, which is really why I start the conversation in the first place. I write lines while they're being spoken so that the way they exist on the page is something between the world in my head and the world in which we live.

It would have been my distinct pleasure to be a child murderer. In some ways I am still a fifteen year-old sitting in my room listening to R.E.M.'s "Gardening at Night," singing the wrong words with all of my lungs—*"they said I couldn't be a man"*—clearly a story I am telling myself while my mom battles through her second divorce. I still tell myself, you score, you fight, you drag, you drain, you make yourself vulnerable, you make yourself courageous; your heart sinks and rises; you find a logic that rules your life, that rules life in general.

Dad says that his grandfather used to raise pigeons. I did not know that he lived together in the same apartment as his grandparents. I guess it probably cut into his adolescence. Apparently he would spend hours watching those pigeons. Then one day when he was fourteen he came back from school and his grandfather was sweeping away their area. They were gone. All but the two remaining in the fridge. Dad says he didn't eat them.

2

We pass the defunct Santa's Village and scars from the 1980 Panorama Fire and are almost down the mountain. Dad is the driver. In a couple of hours we'll reach the place where he retired in *always* San Diego. Above the haze is a layer of brown smog shackling the dry grid-patterned valley floor. There are billboards on the banks of the build-ups along the freeway that scream *Marble Granite, Jim's Lunchroom*, and hundreds more listless offerings. I'm in the back seat singing, *"How many miles I roam just to make my home,"* watching the redundant signs come and pass. I've been on every one of these exits and on-ramps. They put me in a state to reflect on scenes from the past: the summer we met in Ireland and drove out to Doolin hoping to hear Weile Waile and everything we loved from his records; the time we took on water and sunk his two-person kayak in the middle of Arrowhead; our hike in Zion where the science of gravity kept us going up a narrow path flanked by crumbling rock and a thousand foot drop; our last camping trip when the Rockies got so cold at night we had to spoon under our sleeping bags. The view shifts from retaining walls to wild cover, forest and desert; in the back yards of some nineteen fifties-style houses there are Italian cypress, pine and eucalyptus. Out east the snow is falling and here people put their windows down as traffic slows. See the people in great asphalt parking lots dotted with planters of waxy bushes and birds of paradise, the tall palms leaning the same way along the side of the road.

I restate the obvious to my dad: This place is sprawling. He says, "What're you gonna do? You can't have public transportation for a city that's all over creation. It's not like people are gonna be in their little town and that's it." I imagine this place in the nighttime, skunk dark with the occasional streetlamp.

If I never came here again I might be able to let go of the past, but this is where I'm from and it's always going to be a part of me, especially the part I can't explain in words.

3

Hannah, my belle, speaks to me by telephone from Paris and I imagine her full lips, the rigor in her beauteous eyes, high cheeks that smell like cream, her free hand pulling at her bangs: "I feel guilty. Everything you want, I'm against. I'm turning crazy. I don't understand when I talk to you. There's nothing you can say. I'm just so tired of being by myself. I'm tired of it. One more month. I'm envious that you get to be in vacation mode. Obviously my way is the harsh way because there's a lot around it. I told you you should go even though it sounds like I'm telling you shouldn't have gone. I have two battles instead of one. I'm alone with two big battles. But your life is in the middle of both of those. It's painful. Maybe I'm totally ruining everything. I think it's you, but maybe it's me. But fuck it, I'll eat it."

This is a person in the mire of exam preparation. I'm engaged to be married to her in eighteen months. When I met her she was twenty-four and I'm still seven years older.

"I fear I'm going to lose you," she says. "I have fears about what you're capable of doing. Maybe I should just be more mature about it. I just want it to be you and me. I don't want no Hollywood. I have no idea if I'm capable of this. I'm a homey girl. I need my house. Maybe I'm wrong. Maybe I'll change my mind two weeks from now. It's very dark in Paris. I guess I'm not in the best scenario to be super uplifted. I'm getting sick to my stomach with stress. I don't know how far you can go with your goals of being an independent writer. I fear you can just go away. I need to be reassured. You know, you're very often in your own world. We are connected but you're the kind of person we can lose in a conversation. My feet are on the floor, they're not going anywhere. The more I express myself, I feel like I'm putting you away and I'm never going to hear those nice things again."

SEPTEMBER 2011

4

My plane is about to land in Tel Aviv. I'm reading over some papers, taking notes, anticipating my dad at the gate. The work is laying in my head going pinball crazy. Mordechai Campbell's *Primogeniture*? Back in California I'm orange groves and subdivisions, here I'm a cultural legacy. The last time I visited Israel you still took the stairs down to the tarmac. Out in this new terminal I feel disconnected from the shiny marble and glass and the duty free shopping they planted to say that the nation's been properly suckled.

There's my dad waiting next to his brain surgeon brother, his eyes smiling behind his glasses, his now close-cropped grey beard, chest hair pushing over an open collared shirt, small protrusion at the belly, skinny legs. He calls out whatever diminutive comes to him, his mouth fully open showing the two teeth that crowd in the front.

"Ghi-Gee!"

I'm lucky he doesn't force affection into the name; it comes out that way.

We planned on meeting in Israel for the Jewish New Year and here I am. Thirty-six and my first time ever alone with him here. It made sense for him to pass by Paris first, but he didn't want to. He was going to Israel for a month. He said he would be in France next June for the wedding.

NOVEMBER 2011

5

I make a routine Sunday night call to my dad to confirm my plans to be in California for the first six weeks of the new year to finish writing *Document 120* at his place. He flips open his phone — "Hell-O" — and straight away I hear an unfamiliar concern in his voice. He says, "I have shitty news." He uses his favorite word. I stop talking and take a deep breath. I am rocking back and forth in my sealed universe. He says, "The melanoma crossed my blood-brain barrier and the doctors are giving me six months to live."

The facts come out like you hear them on evening television dramas. The deferral of the threat blends in with the medium. My seventeenth-century apartment is exposed beams and plaster, an empty fireplace, a view out the window of zinc rooftops on fire. It might have been a convenient omission on my part, but up until this moment my dad's cancer couldn't be serious. It's my dad.

My first reaction is to try and frame what he's telling me.

Statistical data says his cancer isn't going to hold out until he reaches a hundred.

I make no response until I can register the frequency. "Wait a second," I say. "I thought that you were clear of cancer after the last surgery."

"Melanoma is particularly aggressive. But I don't want you to think that this is the end. There are excellent treatment options here. I'll do whatever it takes as long as it doesn't diminish my quality of life."

"What do you mean?"

"You'll still come to work on the mountain, right?" Dad asks, with reservation in his voice.

I can't admit any disappointment about my plans being broken. "There's no way," I hear myself say as if I've rehearsed this moment.

"I'm not going to miss out on this time with you."

"There are some tests that I have to take that may make more effective treatment possible. I may live much longer than they say I will."

I'm on the other side of the line, twisting the cord, eyes warm with tears, desperate to make this emotion sink in quickly, before I realize that I'm reacting and distract myself with patterned predictable thought. Why did I bother worrying about this day if there's nothing I could do about it anyway? I start re-imagining this upcoming trip.

"I'm not going to the mountain," I say. "I'll spend the time in San Diego with you."

Dad gets excited. "We'll have fun. We'll take walks, we'll eat, we'll explore. We can go to Las Vegas. I want to get up to the mountain as often as I can. I love it up there."

"I know," I say thinking ahead six months. "We can do it all," I say, meaning it as I start to escape.

Dad tries to carry on with our typical check-in. He makes sure that I'm not upset and I make sure that I'm not transparent. I'm hollow. Every emotion might have its word equivalent, but I don't understand these feelings so I leave them where they are in my empty cavity. I'm going to hang onto hope like an idiot kid.

PART TWO

AUGUST 2001

6

I wake up stoned. How I wake up I'll never know. I am in northern Brazil, in a big home, downstairs on the living room sofa. The night before I couldn't sleep on the concrete floor of the silversmith's house, so when he went to bed, I went out into the half-built streets looking for nightlife. It's possible to find this in a small Brazilian beach town. I knew it would be. How I knew I did not know. You just feel it. You feel the energy you send out coming back at you. Or you look for lights. I was looking for lights. I had a book with me. It didn't matter to me what I found. The night had gone dark and dull and I was uncomfortable deep inside my skin living the life of struggle with a poor drunkard of a lonely man who once in a while sold a few silver rings to pay his rent and every so often took in strangers for beer.

I made my way on an inclined dirt road, looking up at the stars, listening to the ocean below, passing weeds and construction materials until I got to the main bend and found a place to sit on a doorstep next to the only open cafe where a group was sharing the last drink of the night. They were talking fast and laughing. The street light was bright and cold and it lit up the pages of my book. I barely read a short chapter before they invited me to join them, and I hadn't expected I would, but I did. Above all, I was on this journey around the world to have experiences.

When we all left, the two most beautiful ladies took me out to smoke a joint on the concrete side stairs alongside the café, and when I got good and high they brought me home to their bedroom. We were getting along well so the one with the yellow tee-shirt to her knees wanted me to sleep with them and the other wanted it, too, but she said she couldn't because of her child.

Nothing to do for natural disappointment, I took to the sofa and sleep came over me anyway.

Then I open my eyes in the morning and I'm fighting the thickest haze. It takes me a minute to drag myself to a seated position and get my bearings. I cannot process the whinnying noise grinding on and on, but I hear it before I see it, so I'm thinking it. On the steps to the second story of this well-designed house where this half Swedish, Brazilian mother lives, a little boy sits with his eyes wide open, set staring at me in fear, making the strangest noises. It's difficult for me to communicate at all and it doesn't seem that there's any neutralizing this situation—I'm obviously where the boy wants to be—so as soon as I really come to and get a good look at him, I get up and let myself out of the house and through the gate in the front yard. There are big dogs in the yard barking that I don't mind because I'm on my way out. But then in all that heavy haze, on the other side of the gate, I remember that I left my bus ticket in my book and I have to turn around. I don't have any time to think. I'm facing the red sand cliffs and the beach and my bags are down the road at the silversmith's. My bus is coming in less than an hour. I know that. This is one of those times I tell myself you just go with the experience provided it won't get you killed.

I pass the big salivating barking dogs and get back into the house, and there is the boy on the stairs where I had just left him. I look at him and see that he is still afraid, so I think of everything I can tell him with my eyes. Me, a stranger with no identifiable reason for being in his house. He's around five years old and I start to see my reflection in him. Before I know it I'm climbing the stairs to pick myself up.

DECEMBER 2011

7

I call my dad at night, nine hours difference on the Pacific Coast, and talk to him for a half hour or so.

"Dad, I had that rotten bad dream again last night. I dreamt someone was coming to kill me in my bed."

"No. What's the trouble? Did you fight?"

"That's just it. I'm asleep and I know it so I have to wake myself up."

"Well that's good. When you do struggle that's only a sign that you value something in life. That there's more to it that you want to discover. All you've got to do is figure out what that is."

"My belle says I worry too much. I think I'm getting used to feeling powerless. I should take whatever future I can get."

"You've got to be better at using your resources," he says and then he backtracks. "All anxiety is death anxiety when you trace it to its roots. You have a nightmare where you're going to suffer the final blow? These probably settle in and start before age seven. People with anxiety disorders suffer conditions that make them feel vulnerable in certain situations. The mind defends you by waking you up. The most primitive anxieties show up in your sleep. When you are awake and you're a rational human being the defense mechanisms work. It's when they don't work and you are awake that you suffer from total insecurity and fear. Fear of the unknown in most cases. That fear may crystallize a more generalized anxiety in life. When you sleep you go into a more base level.

"You can manage anxiety with a good diet, exercise, by identifying what makes you anxious and by eliminating anxieties to the best of your ability. You should share it if you can. Everything comes at a cost. Talking about things that make you anxious with people who won't use it against you can help. I have a recurring dream of losing my wallet. I am very sensitive to losing money and being lost somewhere you don't know. That's why I need a wallet. In the jungle there's another law, but in America, as long as you have your wallet, exercise, good food, good relationships, and an income, you are alright. You can also make lists: things you can't control and things you can. What you can't, don't worry about it. Things that you can, make an action plan."

8

What happened was that I didn't receive life training from a head to tail kind of family. We went forward with our hearts. That's what my mom said on the phone from the Atlantic Coast last night, that she and I are different, we think with our hearts. Other people go directly from their minds, so they prepare to face new frontiers. We go with the heart.

So what does this mean to a guy who's thirty-six and living month-to-month, one word at a time? Should I go back to measuring days in installments and planning incidents by the clock?

Between looking to stretch my heart or stopping believing I can touch just about anything with my heart, I know I have to decide what it is that I really want to do with the news about my dad. I'm not sure how to make this exchange from heart to mind, or if I have to at all.

9

I won't give up on writing *Document 120*. In fact, as I push the content harder, I might be forcing the issue, but I regularly ride the metro out to the edges of Paris in search of adventure. I go where I don't recognize a thing and try to work my way back without a map. Every time I get lost like crazy. My day job leading walking tours is a much better source of creativity even if I barely have the chance to write while we're on the move. Sometimes a new character sketch triggers old chunks of memory. This is one such sketch.

He was a man born out of time and place. He could master others but he could not master himself. His wife was a large, overfed Chicagoan with strong hands who walked with a baby stroller to give herself back support. They'd been married 33 years and she was still an idealist in love with what devours men, pock-marked, smoking cigarettes, wearing no nail polish on her toes. On holiday she would tip the guy standing statue-still to see him move his sword, but not the guy working overtime taking her photographs. That day he lectured to a crowd of white faces who had never heard of, "Internalizing a racialized self-identity." He told them what he had to say about getting good and drunk and after admitting he had gone adrift, made certain that they knew how African American literature at one point manufactured conventions: character types, genres, language styles, predictable patterns of behavior, strict limitations of intellectual and moral capacity. He wanted them to understand that internalizing a lost and failed, troubled identity, internalizing any identity, comes through reinforcement from the environment.

AUGUST 1995

10

The summer before I leave to study in Dublin I go out twice with a Puerto Rican girl whose stepdad is a regular at the place I wait tables in Brooklyn. I think he introduces us because he believes that I'm hard working. Though this guy has a huge anchor tattoo on his forearm and I figure him for a navy man, he's actually a professor of American Studies. But I never ask. Actually, the context we have between us is the extra anchovy sauce I sneak out of the kitchen to him. The day he brings in his wife and his stepdaughter for a meal, she looks a little plain hiding innocent under a sailor hat and I don't make much of her.

The next time I meet her, following the professor's suggestion, I get off work a little early on a moonlit Friday and she comes to the place looking like a dark mermaid wearing a low-cut white tube top and a flowing black skirt. We are still basically inexperienced teenagers, meaning, we are awkward because we don't know what the point of this is, but we're also too absorbed in pop-rhythms to consider that to be a problem. We're a boy and a girl who don't know each other and probably aren't going to have more than a month to get to know each other. So it's obviously a bit of fun. We don't discuss any mutual understanding of what fun is. That's the fun. We walk to the waterfront and around Brooklyn Heights and that provides us plenty of time to connect for one night.

At some point I stop this girl on the sidewalk down the street from a chained up YWCA and we lean against a locksmith's storefront and start to kiss. It's nice but I'm not very tender. She's receptive to my intensity and I'm quickly getting overheated doing the things that make me too light in the head. I know that I can control this if I want. I forget that I'm a hypochondriac and imagine myself as some kind of sculptor shaping something beautiful on this storefront. This is my life. This is the life. This and not the shiftiness and small talk and petty ladders to the top. This is the top. I am exclusively aware of this in the cells of my body, wrapped in tension, not seeking a release so much as an expression. I have no strategy for turning the corner in a legitimate profession, no way of thinking about how to make myself normal, and I've been moving ahead minute-by-minute for so long it's how my brain works.

So here I am breaking open at the ribs, the light inside of me shooting from my lips, holy hands caressing, and I turn her back against me so that I have my arms around her. I look out at all the heavily bound atoms in the summer night and peck at the base of her neck. It's hot and humid and she has a face that makes little impression, but a body that scars my boy brain. Even the short absence of touch is a strain. I close my eyes and feel as much of her as I can. There is no place to go and the night is now. We are part of that sidewalk for five minutes not facing each other or insisting on words. I kiss her some more. Then I hold her and I take her top and slowly pull it down below her full breasts exhibiting her to a vacant lot. The street is empty of all but greasy gutter papers, overblown signs hanging opposite the tired asphalt, the sky above perfumed with stars.

She doesn't call me for three weeks after that.

SEPTEMBER 1988

11

Halfway through middle school I was becoming an arrogant kid and my dad looked down at me one night through his thick-framed glasses and flat out told me to "have some humility." I didn't know what that meant. We were at his condo in Rio Seco, like any other Wednesday, waiting for his subpar split chicken breasts to cook. "Be humble," he said more slowly, instructively. I was boasting about life after class—specifically, the girls in bikinis. It was 1988. We were strong and energetic and there was always a lot of sunshine where we lived. That was the year I started to be afraid that it would all end someday if I didn't discover the secret of successful living. I had no way of knowing I wasn't ambitious enough to allow myself to fail and grow from that failure. The more I thought about it, the more I made my dad's rare advice into my truth. After that trip to the dictionary, I would not allow myself to overindulge in what some would consider the highest heights. Personal victories reminded me to consider those who achieved more. Deflecting the pleasure principle elsewhere, I went inward and adopted a more modest departure point for success. That was the end of any purposeful social climbing or most of my desire to rise above competition, and the beginning of my passion for poetry that instructed the reader to take advantage of life.

12

As for my relationships, I wouldn't let anything last too long or get too serious. I was never a moderate. The speed at which my cells collide would grow your mom a moustache. My version of coupling was unsustainable. You want me to remember your face, you better connect it with some action. I like the thrill of human exchange. I like to be traumatized by beauty. Oil is boring. To be liked is stimulating. A surprise early morning ride to a nude beach with smoothies waiting in the cup holders brought out the contrarian in me. I would like you exactly how you are, but then your flat ass or shaved head wouldn't get you too far. Please understand, it's not what I'm saying that matters; Please, it's the stuff that cycles through my mind; it's the fact that we only have one life. I truly want all the parts as the package came from the store, the broken pieces still inside. That's how I found Hannah, my belle.

She was a woman to be kissed upon the eyes, an old-fashioned love-song. Her moods were similar to the spice trade, scarcely conveyed without transforming your world. She worked her media job like an awkward intellect takes to the dance floor, pushing deep into the night. Her early struggles tended to be more interesting than her later successes. She grew up for some time in a hotel where she spent one summer in the arcade beating the only video game I ever beat. Thus the secret message I sent her referencing "an overwhelming desire to make America proud," which began our relationship. We were bad. On our first Bastille Day together we rehearsed a line — "If we can let off a fireworks bonanza in your back yard for about an hour" — and we went door-to-door until we just let loose in a field outside of Lexington, Kentucky.

JUNE 2011

13

"You're a poulfranc," I say.

We're late out of the rented house, the sky is partly sunny, clouds are forming about Brittany like fairytale castles. Our trip is a pilgrimage around the Gulf of Morbihan in search of a type of brioche called gochtial.

Before I say my line I am thinking about my theory on her moods. Can Hannah be unhappy for such long times, flipping when she wants, into and out of intolerable, saying 'without you two annoying me, I'm fine'? Yes, we are a kind of hell and life is all about adjusting to the immediate heat, but she is simultaneously fixated on some point of injustice and her mood is a ball of all that disturbs her now and before.

I am tense. I feel it in my nerves, my veins, in the clamor of my arteries. I sense a stopping of breath. All this pouting just to come to another point — a switch — any minute any hour. Some decision that this isn't as she wanted it to be. That's what my line comes after.

"You're a poulfranc," I say to this Parisian *pzatza*, advanced in the art of intentional loving, whose real name evokes every image you have stored in your mind to the point that reconciling life with her above the boulevard destroys you. "Aren't you coping in your way, taking a little power by holding those discs in your hand while your mom is afraid of your driving?"

She puts a disc in and removes herself back somewhere deep. I'm on the page, this surface not yet in anyone's life. As soon as I try to lighten the mood I knock around another line: Thank the living energy that I'm not tone deaf. I can rock myself out. She's the driver. I'm the perfect one.

"That's it?" she says.

I think no matter how you look at it, it will change. Here she is hitting buttons. With every forwarded song I want to bite my lip and spit the blood on her. I want to hurt her into changing, into looking at how I must feel. I come down here and my heart is in clamps. I calm by writing, by anticipating her fingers finding that one song.

"Who are you talking to?" I ask.

"Who are you listening to?" she answers.

She likes the song. She's talking to the air. I can't ignore these moods when I should. They affect me. So maybe mine affect her. Maybe she'll ask what I was writing or justify her mood because I hadn't tried to make it better. Well, what am I supposed to do? I don't believe there's any great reason to be upset and lose an hour of good feeling. At least time will never be boring with her.

OCTOBER 2003

14

Before I left New York for good I dropped a letter in the mail to an old friend. This is from the first page.

You're in a period of uncertainty. You do what you think others will like, you work on the image that others carry of you. Soon enough you'll know yourself —at least know enough to know what you've been doing for others and not for yourself.

Do you really like licking the drops of semen that fall onto his belly or is that *your move*? You don't register the impression it will make on him, but you know he now speaks highly of you. You know that has to do with the things that other people know about you and the things you know about yourself. You know that you play your position better than anyone else in the league, that you've studied in the world's finest classrooms, and that you stay feminine because your eyes shine like two stones under a moonlit waterfall. You know you keep cool in summer walking around topless in your high-rise apartment and that proves you're not frightened to be seen.

This is what you think you need: A guy to come along and take from you what you have never given anybody. Even you can't sleep in the night for wanting to give.

You register that moments are brief and that he's a fallen star. He is almost caught up to himself and you will not allow him to because even though you have just arrived in the big city with a great resume, you have this thing: to see you on the street, you can barely distinguish yourself from the rest of the living. The shocks you need to deliver the waking world to make your mark day-by-day rank and place you among all other men and women.

Now you are looking for the death of your acquaintance. It does not help to delay. There isn't much to be said. Speak up quickly and start making yourself more than the sum of your features. Until he requests something of you which does not come natural, you can be sure that your expression is unique to every unique molecule of you, but then again, maybe you need to be out of control. Maybe you need to submit to the desires of the partridge.

15

On the metro people ignore each other, avert eyes and try not to touch the living part of you in any way — that part in which you register the mint of your existence. This sometimes currency of skin-so-close reminds you it was once greater than it is; the narrows, the swells, the apprehension of the soul's work, fiddling over exotic problems, complications, anxieties. Mine is an anxiety of separation. I can't see myself going through the machine movements anymore; I want to lose touch with reality and let play the twisted inner feeling of infatuation with my wife to be. I need to get out and run. I need exercise. What was it that we did together once? I have to remind myself. After getting so far into the dreams of things that I was accomplishing, I have to reconsider what isn't going well for me. I think I've reached a point where I won't be able to handle the next living room I go into. It's natural feeling that I'm after. I don't want to admit that I might have an ounce of forced feeling for anybody.

SEPTEMBER 2011

16

For the first two days we are in Israel together, Dad and I leave the house and explore. This Tel Aviv I don't know at all. Dad shares his memories of foot soldiers and other troops with recoiler cannons in Neve Tzedek. This is where he lived when he was born. It's now the most fashionable area in town. Old growth fig and palm and eucalyptus canopied over narrow roads full of art, flowers, coffee shops, broken ends where modern architecture meets original concrete foundations. This is like home. Dad tells me that his grandpa had his hotel there. I didn't know his grandpa had a hotel. We stand in front of the spot where the hotel used to be in the 1940s and he tells me about an English Smith clock he remembers in the breakfast room. He tells me about how during the War of Independence his grandpa would make him something to eat when the bullets frightened him. Then we talk about Etzel terrorists and the Stern gang. What I hear Dad say is that someone's son went to school with his aunt and the British caught him and hung him. It is the first I hear of any of this stuff. Maybe my Hebrew grammar is bad, but my dad never told me stories about this history. I learned Hebrew by listening to my mom's long phone conversations. The only bit of this story I recognize is about the Haganah movement of which my grandfather was a part.

"They were firing their guns from Yafo (Jaffa) the year I was born," he says. "Arabs used to live behind walls."

Not these walls, not those walls—walls.

"What do you mean?" I ask him.

"You open the door in the wall and you'd be in the house."

If I wanted to break some ground on my heartstrings I would read about that because nothing I ever see when I go to Israel says anything about that anymore. It is not a land of sentimentalists. The society is evolving along with the market.

Walking on Abba Eban Boulevard I bring up the subject of Em and her wealthy father because I'm interested in how he left Romania before the Second World War and settled in Mexico. Last year Dad moved into Em's house in San Diego after retiring from 35 years of work as a psychologist with the same San Bernal-based medical group. It was all very much planned. They had been together for about three years already. Their first date was at a grill restaurant in Temecula halfway between their houses. Em is a painter, Jewish, with a strong Mexican identity; she's tiny in stature, physically fit, has short black hair, likes to read, take walks, travel, and listen to opera.

"Hal is narcissistic," Dad says. "He bought a machine at an auction and they gave him the factory. Sometimes you get a deal out of life. He knew how to take advantage of it."

I immediately think I want to write his story. If I could. If I could write fifteen different stories at once. But you can write it instead, dear reader, if you wish.

Later in the afternoon, after our lunch of chicken and plums, we take a bus to the neighborhood where my dad was raised, near Dizingoff Square. He moved to 16 Zamenhoff Street when he was four, the year before his twin brothers were born. Back in his old neighborhood of concrete apartment buildings, the setting sun overhead, he gets a rush of memories unlike any that I've ever experienced with him and I think no wonder he loves stories about boyhood. They were kids whose parents survived the concentration camps. Their families were motivated by traditions that now were a part of a national identity. It was a nation becoming with each little pulse running its course, each high on nature's laws and each with his own sense of personal justice. In an era when the people were so unsettled, common goals could be pervasive; the individual took a knee waiting for overall security; his sacrifices were still fresh, a single logic could be employed to destroy his counter pulses.

We stood and stared at Municipal School A and Dad told me about his childhood in a way he had never done. Maybe it took visualizing the place to get into it. Like he wasn't telling me so much as reminding himself out loud.

"Zvi Sternfeld the Romanian and other classmates hung out and played the game of the season here." He pointed to the building with his square pink finger. "Just down the street, Yehushuah Cohen's grandpa owned a building. He used to sell the red variety of mulberry. We would sneak in and eat them.

'Dr. Becker was our dentist. His daughter Hannah had homing pigeons. I would see her when I hung the laundry. We had neighbors. We liked to hang out. Herziliyah Dolitskaya—my preschool teacher—did theater and played Golda in *Fiddler on the Roof*. Michayal Kaiserblatt moved to Argentina. Zemanenco is now a doctor. His father lived across the street from the school. He became a doctor in Vienna. His father went senile. He used to stand on the balcony and pee. We were laughing. Doba Alperc was the principal. Mr. Strauss was the driving teacher. Tzvora used to do accounting out of his house. He had a school where he taught. The drycleaner's son, Ellie, became a veterinarian. Sonny and Roni Bar-Kochva threw their cat from the third story," he pointed. "There was a boy's religious school at Moriah. At three Zamenhoff there was a music school under the post office. Mira had her own private library. Hinga the math tutor was major ugly."

We spend the next day walking up and around the beach in Tel Aviv and then for the rest of the week we wait for things to happen to us, visits and such. We eat potato salad and soup and lots of Ashkenazi food with tons of mayonnaise. On Rosh Hashanah we do a festive dinner with a patio full of faces I'd never seen before, a total variation from the tonic rooms of aunts and uncles on my mom's side who I met when I was five and spent a summer here awakening. And then a few days later I leave for Paris and Dad stays for three more weeks. The only thing he wants to do is go to Jerusalem and nobody ever takes him.

17

In *Document 120* I'm trying to re-design the world.

> An elderly nurse approached just before the building
> inspector. "The doctors have all gone underground,"
> she said. Cigarette smoke was so deeply pressed into
> her leopard print pants that it recalled the abuse that had
> been perpetuated on me in my crystalline phase. Once we
> heard that the inspector had been a housewife before her
> husband's death, we understood why she stayed silent.
> "There's been a new system in place for a while now," the
> nurse continued shoulder-to-shoulder with the inspector.
> "Alternatives to sickness. We're back to dying. And not
> dying. The DNA replicator can insulate the structure of
> certain elements inside you, certain paths, town blocks,
> villages — certain metropolises — and map out a critical
> restructuring. Some require many months of hard labor
> and hope. Others are spoken of very minimally because
> they are impractical. The geometry is skewed. One can
> get bad information from anybody who has the incentive
> to perpetrate a misread."
>
> The inspector was picking her nails, smelling the garlic
> and shallot bits that came clear out of the clicking plastic.
> I wanted to break her hand.

Later in the story, the supporting character, Mario, spins a super-
hero comic book question:

> 'How can you be interested in love at a time like this?'
> I tell him, 'I'll give you a hint. Risk, risk, risk, risk, risk.
> I get away from myself. I forget that I'm going along with
> anything beyond instinct. You should try disengaging for

a while. Make yourself move past the place where you're stuck. Just keep going forward through the cliché and the chorus and the troubled mind. Let go, man. But use logic. Don't stray from sense. Sing to yourself. Put some sound on your lips. When your mind is all beat and riff, it's an entrance; then you push a lyric out and even if you didn't write it, it's like you're living to it.'

I'm not sure that there is a point to hiding myself in fiction. I decree that we are all a generation of fiends forever scandalized by the subversive. The natural act of love is not dead, but it has endured the many filtered lenses of popularized feeling. What enters my imagination might enter yours. What exits is altogether different, though. To be capable of discovering what it is that we really are to each other is life altering, but it's desire that gains strength by remaining unfulfilled. Consumers who are catered to and flattered discover that they can have what they want when they want it without making any effort, yet what influences our behavior most is our desire to behave. Even if our lives are marketed to us, the suggestion that we make our choices makes us feel significant, like we know ourselves. Imagine being able to determine our preferences without commercial interference — when we're not exposed to the same shocks, the same repressed energies; when we don't know how to behave; when we are truly ourselves.

JULY 1981

18

Six years old, solo on my Dad's weekend, we drive out to Long Beach to spend the day with Atikva, his only old friend (that I know). In the afternoon we go to the movies and I fall asleep right as the opening credits roll on *Chariots of Fire*. All I saw on the moving screen was a pack of young men in short white shorts running slow motion along the beach, sand kicking off their heels to music with the sound of melancholia in it. That was the year of my parent's separation. I believe that I understood what it meant to be loved and I remember taking no issue with their choice, but what I didn't know was how deeply I would empathize with my parents. It was obvious how hurt and alienated my father had been. Though I would later learn to associate the piano notes with triumph, the slow motion brought only sorrow to my mind.

Chariots of Fire would go on to win the Best Picture that year. I would always feel like I missed out. The dark stadium seats were modern and very comfortable. You could have taken a fresh breath of the ocean into that movie theater, it was so close to the coast, yet some of me would have carried the troubles of landlocked living into my cushion. My dad's friend Atikva was tall and thick chested. He wore his loosely curled auburn hair slicked over the balding spot at the back of his head. He had long hairy arms. The tip of his right thumb was crushed in a construction accident and I used to stare at it noticing how flat and stubby it was thinking how much of a difference it made to have the whole thing. I sat beside my dad. I looked up at him often to see how he interacted with his friend. My eyes were wide open. The two old friends talked in Hebrew about things I couldn't follow and the idea of the movie didn't grab me. I didn't know what it was that I should do, so I gave in to sleep.

I never forgot the first thing that came to mind when my dad woke me up: It's all we had and I wasted it.

PART THREE

19

Hannah and I fly to New York City so that we can take a break from the All Souls exam and spend some quality time with friends. We stay with my mother's sister who is always a breath of fresh air, especially in the morning.

"A person that's only got six months has got to believe in everything. Ah, look at the sunrise. There's this new medication calls SMS, SMC? They don't sell it in the US. Dros knows a guy who took it and survived. Well, he knows the guy who knows the guy. [Gets up, looks around the living room, hands in pockets, sits back down, opens magazine, looks at a column, lifts a corner of the 30-page spread, ten of the pages in her hand, moves it closer to her face and reads.] They have it to 75,000 people. America is stupid. All of this research and they came out with nothing. It cleans the cells of everything bad. Not only cancer. AIDS, everything. [Continuing to read the column] — Wow, I would like to do that, too. Take a cooking class in Italy. Fun."

"Where is it?"

"It's in Positano. It's only one week. Course I would do it. Fun way to meet people. Turn around and look at the sunrise. It's absolutely gorgeous. Look, It's gonna be very cold today. Very cold. Twenty-eight. You want to open the thing better so you can see?"

"I've seen the sunset."

"This is the sunrise. I want to tell your father but he's going into radiation and I don't know how it can balance. The medication and the radiation…I don't think he's gonna want that."

One week later it's a new year and I'm on the plane to San Diego thinking don't hit a man with anything heavy at five o'clock when an article about Jim Humble and the Miracle Mineral Solution (MMS) appears in my hands. Shit. I feel full in the belly, sore in the lower back, my eyes are puffed up and I need rest. I expect a lot of hard talk up front to bring me to speed with the facts and the responsibility before me. I guess they'll come to the airport at 8:08 and I'll find out what they want to do. They'll be the engine and I'll be the occasional fuel.

JANUARY 2012

20

The first days of my arrival are the easing in period. I get acquainted with everything. I sleep in the spare room at the house in Kensingstoke. Until about eight years ago my dad was largely deaf in his left ear due to the military and he used the constant refrain, '*I cannot hear you.*' Now we talk normally and the first thing he tells me that sticks in my eye is, "I cannot bet that I'll be in Paris for a wedding, but I can bet there'll be a wedding."

I go into the small bedroom with that one. On two walls of this room there are bookshelves stuffed with the books Em has already read. It's the kind of trophy room that would make any reader envious. Then you find out Em has never had to work. During the day the blinds are slightly parted so the sun shines and warms up the fifty degree house. Across the street there's a lady in a black Chevy curling her eyelashes in the driver side mirror in front of the only house on the block whose roof is caving in. All the bushes and trees seem to be growing out to it. There is a small desk below the blinds. This is where I put my computer. I don't imagine I'll use it much.

This is a Hacienda type house with a tight footprint. It has a flat red concrete driveway, citrus and avocado trees, a garage that's been converted to an atelier, and a casita in back where Em's son lives. Nobody uses this room. The bed is high and firm. I am very close to the bathroom, but I will not use it. Em likes her privacy. There is another toilet adjacent to the kitchen, which is opposite the two bedrooms past the dining room. At the front of the house is the living room where we'll spend most of the time watching TV and ignoring the spines of more books. Everything is neatly placed on bookshelves, in refrigerator drawers, and any other available surface. If I leave my glass by the sink during the day it disappears. The placement of things is important. The Oaxacan pitcher on the tapestry that lines the center of the table, the remote parallel with the couch, the heat in the off position. Our backs on the couch in the living room are against the adobe painted plaster patio. If you sit at the edge of the couch or on one of the two square leather chairs you can see the landscaped back yard with its cacti and large grey pebbles. There's enough room to build another house on it. The same-sized lot next door has a two-story apartment building sitting on it.

Down a few blocks is a small neighborhood commercial strip, very well designed, just off of the freeway exit: classy restaurants, an old bar, family owned video store, the library and public park in tandem, a couple of coffee shops. The action ends abruptly at a dentist's office and some single story apartments. Apparently houses are of less value south of the strip, towards Mexico. On the north side, there is not one front yard or lawn left unmanicured, and rarely can you spot a human being.

There isn't much to do during the day that isn't medical and since Dad can't drive because he can't read or see well, I am taking him where he needs to go. The thing that he likes to do is go for coffee or a bite to eat in the early morning and I try to get him to do it again in the afternoon. My dad is very much a routine man.

For thirty-five years he took the same turkey sandwich to work for lunch. You know what you are going to get with him. Otherwise there is a lot of television, at least two walks with the dogs around the neighborhood—a short one in the morning and a long one in the evening—the 6:30 news from New York, and errands.

Dad never really had the room for birthday celebrations or holidays. Every day is whatever is on his mind. This often comes out unfiltered and in the form of a concern. He takes a lot of naps. Every night he falls asleep watching television and then he put himself to bed around 11pm and wakes up in the morning about six or seven. He sleeps like he did in the military. Flat on his back in his European underwear, chicken legs sprawled out before him, blanket over his head. He is saint white, hairy, full of skin tags and sun spots, and though I couldn't say where each of them are, I recognize him like that from camping and from the pool at his old condo. We never went to the gym together because he didn't go to the gym, but sometimes we shot hoops by the pool. I always pretended to be my favorite Showtime Laker and feed him the ball. He didn't dribble much. Neither of us were spectacular.

Dad had a period when he ran long distance. He did two marathons. On his weekends sometimes Toots and I watched him train around the golf course from his parked red 320i. Usually I joined him for the first lap of the course and my legs itched tremendously in the early morning cold. I ran when I played a game or practiced for one and was not very motivated otherwise. I don't remember how I spent the remaining hours waiting for him, but I'm sure it was with the snow-capped mountains and the eucalyptus lined boulevard, when the sound of the wind through the shallow-rooted giants got you absorbed in daydreams while the sun went higher and brighter in the sky. And with my sister's big head.

Kensingstoke is a couple of hours drive from the old house and things are much different in my breaking heart now. I interview

Dad over breakfast. We talk about judging character. He says, "I'm a private person. Judging to me is innate, it's not a science." I tell him stories from the days where I knew I was making him proud, working for the City of New York and then in Holocaust reparations. I tell him my version of the scandalous.

21

The first time I ever drive around the complex freeway interchange required to get to Kaiser Hospital, I'm a little confused, but I'm following Dad's directions. "Make a left," he raps his fore and middle knuckle on the passenger's side window getting me to Dr. Chow's office. I'm not in love with this transition, but I'm here and I'm keeping my mouth shut. To date I haven't been involved with my dad's cancer. He kept most of it in passing comments, like, 'I had a procedure for this melanoma, but everything's alright.' Maybe he didn't want to bother us. Maybe I was too bothered to listen. Even when they started removing tumors. In 2001 he had melanoma on his back and then didn't have a checkup until 2009 when he shaved his beard and there was one by his ear. Then they found it in his lung. Now it spread to his brain. Two months earlier he had the flu and resisted the doctor. They told him it was meningitis. The melanoma metastasized in his brain for over a year.

The first caring word I hear in Dr. Chow's office comes from the waiting room. "You're doing good, huh?" this death-mask wearing cowboy asks a kidney transplant patient missing teeth. Dr. Chow is a reasonably frigid guy. Dad and I walk into his office to discuss the radiation treatment and other options. A lot depends on whether or not Dad has the BRAF mutation.

We are just about at the administrative offices where we need to chase down Dad's medical records when we get the call that the BRAF mutation test results came back. "You probably want to see them," Chow's administrative assistant says. This is wonderful. We have Dad's cousin whose former employer was NIH and Toots and my connections trying to help us get into medical trials and to see the best doctors, but this is more than an option. This is proven to prolong life. We turn quickly into a construction site with all the cement trucks parked side-by-side and the barbed wire fence. I can see Dad bubbling and it's harsh of me to resent this clutching on to the life that has not yet left him, but it occurs to me that this secretary is interpreting a medical exam. I start questioning what she believes is a good result. "Dad," I say, not rueful enough, "try and hold your excitement until we see the proof."

The road ahead of us is full of used car lots and the flags you see spanning them. I'm focused on my dad's reaction and I miss the turn at the fast food chicken place, which aggravates him terribly. I think, right now a Kaiser administrative assistant could be crushing our hopes, so I extend a consoling hand towards him, hesitant to admit to myself how serious I know this is.

We get to the office and there it is in red print on the page: negative for the BRAF mutation.

I think having the mutation is a good thing.

I request the doctor come out and tell us what the report means. He comes out alright. Cold as the liquid in an IV drip, hands in the pocket of his white labcoat.

"You do not have the mutation. You do not qualify for the treatment."

Dad acknowledges this with an exaggerated smirk and he starts to hum like he often does, same tune he was humming in the car earlier when we turned into the construction site along the San Diego River. It will take me a few weeks to realize what he's sounding out.

He says, "I guess I just have old fashioned shitty tumors." We laugh.

The guy without teeth or a kidney, who abused drugs for years, he has the mutation.

22

We leave about an hour early to get to the Moore's Center. The parking lot opens up to a building that looks like the hull of a ship, an enclosed space for anyone seeking forces larger than self, the material reflecting sun, earth and water. It's under this roof that people speak in genes and amino acids. We head to clinical care where a technician is prepping the first radiation treatment of twenty on Dad's brain. He has already been fitted for his mask and thermoplastic mold. He says, "I'm very level, emotionally."

By midweek he says, "I think I'm losing a little bit of weight, I feel my waist. My pants are dropping." He has been given a steroid to control the swelling of the tumors, one that is the size of a walnut and another that is the size of a marble. Dexameth usually creates increased appetite but it also strips the body of muscle and Dad knows this.

In the high-ceilinged waiting room there's a man in an old Padres baseball cap talking to a lady in a straw hat who still has a pony tail. She says, "It's your last day, are you gonna ring the bell?" The man says he will. A towering guy sitting a couple of seats away starts talking. "Pretty nice place to come, though. They got nice people. Pleasant people. Pleasant people make the world go round." Dad and I get a look at this guy. In the room of one of the finest research hospitals in all of the United States there are some sunken, visibly distraught patients, a couple who have been brought in on gurneys with oxygen tubes up their noses, and most are not much for conversation. Everything is meant to reinforce tranquility and distance from the situation. There's even an outdoor courtyard garden with tall plants lending a calming effect.

Dad says to me, "Jolly place."

"You miss the people. It's gonna be sad when I go. You just miss the people. It is a nice place to go. All these nice people.

Make the world go round." This guy turns to a thin young lady in a dark wig who is clearly distant. "Is this your last day?" he asks her. She doesn't reply. "How's your brother doin'?" he asks. This time she answers, "I don't have a brother." He keeps tending to her, "This your last day?"

The man in the baseball cap goes up to the bell and is presented a certificate by a technician. He rings the bell.

"This is a nice place. You're gonna miss the people."

The guy says, "I'm gonna miss the machine," and laughs.

"It's a nice place to come. Nice young ladies."

Nobody left wants to interact with the oversized man-child. Six foot six of bird feathers.

"I guess I'll go see how many pounds I lost today," he says.

A technician comes by and asks the woman in the straw hat, "They call him in?" You can hear him going *'Dee dee dee dee'* in the distance.

"He's on the weight thing. He's gonna see how many pounds he lost today."

"You dropped your glasses," the technician tells her.

"What they give you?" she asks the man who rang the bell, realizing he's opening a gift that came with his certificate.

"Fifteen dollars worth of coffee."

"Don't waste it all in one place."

The manchild comes back into the waiting room humming, *"I could have danced all night…"*

In the Navy SEALs you ring the bell during hell week and you're done, no questions asked. Here it's graduation. Dad says, "All these people under siege and I want to live just as much as anyone." Meanwhile, manchild is bothering the young brunette again and she puts him in his place, "I got what I got, you got what you got, let's keep it that way."

Back at home Dad and I catch some afternoon 24/7 News and it's putting both of us to sleep. When he wakes up he tells me,

"I dozed off and that's not normal for me. Normally I don't doze off at this time." He's waiting for the radiation cumulative effect.

23

The next morning during the car ride, while I'm watching the road, I describe to Dad how some of this feels like it's not happening. He explains to me that this is derealization. "Everything looks like it's out of a movie. It's a defense mechanism of the mind. It distances you from stimuli. It's like you're watching everything happening around you. You're there, but you're not there. But you know you're there. In dissociation, true dissociation, you don't know that you're there."

At the Moore's Center the nurses are exchanging "happy Fridays" while my Dad's inside the machine, cooking. I'm over-thinking and over-tinkering emails and text messages. There's a short afroed lady in white-rimmed sunglasses, protesting the groove hitting her headphones, disbelief coming like rainfall in a living room. "Lucky me, lucky me, I won the lottery!"

After radiation we go join the crowd for a coffee. According to Dad's encyclopedic mind, "Lines in America are social occasions, acknowledging room for pleasantries outside the cubicle." We're waiting in line for ten minutes when Atikva calls the flip-phone and it's, "*Lo human cama pitzooz ze be Buckbucks.*" Lately Atikva's been talking about his move to Napa Valley. He says on his property they don't have curtains because it's so private. He's known to speak as if it's the word from Mount Sinai. My dad is the opposite. He doesn't need to talk. Atikva lectures. Usually about something he read that day in the paper. Or his new coffee machine. Or the plunger he got for his toilet. He affects his accent to sound like he's making the most important declaration.

When he gets off the phone Dad announces to me, "I have a slight sense of burn on the top of my skull." Minutes later we're sitting with our coffees and he says, "I hate this thing."

"What thing?" I ask.

He gives an upward nod. "I wish it would just go away."

24

We are about to leave to the mountain when Em tells me that Dad is happy I'm here, that he feels very safe and loved with me, and that breaks my heart and makes me bleary-eyed. On the road I think of the Inland Empire's linguistic cleansing movement that I read about in the *L.A. Times*: Bathing everything in the sunny light of superlativity and using an economy of expression, language is wiped clean of almost all content and nobody has to risk expressing a real thought of sentiment. The mountain is all frozen, too. That first night up there I don't tuck my head under the cover because I don't know that the vent is closed so I sleep poorly and my neck is sore. I figure this out when Dad knocks early and says, "I'm gonna open the door so you'll get some heat."

Saturday morning, I put a pill in my mouth and lean over the open faucet. My hamstring's sore for some reason and I think about it while I'm leaning over taking water, counting one, two, three, four, five. I haven't taken a shower in a couple of days and after just cleaning my teeth and flossing I consider how rotten I must be. A thin shield of shit particles, dust and dry skin. It's so dry up here. And what was I coming to write, anyway? I can't get into any rhythm. I have no solitude, no discipline. All I need is time. TIME. All this balance business. All we've got is time. I don't think I took in enough water so after standing up I lean back over to drink more thinking of the Coleman thermos and all that Country Time lemonade we tipped to our mouths camping and I do it for three seconds and I'm happy. Why shouldn't I be? I mean happy and ecstatic are two different things. At this moment

I'm alright. We're together as we have been many times over the years. Nothing changes. I still love you and I'm still compelled to tell the *Document 120* story.

Television, television, television is going in the living room, commercials lacking necessary images, product messages and pop songs attacking my brain. The adjacent kitchen has a little square table that's good for working, full of afternoon sun coming though the bay window. Dad reminds me that he's got a pair of gloves to give me. Next he tells me, "I'll be happy with nine months."

It's getting late. He checks his watch. 10:55am. "Yeah, I'm still resting," he says. I anticipate the day going like the last of the popping corn.

Over lunch, Dad offers, "Maybe you want to put out your own version of world order and human condition and crystallize it into thought." He opens his mouth so wide over the soup bowl that his face shakes. He's onto something, but I don't know if I have the focus. He loves potatoes and can't wait to get off his steroids to eat buckets of them. "When I'm sitting on the table [he means laying], I say, do it! Do it, you sucker! Two weeks after radiation, they'll see what's going on in there and then they have the gamma knife option if they think it will do anything."

After noon we go on a walk and see some nineteen-fifties frame houses. Dad reminds me that some people have no place to go, no job, no money, no food. "There's a certain pride knowin' you did your bit and you did it good," he says. "I always felt it's me against the world. Beat the system. Survive. My children will never go wanting. The worst prospect was that I would push one of those shopping carts with all my stuff in it. That's part of the human condition. You live and then you leave. Am I happy about it? Nooo. Do I accept it? Sort of. Not with happiness. But I lived a good life. I have nothing on my conscience. I'm leaving some money to you. Pass it off one day to Nimrod."

"Who's Nimrod?"

"Your first born. Just don't name him Francois. It's too French."

He mentions having to cash in some stock to make funeral arrangements and I ask him if he wants to be buried in Israel. He says, "I don't want to pay thirty-thousand dollars. I would rather up here on the mountain, but there's no cemetery."

That night my computer isn't very fast to process the printing job I send and so I make my complaint to the walls and Dad says, "I hate that you're poor and you have inferior products. When you make decent money…" I tune out the rest because I can.

I have a dream that I wait until the day of my wedding to buy my suit. It's not great.

25

Back in the radiation center for the seventh time, we have a baby in front of us.

"Big boy," Dad says to me.

"Boy?"

"I don't know."

"Pink pants?"

"Girl? I'm next. I better be. They're not on time. They're fifteen minutes late. Today they don't even tell you there's a wait." He goes on humming. Finally gets up and checks on them. "They're really running late today. They didn't even have the table set."

"Who, John?" I ask, randomly assigning a name.

Dad says, "John? *Get away from me*," with that higher pitch. "I'll go in in a minute."

The manchild appears down the hall wearing a baby blue Kangol cap.

"Here comes brother Rick," Dad says, screwing up his face, mimicking him. "I hope they give him an attitude adjustment. Bring him down a couple notches. Six feet five of Dumbo."

Rick heads right to the table. "Hey there young lady," he addresses the first woman he sees. "How are you today?"

"Fine," she answers.

"You have a good evening?"

"Fine, thank you."

"What's your name?"

"Tara."

"Tara, you have a nice name."

"Thanks."

"Come on Rick," the lady accompanying him says.

"She's very pleasant. Nice."

You ever get that feeling that something comes together and something comes together and it works the way a miracle might work: voices, all voices in harmony, and the structure flows and it flows and it flows.

Dad says, "You gotta be realistic."

I mumble, "I'm tired of being realistic."

26

We're in Davies' office talking about gamma ray and the psycho-pathology of everyday life. Dad tells me, "I don't go after fateful or futile arguments that mean nothing," and hands me his hat. "You better hold that," he says, "because he may want to check my head. I don't know for what."

"For lice," I say.

Dad laughs. "If you want to be rich in America and you have what it takes —"

"What does it take?"

"Ingenuity, vision, guts, ability to touch on a nerve of what's gonna work. Identify the needs of the society you live in. After products. — You just have to hit something nobody else has."

Dr. Davies comes in and asks questions. "I feel fantastic," Dad tells him. "I dropped one dexameth so I'm not hangry anymore. Now I feel fine, I eat better. I don't pig out too much. I feel great and I have my faculties back. I'm not confused. The only side effect we see is fatigue."

"We want you to continue with the activity."

"It's my life!" Dad's says with boyish excitement. "He's getting married in July and my girlfriend's daughter in October. I got to make it."

On the way home from the doctor's office we go see a movie that neither of us understand. Dad tells me, "You're gonna get a book out of this. You need some distance, perspective."

I start to tell him, "My bald spot's really bad."

"Well, what can you do?" he says

"Cry all the time."

"Everybody's crying," he laughs. "You better get married while you can."

27

I'm excited to see Toots. We've lived through a lot of our family affairs together and we need each other. I just hope for one strong dose of healing before we start on the tears and pain. I pick her up at the airport close to midnight and on the drive to the condo where we'll be staying, we reach the situation that stops me from getting too invested in this heartfelt mumbo jumbo: I don't know how to get to the condo and the freeway interchanges are rapidly approaching.

While I take the wrong exit I hassle Toots, "When you say move to the left, I need you to tell me how many lanes over."

"Don't drive like a Nervous Nellie, Ghi."

I rev the engine and make a hard U-turn.

"Ghi, what are you doing? You're acting like such a dick."

"No. I'm asking you because I need to give you feedback. I should be able to tell you something without it being called fighting."

"Stop talking with me."

"You're the one that's being a bitch."

"I'm not going to fight with you," Toots says, crying.

"No, no. I'm not fighting. I'm trying to tell you something I need. That's not fighting."

"Well then you need to communicate."

"That's what I was asking *you* to do. How do you manage to flip that?"

I'm driving in the dark, depressed, all depressed. I will get the small bed, small bathroom, and the feeling that there's too many people everywhere. The days will go by, the hours will go by, the minutes will be consumed in talk and talk and gossip and sad stories. A man is himself in his element, with all he's interested in and trained to be. A man is himself inside himself.

28

We're in the Shelter Island parking lot. After a walk along the ocean, I'm being told I drive like an idiot again, so Toots takes over. I'm critical of how much she is on the phone. Dad needs to use the bathroom and she's saying hold on, I'm running a company. I rip for the seat belt in frustration. She guns it.

"You don't have to drive like an idiot," I say.

Dad says, "*Shhhh. Shhhhh.* You're picking on her."

The conversation of 'what we need to do today' takes place between the two of them. I'm cranking out passive-aggressive refrains in the back seat: *of course I want to go to a cement plant, check out the prices.* They agree on the bank downtown.

"This car drives well. It's not a formula one," Dad continues, trying to neutralize the situation. "The stockmarket better be better this year. It's flat. It worries me."

Toots says, "I bought a lot of +Z last year and the stock took a big shit so I bought more."

"I don't have a lot of retirement but I like to play. I should have retired at sixty-two. That was 2008 when the market lost forty percent and I wanted to finish out my career." The stock-broker I had was such bullshit. He was making nothing after a year. I didn't want my money to sit for a year. I have good stocks. I have Apricot. It doesn't matter what the price is. It matters if the stock goes up."

"Kind of a stinky day, huh?" Toots says, driving along.

"Well, they said it will clear up. I see blue skies staring at me. Bluebirds singing a song."

"I still think it would be fun to go to the zoo to see the monkeys, the polar bears, gorillas. Did you hear that Exene is having a baby?"

"I hope the baby doesn't have her brother's genes, or her father's. Her mother's no prize, either."

Toots gets excited about how Dad's doing better and she tells him (and she tells me) all the time. It's here, this moment in early January, while each of us is trying our best to come up with a miracle or research remedy, that she tells us about this new diet she saw in a documentary. My brain instantly wishes to produce something to the contrary. Toots tells me, "We'll get along better on this trip if you stop saying every single thing I say or do is wrong."

"Okay," I reply.

"They say protein is rocket fuel for cancer," she continues, all her speeches between peaks and valleys. Her final word on the diet is that it should begin now. "So, I'm thinking about a veggie burger for lunch," she says.

"I couldn't stand a yellow car everyday," Dad remarks about the car ahead of us. "Toots, a little bit of music?"

"Okay. Starting in a few months I'm going to have to get mammograms every month. I'm gonna sign onto Furstman's insurance."

29

Friday morning I put Toots in tears because we're already late to pick up Dad for radiation so I won't stop for coffee.

Five dark suits enter the Moore's facility ahead of us.

"What is it, the funeral director?" Dad says.

I keep telling Toots she's an addict and she keeps repeating, "I just want my coffee. It's all I asked for!"

A white-haired lady in the waiting room announces, "It's the torture chamber in there, you better be careful."

"Nice people," I say, thoroughly pleased with myself.

Dad says, "She wants you to live near her again but you guys can't be together for two minutes."

"The only way to get along with her is to give into her."

"Don't make too much of it. We don't need to analyze everything to death."

"I always fight with her," I say.

"You take the bait," he says.

Toots is holding Dad's medical records tightly. "I didn't get any sleep. I'm just exhausted. I woke up at five a.m. I'm just exhausted."

After the twenty minute treatment, we're back in the car heading to the cold, but not yet snowy, mountain for the weekend. It's a two-hour drive. For the first ten minutes Toots is on an ear piece talking about flights. When she hangs up she says, "It's hot in here." She opens the window.

"Hot?" Dad asks.

"When I smell bad smells I gotta open it for a second." She has a habit of eating the skin out of her nails. "I should take the carpool lane, shouldn't I?"

"If you want to," I say.

Dad says, "Well, it's free, remember."

"You want to listen to music?" I ask.

"No."

"I was asking Dad."

"No, Toots doesn't like music. Not now at least. They've been working on it forever and they're done. Of course, they were hoping people carpool, but Americans are stubborn. Everybody wants his own car."

"Dad, you should sit in the front so that you can talk to me. Ghi's writing a book."

"Is that what you're doing?"

"No, writing in his diary," she laughs.

"I'm not going to tell you what it is. It's not writing, though. Writing requires thinking. I can't write around people."

"I don't care what you're doing," Toots tells me.

"Talk about stocks or something," I say.

"Did I tell you that Kohup's accountant did a Madoff on him?" Kohup is Dad's former employer, the man who bought him a cheap clock to say thank you for 35 years and thousands of patients. "He embezzled about six hundred K."

"Did he take from anyone else?" I ask.

"You sure you can trust your guy?" my sister asks.

"He's not doing it on his own. Let me brighten your day a little. How much do you think I have in my account?"

I continue writing.

"It's better than a poke in the eye. It would have been fantastic to travel in my retirement, but at least it will grow."

Dad hasn't travelled much. I've often asked him where he wants to go and the list turns out short after many screwed-up faces and nahs.

30

The dump up on the mountain is a pretty serious disposal operation. Dad surrenders his awe first thing Saturday by repeating our purpose, "Put the garbage in the garbage and the dump at the dump." He tells me, "You know apparently this one time a guy brought his son here and the tractor got him. He must have gone inside and nobody saw him." Back home Toots is preparing lunch using a recipe book compiled from a major newspaper. She goes from, "I'm going to cook everything in the book," to, "I think these recipes are meant for vegans, this isn't Food Section food, there's not much flavor going on there." On the way home we take a detour past a house where a young girl believes that the man in the framed painting in her parlor is her estranged father and not the late totalitarian dictator of Russia, Vladimir Lenin. Dad leans the passenger seat back, "Right now I'm resting and I feel like a tiger. That's why they do the treatments. It gives you the gift of time. The challenge is to think one day at a time under any circumstances."

At home he shows off his energy unlocking the front door and hollering, "We're back! That's right, we're back." Then we walk right into a vegan lasagna lunch that hurts our feelings, so to speak. Dessert offers little redemption. It has to be sugarfree because Dad is a type II diabetic. He can't have sugar *or* salt, actually. I try and understand how it came to this. You never pretended you were into cooking, I say, knowing since his divorce he ate corn out of the can and processed lunchmeat. "One thing about me," he says, "I'm not a pretender." He continues to justify the unspectacular instead. "It's not great ice cream, but it's cold and it's edible and it's sweet. Once you eat it long enough you forget."

After lunch I play some Parvarim Ladino music for Dad, *El Norah, el norah.* The awesome, the mighty. He says, "I heard it at the Smoochas in 1970. I can see Saba Smoocha's face right now like he was sitting in front of me."

"Why?"

"Because he had a memorable face and everybody was afraid of him." There's a little dance in his eyes as he recalls his first and only wife's family. "I know Esme since she was thirty-five. She was divorced. She was dating some people. Natalie was dating a guy in undercover military intelligence. Tamar was living with a pottery maker in Yaffo, helping him out. That was where she met Ud. Orly was thirteen when I met her forty years ago. She was a high school kid. Dros and Jacob were in the military. Esme and Yasmin were out of the house. Rodolfo had kids, was married. Darom was still at home, dating Elana. They were childhood sweethearts. She was schizophrenic. They divorced and he met Mere. She got fat. All the girls in Israel get fat because they eat like pigs and don't exercise. All of them after they have kids become blimps."

Having your Dad reframe the frame of your life, you stand back and look at your own version. There is little I have ever seen that compares to my mom's family altogether for Friday night dinner. Everybody in their own crazy world, crazy in love with you, wanting to devour you, and you without recourse at all, just taking it all in and doing nothing with it.

Before the winter light gives out we take a walk on the zigzagging Burnt Mill Road. A neighbor that Dad knows is out with his dog.

"What happened to the sun?" the guy asks pinching the bill of his blue Dodgers cap.

"The wind came and it's gonna be a lousy day from now on," Dad says.

"Might bring the snow. The young people like it."

"They can keep it."

We part ways after another couple pleasantries. Dad tells us that this man is a contractor who built the house down the street from him. I'd been wanting to know what residents do up in the mountain. Dad says, "People who live in Lake Arrowhead permanently either clean houses, build houses, or sell houses. There are very limited services."

31

Sunday morning we're out the door waiting on Toots in the rocky driveway. I let her drive but I give her a hard time for the delay.

She screams, "I'm sorry I was late three minutes!"

Dad shakes all over, "Ghi-Gee, why do you have it in your nature to act like that? To egg on?"

The car swerves on a stretch of backroad behind the highway that overlooks the valley. "What are you doing?" I ask the driver.

"I'm trying to heat up my hands. My hands are freezing and you're heating up the window."

"No, I'm heating up the sides and feet." Her hands are on the wheel now, open palm.

In a subdued voice, she says "My hands are freezing."

I want to say: You can hang on: Two miles: Two minutes: You can make it.

At The Mountain Coffee shop, Toots is the one giving unfiltered feedback, "Their smalls are really small." I tell her to order one size bigger so she does, but when she gets it she says, "This is so big, I probably should have ordered a smaller one. My depth perception made that cup seem so much smaller than it was. I thought it was a Dixie cup. I'm not used to these glasses."

Later, when we'll be in the parking lot waiting for the car to heat up again, I'll make a suggestion and she'll tell me not to micromanage people.

We sit down with our coffees before driving back and I start talking about the woodpeckers making holes in the house, confusing the fact that a bird is hollow-boned with the thought that it's cold-blooded. "Ghi-Gee," Dad says, "what's wrong with you? A human's temperature is ninety-seven. A bird's temperature is one-oh-one."

"Wow, I make one mistake..."

Toots says, "That was very satisfying."

I use this opportunity to talk about the erratic behavior she has been demonstrating lately.

She admits, "I'm not afraid to say that I'm crazy in a good way, and in a bad way. What can I say, you gotta take the good with the bad."

I sound out Dad's phrase, "Put the garbage in the garbage…"

Dad's sleeping on a fauteuil at the center of this empty place, hands folded together, arms across his belly, head down. When he pops up I get him talking about his parents.

"My mother was standoffish. My father was more demonstrative. I never had any complaints. I accepted who they are and how they are and they loved me totally. And if they loved me more they would have given me more materially." I'm not sure that I hear this right, but I'm not sure I hear anything right. "The temperament and cultural differences between the Smoocha and the _[illegible]_, were extreme. The Smoocha boys were chasing to kill each other by the end of each meal. The girls were more tame. Your mom has a lot of things she remembers but she was ashamed or embarrassed. She was never quite accepting of her family. Your mom grew up in Israel in an apartment that was two rooms and a kitchen. At night it was one big bed. Thirteen kids grew up there."

I have one last question and then we can leave like Dad wants to. He sees 10:30a.m. and thinks it's late.

"What's the difference between psychology and psychiatry? About two-hundred thousand. Psychiatrists write prescriptions. It's boring as hell. I couldn't, I couldn't. Frankly, I couldn't pass physics and chemistry. But there are ways around it." He begins telling me writing isn't a career and it's not a profession. "Seems to me you made your choices in life. You can still teach, but that's it. If they give you a college job, you take it. It's a good decent life. Maybe the tours will work, maybe they won't," he says with a lot of reservation in his voice.

We head home and throughout the day he keeps saying "I really love this place, I love the mountain." After lunch, most of the ambitionless lasagna thrown down the garbage disposal with an atypically stingy put down (*I didn't like it, it was kind of soft?* Hands-down the worst food item I've eaten in two decades), he studies the space in his kitchen and the logs in the fireplace. "I did everything I was supposed to do," he says, "but it goes back much further. It was already a done deal. I always knew I'd die of cancer but I thought I'd live to my parents' age. I treated myself nice, I can't complain. I lived a nice life, just a little short. But I always joked, after fifty it's all reruns. I sure wish I could go to the weddings."

Even with my eye for detail, his collection of glass chickens doesn't register when we are in his living room staring at them with the TV on, but right now I have them in mind. It's a difference of personal aesthetic.

Dad gets a call and is debriefing Em on the phone, telling her, "Today is dark but tomorrow may be better. I have pressure around the left eye. I only had nine treatments. I have eleven to go. You wonder what happens if I stop the treatments," when my sister makes eye contact with me in the kitchen and says, "It sucks." Instead of giving her a hug or a squeeze on the arm, I go and write everything down.

Later that day Dad tells me, "The more I think about it, the more I think, you don't need to pay the rabbi or pay the cantor to have a funeral. It's not in my nature. You remember me in your heart."

32

Just before leaving the mountain I remember a mathematical formula I wrote a decade earlier after a dinner date went bad. I want to have it verbatim. I know somehow it still applies. It just needs a bit of tinkering to make sense. I go down into the build-up under the house and find the box without any trouble.

The thick parchment in this particular notebook smells of mildew and reminds me of the night with that lady friend, how I spoke before considering the fault in my words. We sat down to eat the spaghetti and meatballs she made and I opened my mouth and asked, *What are we doing?* Then I obsessed about how it ended. I had to understand the thing in a deeper way, by connecting it to all the print and pupils and footfalls. I wanted very badly to believe I was the continuation of a long line of mystics. Now as I pushed the parchment to my Roman nose, I saw the woman, her moves, the things I missed out on, the decision I made before I made the decision. Nothing seems to come of waiting. This was my connection with Mordechai Campbell. There was something to find in here.

Pulling the Curtain on the Wizard — the central operating dynamic in the universe of relational matter.

Y/X, $X+Y=Z$ the wizard (relationship cohesion)

$Z+$(time)$+$(external world-matter)-finality/utility$=$curtain

But there's an internal contradiction because $X+Y+Z$. Z is an absolute, an ideal. The curtain is the screen, is imaginary, romantic.

If $X+Y+Z$ where Z is 0 (empty set) anyway, then X and Y have their unique properties and they never enmesh or become a single entity — they only connect and maintain due to the necessity to follow the rules of the game and thrive. Not everyone necessarily thrives, though. Especially not those who lack the instinct to recognize the games at play or the rules. For example: higher being rules (consensus reality) vs. there is no higher being.

Don't take anything for granted. Be aware and don't take
for granted that the world encourages you to do things
a certain way; try to do things your own way. There is
no right way.

On the drive back to San Diego we talk about the gamma
knife surgery and how it can help remove the tumors. "Depends
on the size, you realize. Chicky had a surgery. He recovered, he
came home. At home in the shower, he slipped and fell, he hit
his head and died. My thinking is very sharp, my memory, my
circulation — but it's because of medication and treatment. It's
about the swelling and maybe there is no swelling. Well, that's
too early."

I can now admit to myself that *Document 120* is story of heartbreak
and overcoming lust addiction. After the crushes, the rushes, the
pushes, the crossings into unknown territory, and the new discov-
eries, I want to convince myself that the actual thrill of living can
be replaced. The main conflict I can't shake is that I am purposely
becoming demure, dulling, dull. When my sensory awareness is
up I'm telling myself that there is no need for action I've already
had. The thing is, exceptions are what I seek. I can adapt but I am
still the same animal of the same fiber. I have to teach myself
that my highest pursuit is to be content with the contrary of what
I am. Maybe that's too high an aim. I just want to be able to overcome the challenge. Consequences keep your nose clean, I need
challenges. Not bungee cords but skydives — looking out above
the world with life on the line. That's what every day should be.
I think of my Dad's jump when the chute didn't open — and the
lucky break he got when the backup did — and the seconds after
when his first chute hit him right in the face and knocked off his
glasses. It was a jump in the middle of the desert and somebody
found those glasses. There's always something — but then there's

skill and there's chance. And what's chance to a boy in this world of real skill?

33

The waiting room of the Kaiser pharmacy is packed. This sick woman stares at me like, "What are you looking at?" and I respond: you're over there groaning and gurgling like a short-breathed bear-fox, I think you'll find it acceptable to have a little curiosity about a sound like that. Behind us in line is a fat-faced Sudanese kid with a head covering and little pink lips like life savers. Just in front of us a Filipino man in baggy black sweat bottoms and a tight zip up top on his love handles whines to the counter person. Dad overhears the pharmacist explain the use of his medication. He says to me, "I would take shingles all the days of the year if they could take back what I got. I'd trade them in a second." We get to the front of the line and ask for our order. Dad tells the pharmacist he is familiar with the medication. The man looks at him and says, "You stop suffering when you're dead."

On the short car ride down the street to the hospital, we pick up Toots from her bank and Dad arranges for Ron the broker to come to the Hacienda for an appointment. He tells him, "I manage to keep my memory but I'll lose my hair."

I'm trying to remember the turn but I'm so fixated on getting it right I miss it. Anyway, we're still on time to the meeting with Dr. Chow to discuss options after radiation treatment. We're still hopeful for the path to cure. You do any research that you can because it's your dad and you will do anything even if you are not scientists. Dr. Chow thoroughly reviews what we already know, that daily Themozalamyde has almost no side effects and is unlikely to help and that we may qualify for NIH cell-based therapy if we write Dr. Davies. We tell Chow we've already met with him. He asks if he's our friend. Dad says, he's no friend of mine but I got friends in high places. We all laugh. Then Yervoy is brought up as an expensive chemotherapy with a lot of side effects and Dad says no, I don't want any side effects. When we walk out of the office he's humming Garth Brooks.

Dad says, "I think somebody got to him. Somebody got to him through the connections. My short term memory is not so good."

"But it is good," I tell him. "You remember that you said 'I got friends in high places.'"

"*Y-e-a-h*," he says, like a revelatory wind.

"It sounds strange to say 'I got friends in high places,'" I tell him.

"Well—" Dad lets the thought circulate.

"You're the one who told me to have some humility," I say. "That's the defining advice of my young life. I was thirteen."

"Ghi, leave him alone," Toots says, watching the road.

"Just shut your mouth and drive," I say.

"You treat me like an asshole."

"But I resent the double standard," I say, not realizing that I'm upset for another reason entirely.

"You treat me like a jerk and hurt my feelings," Toots repeats.

I say, "You're redundant."

It's last man standing in here. Dad stays quiet. I don't have to worry about hurting his feelings. He is very methodical. If he sees any flaw in my logic, I can expect a laugh out of him.

34

One morning the following week Dad is sitting in the sun trying to button his sleeve. "I can't close it, so shit on this," he says. Em has Housedog at her feet, looking for food, licking his narrow snout. She says, "Yeah…too bad your dad got sick, really too bad." On the expectation of walking the dogs in an hour, I want to steal Dad away to a new coffee shop in another section of the city where we can talk about some more serious stuff like the psyche, a term I use without knowing its precise meaning. Coming back in the house Dad says, "Isn't it ironic that the thing that I love the most, that gives life, can also kill you?"

I had a dream that a duffel and a backpack go missing with my wallet, library books, writing, and I don't know what all else. Apparently Dad is lying on the bed in our hotel room when he nonchalantly tells me he let the men in. I can't handle the theft so I'm yelling at him and he starts laughing at me and finally I just lose it. Fuck you, I say. He gets up out of bed and is standing on his feet. *Fuck you?* he repeats, still kind of laughing. It's the first time I've ever said that to him and he's standing. I admit in near tears, all I want is you and I feel so guilty caring about these other unimportant things: none of this had to happen.

On consultation in the coffee shop my story gains some headway. "Psyche means mind: the sum total of neurons of all parts of the brain. It's really a wonder that we have awareness. Not all animals have. We have five billion cells and at any given time we can only use five percent of our brain. There are thinking and feeling parts. Where we feel emotional pain, those are interconnected parts. But some try to create systems based on the dichotomy. Words shape thought. Psychic pain is based on memories ongoing, subjective, oppressive and noxious."

Words.

Later on in Balboa Park, Dad's got Kimbo on a leash and Em's got Housedog loose. She's worried about someone stealing him and Dad tells her people don't steal dogs that look mixed, they steal dogs that look like showdogs. "Good girl," Dad announces, picking shit up and inspecting it fully before it gets all the way in the bag, holding it in his palm, twisting and tying the bag off. What love ruins in a man invested in knowing his beast.

Em sees some old ladies watering their lawns, "with their chichis like that." Too much cream and fat, she says. Dad starts talking about how if I lived in California I would have his car pretty soon.

"I mean not too soon. You and Toots are going to have to figure it out. You'll probably sell it." He says, "when we get home we have to do the survey, the advance directive, and I have to show you my guns." Before I protest he asks, "Is there anything you'd like to do?" and I feel a sense of relief because there is that Mexican popsicle store I really would like to go to. I don't want Dad to be home by himself, though. What if he's frustrated by not being able to read?

I say no, it's alright. I mention an upscale Mexican restaurant instead. Dad says, "After Toots leaves we'll go." Now I'm the one making his diet the issue. Dad says, "I'm not just going to let go, but we can get a burrito. Toots is so intense about it. She's controlling. I don't want to argue with her so I don't."

Back at home we talk about Gagliani, 'the initial idiot Kaiser doctor,' through the end of the Laker game and the beginning of an episode on the art of conducting.

"You don't choose how you die or where you die," Dad says.

Em says, "I like this conductor, Marinsky. Very good looking. Movie star looks. The Romanians are handsome, no? Not the Jewish Romanians. The gypsy Romanians. I saw some of them and I couldn't take my eyes off of them."

"Melanoma is the lowest incidence of cancer. They don't put billions after millions in pharmaceuticals. Well, every dog has his day," he says and laughs, classical music on his lizard brain. Marinsky is conducting hands only. "I could never do that," Dad says. "He is in the music, you know? He feels the music. Like it was a three-dimensional object."

35

Toots and I wake up early and get a late start. We drive to the Hacienda and stand in the living room for the first few moments of our day to be. The morale machine is cutting its teeth. Em is pulling chunks of Dad's hair out while she massages his head. 24/7 News is scrolling on TV. "Something's coming down from San Francisco," Dad says. "We need to fill out the advance directive. As soon as you leave," he says to Em, "I'll go over my guns and the safe, which may take all of ten minutes."

I express a severely limited joy at the arsenal opening.

He starts with the Walther PPK and beebees. "You know what beebees are?" he says. I'm thirty-seven years old; this is not exactly the moment to ask me. Next he pulls out a knife in its case curved to the tip. "My father fetched this off an Arab. He was a cop and he took it off an Arab. It's an inlaid mother of pearl."

"I didn't know he was a cop. How long was he a cop?"

"Two, four years." He moves on to a stainless steel Ruger and a Colt Trooper .22 long rifle with a six inch barrel. "This is oak stock."

"Plastic?"

"*Plastic.* Oak! Oak! Oak!" He continues to tell me every detail possible about the caliber, trigger pressure, ammunition, security, but never says a thing about not taking me to the shooting range.

"When's the last time you shot these things?" I ask.

"A long time ago."

"You're allowed to keep guns in your house and kill anyone you like?"

"I was in paramilitary youth in Israel. You live by the sword and unfortunately some die by it," he quietly states. "You have to think of yourself first. There are no live heroes, there are only dead heroes."

This is the kind of mentality one inherits. What you really think and feel matters less. We live on trained responses, looking and listening for what we understand.

Dad has one more gun in the drawer. A Wembley. A British gun. A six-shooter. He's not going to shoot himself. I don't know what

he's going to do with it. He is supposed to feel the best he'll feel
after this treatment so we've been talking about going to Las Vegas.

36

I could do it. Cold steel, quick trigger. Of course, I'd want to
stop short of the implications. Compulsion is a stupid thing.
This is less embarrassing than the thought of fellating one's own
father, which crossed my mind because of the — I can't explain.
It's the Belarussian blood in my veins. I mean, I all too seriously
considered this and it was like a train going one way, just like a
train — the one memory I have of him pulling down his briefs
to pee with the bathroom door open, the only time I'd ever seen
him — considering what one might do to keep a man he loves
living. You see the man all your life but you never see the man.
I think if it would take the sickness out of him; if it meant he
would survive, I could push the train into this disturbing terrain
and then follow the consequences: a father flips out over a son's
gesture, not understanding it. The both of them end up angry
and disgusted.

Hatred is often easier to stomach than being in a loving
relationship.

These are the words and thoughts of someone else. Someone
like me and not like me.

37

Toots has to fly to New York so we drive her to LAX and stop by
some old friends on the way. They take us to Alacala's Mexican
restaurant off Old Ranch Road and my sister orders vegetable
tacos but doesn't like that they are greasy — which she knows
because she's seen my dad's order — so she's going to send them
back. I tell her in a relaxed way, "You can't cancel something that's

about to come out," and she says, "I can do whatever I want."

Over lunch we talk about the L.A. Early Days. I wasn't around for them, but apparently these are the reference points: Steak with mushrooms, Moshe Dayan, *All in the Family*, and the Ginsberg and Wong restaurant. We talk about religious conversion, marriage, failed relationships. Toots relates what she heard someone's mother say to her daughter: 'If he's not circumcised, I'm not coming to the wedding.' Everyone laughs as she demonstrates what an uncircumcised penis looks like by pulling the sleeve of her sweater over her hand. It's all service with a smile, but I bear the crux of the lasting refrain of the lunch: "There's no cure for melanoma."

It's hard to see Toots leave, but I'm used to comings and goings. Our dynamic duo is now just the one good son, so I become a little more closed off. There's no buffer for severe emotions. Van Morrison's "Wild Night" is playing at a Boppity's off the 105 Freeway. Dad's shaking over his peanut butter dessert. He's getting excited about reducing the steroids without having a headache. He looks over and says to me, "It's okay. I can let it go. Let's be happy."

I ask him about his dad's death. He tells me how it started with his mom's death. Saba Reuven was born in 1913 in Vilnius, Lithuania, which is a three-and-a-half hours ride from Minsk, Belarus, where Safta Chaya was from. Reuven used to sleep on the bed and say, 'I'm watching over Chaya.' He said he was there when she was home from the hospital and he would be there when she died. Dad tells me, "When she died, the daily erosion of his mood became unbearable." His voice takes an upturn, "I was there in the last ten days of my dad's life. I was there when he died. I held his hand."

That time I wanted to go to Israel with him and he said it wasn't worth it.

I ask how they met, being from different countries and all. "Well," Dad says, "They had get togethers."

We speak as the fading evening light brings the day to an end.

Sometimes a sunset makes me anxious. One thing is coming up and another thing going down. How do you rise above the end?

38

You take the time to recognize that you can shift your mood with your own brand of alchemy; you take a walk and discover new things, you photograph them. You make plans, eat, smell the air; you indulge in another's ideas, a relationship story, a film; you recognize that you carry an antidote to some of life's miser- ies — that you can love directly and with most that you have inside you, honestly. You can give things a human scale, accept people for who they are, recognize beauty in progress, in the ripple of a horse's muscles, in the power of thinking about someone you've elected to ignore. The universe is a ball, and sometimes you fixate on one curve of the ball in your palm and sometimes you throw it out there and hope that it comes back. It matters what care you give, what effort you make, what enthusiasm you take in smaller, more absorbing moments, in finding the right words when you need them. If you are very careful you may live well.

39

Alone at the supermarket I experience my own crisis: Oh, I really have nothing. Six weeks without a connection to the work, one hour in the morning, fifteen minutes here-and-there, and no accom- plishment — little. I'm trying to live in the moment so I put my headphones back on and listen to Yves Montand's "Actualities" and think, how to delay my anxiety about leaving: extend time, make more of what we have, cancel flight, miss flight — one more night.

In the afternoon Blake visits and rotates my frame of mind. We drink Peter Rabbits made from Pimms #1, bruised basil, pressed lemon, and pickled carrot. I bring up some old blood with our former employer. I listen to what he has to say and tell myself, you want the dream, but you're not a genius; you're one note with a heart on fire.

Filling up at the gas station, brain over in Sandpoint, Idaho, listening to "My Gal is Red Hot," thinking about any little change in Dad's health status, the gas pump flowing hard, it's as if all the inspiration you can muster doesn't amount to shit because the truth is so much more powerful. You'd like to be able to say when it starts and stops, but you can't. So here I am, like Walter Winchell, holding onto everything that's nobody's business. I will make up all my stuff about made up people. The more questions I ask, the less questions I have because he shows me that he is alive, so I have to force myself to see what I don't want to see because it's easy to forget. You look at a man with conviction and call him a dying man?

The food should at least improve.

I sometimes daydream that I'm watching someone else dance with my belle. Right now I'm stuck with the look of amused curiosity on her face, watching the yellow stripe on the road, ears ringing with Beethoven's 13th. Coming back to the condo in Fashion Valley, seeing the old gray drapes, the sheets on the couches, knowing Em's old man owns the place, the empty seventies; This era should make me smile, but the thought of a half-decrepit face turned towards me saying, 'Let's disco, let's love, let's believe in creative goodness,' it's too much of a stretch.

At a certain age we should begin to see each other quite simply, but it is difficult to let go and erase the trail that has been marked as your life.

40

"We must get rid of all of the hairs. She will *kill* me if she finds out. She will have a fit. All evidence must be removed."

We put the dog mat in the dryer and it made a mess that delays our departure. Before we have a serious conversation about divorce (at my insistence) I admit nothing of my hesitation to feel guilt, sadness, or regret. It is possible that those are just words to me. The sensations have always had their advantages and disadvantages. There are some stories you try and write your entire life. It's probably better to find out why you want to write them. In my case, I like to filter a little speculation with some laughs and pepper spray so it seems like there's one more reason to be excited about the cycle of a day.

In the car, we discuss Bach's signatures and hold off on the big stuff, or so I think. "Perpetual motion, or perpetuo mobile," Dad says in his best Latin pronunciation, a little more caricature than old master, the way he accents the "e" in mobile, "is when the harpsichord never stops." He suggests if I want a short example I should listen to "Sonnerie de St. Genevieve du Mont-de-Paris" by Marin Marais. When I do I emote myself into sunlight.

Never mind words, you have to find out what you want to say.

41

"I don't want to ring the bell, I'm a private person," Dad says with conviction. "Besides, what are you celebrating? After that you're on your own." He exhales fully from both lungs waiting to be called into his last treatment. "No bells, no whistles, no bugles. I have these little spasms. I think it's the dexameth."

I say, "I'm having shortness of breath."

"It's anxiety. You're feeling this about me passing. But I'm not. It's the long sleep. I'm not afraid. You should take an anti-anxiety. Are you sleeping well?"

"Okay," I say.

"So you're eating and sleeping well?"

"It's a mild case, yeah. But I know how to sleep."

"It's a little tightness in my chest. First they missed in the lung: one-point-one centimeters, and the next time it only grew by one millimeter in six months. But they admit that they missed it. They only did PET and CT scans. Why? When it's all said and done, take it to a great malpractice lawyer. When I'm dead. Yeah, I won't forget that. If that's the standard case, that's sad. The neurologist said that he wished he saw me two months earlier. They didn't follow closely enough. They did a CT scan of my body. They didn't do it to my head. Why? I don't know. CTs mess up the body. MRIs don't do nothing. I think it's a social medicine decision. You're over sixty-five, we're not going to spend money. But you never talk about it here. You say it when I'm gone. I'm a little bitter about it. I think if I was in a better hospital with better resources—I think, I don't know. Rich people die all the time with the best doctors. But I'm a little bitter. I feel they could have watched me a little closer. What would have happened if they found it earlier?"

42

Then the urine issues start. Dad gets Dr. Chow ("the flunkie") on the phone to tell him his medication is "good for nothing." He's waking up every hour at night, and has had a couple of accidents. "What am I peeping in my pants? What am I an *alter kaiker*? If I'm dying, I'll understand."

Earlier I was taking photos of him hugging trees, now he was hugging me. It was a short hug at first. It's not because I didn't want it to be over that it became long. We are silent. My heart against his. I think about the fact that this is unfamiliar. My chin is over his left shoulder and I can feel warmth between us. After the final treatment we found out that he would in fact be given subsequent radiation at a raised level of precision. He was going to beat this thing. Precise treatment straight to your heart.

"I love you, Dad," I say.

Minutes later Em comes in from raking the front yard and starts talking about an old friend who is dying of lung cancer, who wants her back in her life. She says she realizes that we're getting older and it's not worth it. For some reason she carries on until she starts telling family stories. "My grandfather went with his gambler alcoholic secretary and had two sons when he was in his 70s. Punks. They sold off his tires to make some money. He was a big man in Romania. People in the community came to see him for advice."

I wait a while before going to get Dad's new prescription. The lines after work are like open bar at the League of Nations. I am now certain that Kaiser are a bunch of legal drug dealers. Calmed down from the wheat pizza dough stress of this afternoon—because of course we are still on the vegan diet—I manage to get to the front of the line and back for the State of the Union rebuttal. Dad's lightly guarded opinion of the speech is, "Too bad they don't have this rigged where you push a button and the floor drops and he burns."

43

The next morning at the Hacienda, 24/7 News is on, the dog is barking, and Em is sweeping and vacuuming. In an hour Ron the stockbroker is coming for a visit, then we see the gamma knife surgeon, better known as the Morph. Dad says he lost ten pounds. "By this scale," he says. "I've also lost half my taste buds and my appetite," he continues. "I can't eat what you made me last night. I have to eat what I like." He puts a hand on my shoulder. He loves fried potatoes but he could see I sprinkled turmeric on them for its supposedly strong anti-cancer characteristics. You know why you can't believe in miracles? Bland-ass potatoes. "It's a lousy day. I feel pain all over." Em turns off the vacuum. "Your dad, he looks really handsome, eh?" she says.

This is the horse she bet on.

We haven't been coping well lately. Dad says he gets a very strange sensation when he closes his eyes, like he's losing his balance. He says he's not going to close his eyes, he just needs to relax. The agenda for our meeting is, "I'm going to pass away soon, I don't know how soon." We're on video chat with Toots who is obviously doing something else from the way she is looking all over the screen. As soon as Ron mentions "an investment strategy," though, she questions how he created it. Pretty much from there the fogs start to settle in my mind and I experience magic hearing. "I don't want to wait until I'm incapacitated. One day I'm going to be incapacitated," Dad says, hands folded across his lap, reverting to the occasional "mm hm" when he closes his eyes and "recharges."

When Ron leaves and we get off the video chat, Dad tells me, "I hugged him when he left. I'll probably never see him again. You never know. It makes me get used to the idea." He sits down and Housedog is all over him, rubbing with his nose and licking. "Aye," he drawls, "Don't touch me."

We're listening to Camille Saint-Saens "Introduction and Rondo" on the violin. After a while I go get something from the kitchen for breakfast. Em's doing laundry back there. She restates that we should go somewhere. Dad says we need some Tchaikovsky. Before we look at the advance directive, he tells me, "I talked to Estelle. Everybody's old and dying. We're a vanishing breed. Yizchak just ran a marathon in Tiberias and hiked Kilimanjaro. The doctor told him he has two to five years. He's seventy."

It takes no more than one question about the end of life to decide filling out this kind of paper is a waste of time and upsetting. Em is eating seeds and pistachios in the kitchen and Dad's humming humming humming. "You're gonna have a good long life," she says to Kimbo. "Do you know how long she's gonna live?" Crunch.

"Hm mhm," Dad answers from the living room, mouth full of pretzels.

I ask him what he wants to do today and he puts me in front of this damn paper and the day's so free and sunny. There's nothing he wants to do but get things done. I file. I drive. I cook.

"Why don't you and your dad go to a movie after treatment today?" Em suggests.

"I want to live without being hooked up to machines. No machines. I want no breathing machine. I want no dialysis. I want no blood transfusion. I want no artificial feeding and hydration. I do not want any life support treatments at all, even if it means that I might die by not having them."

He confirms his preference about funeral or burial. "Are you sure?" I ask.

"Sure. I want revenge on that sucker. Burn it." I flash these words against my brain: the soul of a man is what matters, the energy. Dad offers me a pretzel.

"We have to wash the dog."

"Seriously, let's do something interesting. I don't care about the dog. She stinks. Let's do something for ourselves." I look at the open bag of pretzels he has out. No salt. Shit. I take a couple.

In the Morph's waiting room I eavesdrop on a woman speaking to another short hair about how "There is no more terrifying horror than the one that is intimate." The nurse comes to check Dad's vitals. He tells her, "I feel weak today. My back aches. I have pain in my chest."

"Did you start cutting down the steroid to half in the evening?" she asks.

"Tomorrow," Dad says and smiles ear to ear.

"See what Chow says, then." She leaves.

"I don't care what he says." Dad breaks out of the slow morning funk. "I feel sad for Yitzchak. I knew him 40 years. He says, 'come over when you're in the neighborhood.' Invite me and I'll come. I'm never in the neighborhood."

The Morph arrives to a one man shirt-off ovation. He's our hope. He says the plan is that we request diagnostic tests to see the effect of radiation a month from now, then we do radio surgery boosts. Dad is cold. "I bet when I get off the dexameth, I'll warm up," he says. There is a moment of silence when the rest of the team, Dr. Chow, Dr. Davies, and Em, show and bells start ringing. Dr. Chow says it's an earthquake drill. Dad is sitting down hunched over on the butcher paper covered medical bed. We ignore the ringing until it stops.

"So you've had ten treatments?" Dr. Chow asks.

"Twenty," Dad says.

"Oh, twenty," Chow casually restates moving onto a conversation about reactivating his immune system.

The Morph is a family man who wastes no time or effort describing the treatment for which he is seeking approval. Em asks what makes the high-resolution MRI he suggests any different, when out of nowhere I hear a small measure of the lullaby.

"Where'd that come from?" I ask.

"That's what they play when a baby is born," Dr. Davies says.

"They play it everywhere, all throughout the hospital?"

It's what Dad was humming when we got the BRAF mutation results.

Outside of the retro cube-shaped hospital, he looks up at me with his dark sunglass clips firmly in place. "I have three good months," he says.

I didn't know if he was right or not, but I didn't want to hear it.

There are very good days where we sit in the sun and heat up like lizards living the moment and there are days when I see no future in miracles. We are still hopeful for a miracle. You have to realize this. There is no other way to put it. We are not giving up on the possibilities of the tumor shrinking and him living longer.

That afternoon we go out to eat. "I'm in a good mood," Dad announces. "The Butcher (of Baghdad) said two to five years and in June it'll be five years, so I'm on schedule." He shoves in a mouthful of pasta. "Do you want some?" he asks.

I never knew about the five years. "It looks like you have an appetite," I say.

"Yeah, I got it back. I enjoyed the heck out of this."

The tattoo on the smooth side of our server's forearm reads, "Chingada suerte."

"If that peepee pill works and the dexameth is coming down, I'm going to be the master of my fate."

Later on when he's passed out in front of the TV, we're surprised by a video chat with his brothers in Tel Aviv. The skinny twin asks, Did you just wake up? Dad says, "No, I'm dancing."

I tell dad, "All families are dysfunctional."

He says, "No, not all families. It's how you solve your problems."

44

The next morning I wake up and have an itch for Chicago: "Hold me now/ It's hard for me to say I'm sorry." On our way to the mountain, Dad, Em, and I listen to KVCR public radio instead. They're handling the subject of illegal immigration, claiming the unintended consequence of background checks is a racist regression.

We're passing through the core of the Inland Empire on new roads built with federal highway dollars. I see the department store Forever Two One has replaced the old standard. I question the mentality of remaining forever anything. I do like to put off planning, to flake on an event from time-to-time, to spontaneously pump pump it up, but that comes along with other particular thoughts I'd like to communicate.

"You want water?" I ask Dad. "You want water? Hey you, drink."

Dad says, "When I'm thirsty, you bet I'll drink."

There isn't too much snow so we can drive right up to the house and get situated. In no time smoke is going from the chimney and our fire is drawing heat into the house. Dad's looking through the spices. "Oye. Of course. When you come to the mountain you start sneezing," he says to me. "How did I collect so many cinnamon, I'll never know. I like it up here. It's a good change of pace."

I bring back the subject of wedding preparations to engage in something other than Home and Garden TV. Hannah is busy coordinating all the individual services, down to spoon selection, for our site at a twelfth-century mill in Upper Normandy. I'm not revealing anything about all the little details that hold half of my attention. I'm fixed on the bar, the ring, and my outfits. "You're getting the strings?" Dad asks. "It'll be classy. It'll be so nice." I tell him we're just getting them for an hour. He says, "When people sit to have dinner. It's relaxing, it's soothing. It's not a disc jockey sitting next to me." He leans back on his reclining chair and kicks up his legs. "I guarantee no matter what she wears she will look very good."

"Rest, rest," Em says.

"I don't sleep these days. I just close my eyes."

"So close your eyes and don't talk."

"I can talk. Talk."

Dad wakes up and gets an apple. We're watching what he eats.

"You want some cinnamon on your apple?" I ask.

"No thanks. I had enough already to kill a bird."

"Good apple?" Em follows, a little too quickly.

"Yeah, sure. Each apple is different. This one's a little dry, not crunchy. Give me my money back."

Em suggests we go on a walk or go to a movie.

"I can't do more than this," Dad says, "I'm weak and tired."

"We're not pushing you," I say.

"Because if you push me, you'll really have to push me."

The movies on the mountain are in a seventies A-frame wood building at the fork in the road and it takes all of five minutes to get there from home. We kick open the swinging doors to the amphitheater and inhale the butter and pine smell deeply embedded in the carpet. According to Dad, they usually don't have movies for adults here. Our main feature is delayed so we are spending quality time together with the silent advertisements rolling and I suddenly remember the simplest thing. The man cannot read. We sit in the dark, and when the movie (about love and death, who knew?) ends we keep sitting for a little while longer. I don't believe I can feel this much in the face of another human being, even my father.

Coming down the stairs to the parking lot, he says, "It was like a dry run right there at the end."

That's the way things go. And everyone remains self-indulgent because it's all happening to them and it's impossible to share. When one thing happens, everything else is still happening. You have to give yourself time.

At home Dad's phone rings and he answers it, "Howya doon, Toots? Things are changing now. I feel like an invalid. Like I'm walking heavy on the ground. I don't have spring in my step. I'm clumsy. Every day is a different day. It's an adjustment. I really don't like vegetables and mixed up spices." He passes the phone to me and I tell Toots I'm trying to squeeze lemons in his water and he's doing more wiping and looking for crumbs.

When I get off the phone there's a commercial break in the Lakers game. "You want some choc-o-late?" Dad asks. He's been watching the Lakers since '66. Nowadays it takes all of fifteen seconds for him to pass out after the tip-off. From time to time he comes to and requests the score. I remember him giving me

the play-by-play for games I couldn't see when I was living in
New Orleans. Maybe I live like every day is a dry-run and the
world pushes back against me with easy arguments about the way
things should be. This is the way things are. They crash when
they get too heavy and if you can help it they don't land on your
roof and crush your heart. If I can look at the fire light dancing
in the fireplace and not think of the old campfires and our high
adventures, I can also ignore the image I have of our car plunging
off the rim with the both of us in it.

I play back in my mind the scene from Dad's retirement party.
He had worked and saved to live until his eighties and they ordered
barbecue and applauded him when he opened up his clock. He was
sure he was going to get a check. It reminds me of the video games
he got me for Hannukah the year I turned six, after he moved out
of the house. I ripped open the wrapping paper to find one of
the games that came for free with the console and the other so
obscure that all it did was confirm for me how detached he could
be. I hated myself for reacting that time and I never stopped feeling
guilty about it. Everything Dad was going through was tough and
I made it worse. I wanted to be good. Toots and I gave him a hard
time about anything that made us feel broken, like the fact that
we slept on camping cots in the bedroom of his bare apartment.
It was hard to know exactly how we affected him, but sometimes
we knew. After that year most of his gifts were checks.

Hannah calls me two minutes into halftime. She's going to sleep.
She says she wishes she could help me but she can't offer much
perspective. She's right that I don't share much. I think that I have
power over my emotions.

45

In the morning Em pulls me aside and brings it to my attention
that Dad had a stomach problem last night. She stands at less

than five feet, posture crippled by knee surgery, and looks up at me with her small dark eye. She says I have to adjust the meals. "He told me that nothing hurts, but he feels sick inside," she tells me in her Mexico City accent. "This is the first day he feels sick inside. The radiation accumulates and the pills at the same time. You try to keep your life normal but this is not like normal. This is not the same. Mentally he feels okay. The reality is that this thing is gonna hit us. When, I don't know, but it's gonna hit us."

On our walk, the roads are covered in tiny rivulets of melted ice and Dad is clearing rocks by kicking them aside with his feet. Out of a nearly perfect silence he asks me, "How do you write? From the heart?"

I say, "With the heart and a lot of practice."

I think about what else Em said earlier, "You haven't seen him without his clothes. He's lost a lot of weight."

We walk up past the high school on the rim of the mountain. "Oh, your muscles are going to hate you," I tell him.

"What muscles?" he says. "Whatever is left of them." He starts humming another tune: *"Those were the days my friends…"*

46

Dad is in the mirror saying, "I think I have cancer all over me. I'm sure I have cancer spots. I think I have cancer in my ear. Aye aye aye, maybe it already went to my liver. My legs ache, maybe it went to my bones. I lost my peace of mind."

Em reacts in her way, "After the scans and all that, our lives changed and they will never be the same again."

I'm thinking this is happening to other people.

Twenty four hours later, January 30, I'm in the master bathroom at Em's dad's place in Fashion Valley looking around the seventies yellow plastic countertops, mirrors, and fluorescent lights, writing all over my left hand, saying to myself "how is it possible, how is it even possible?" One week we are the best and the next I do all the wrong things. The stress of planning is getting to us. I'm upset that Dad doesn't want to eat. I'm prepping a letter for the wedding invitations, considering vegetarians and vegans, jumping up and down when I'm on the phone with Hannah. The phone is stressful. I want to tell Dad that things are going to be alright, but he knows better than me. One thing I know is that we're going to Vegas in a week—show tickets are booked and the hotel is booked.

We go to this restaurant called Cardamom by Pioneer Park for lunch. Dad's attracted to the chicken in peanut sauce on my plate. I tell him it's the worst thing for him and I refuse to share. Afterwards we go to the Morph's office. Dad wants to know when he should expect a surge of energy. The Morph tells Dad, "I can't follow your case, but I'm going to miss you. You're a cool guy. Take care. See you in five weeks for a follow up."

47

Em is showing some more new signs of strain. We're at the end of treatment options if Dad doesn't go to chemotherapy and she is worried about him dying at her house. He wants to do something about it. He doesn't want to die. "Well, nobody wants to die," he says and reflects on everything but that thought. His suggestion about Housedog's ailment is that he would take him to the vet and if it was more than $500 he would put him down. With him it's a little more complicated. He says, "Yitzhak"—the famous Yitzhak—"is that kind of guy that gets things done and he was given meds that killed all the testosterone in his body. It was a chemical castration. He said it had him crawling up walls." Dad tells me that Em could be making the choice between him and her dog. "You don't want her to make that choice. She loves the dog more than her son."

The conversation turns to Dad living out his days on the

mountain.

"Who's going to visit you up there, Yitzhak?" Em says.

"What about Atikva?" I ask with a churlish squint knowing this man and his ego. "You say he's not your friend. Are you his friend?"

"No comment."

"With a hole out of your Dad's lung, Atikva came by and gave me a lecture about coffee." Em mocks his inflected gentry pronunciation with her own Mexican version, "'You come over. But I don't really care if you come. I want you to see my stereo.'"

The subject gets dropped.

Sometime later Dad asks me into the small bedroom and shows me a cardboard box full of files. "This is my office," he says. In the middle of figuring out his bills he mentions the need to find a home for his dog Kimbo. I ask if she barks and the answer is no. So, if she's in a predicament she won't bark? "She used to bark when she was younger. She realized I wouldn't let her bark, so she doesn't know how to bark. She's not a barker." I say, is Bob Barker a barker? Dad winces.

Em interrupts my check writing, which is to say, chisels into my reputation as a reliable provocateur and miner of fresh cultural territory, to tell me, "For you the anxiety about the PET scan is new. I'm really nervous." I feel like all her concerns right now have a homogenized quality to them.

Dad says suffering can be meaningful only if it is unavoidable. The biggest part of his daily life was his profession. What he did for other people, I never thought he had to do it for me. I ask him what it was like when he came to the states, how he lived his life. He tells me, "We raised kids, had friends, ate at my uncle Joe's restaurant on the northeast corner of Sunset and Gardner. He lost all his money on the horse races."

He proceeds to tells me about the members of his mother's family from Belorussia. "There was Meyer, Nunny, Joe, Jay, Chaya, and Estelle.

"Meyer died before I was born. He went to Hadassah in Jerusalem to take off a bad toenail and they gave him too much
chloroform. They put him to sleep like a dog and he died. Twenty-one years old. Nunny died of Parkinson's, age sixty-five. He was
born in Russia." Did he drink vodka? "Don't be silly. They were
kids." It's Russia. "They were kids. Joe was born in Tel Aviv, as
was Jay. They both were in the War of Independence. They were
in paramilitary groups before the IDF. Joe was wounded. He took
a bullet to the head in the Battle of Latrun (1948) fighting the
Jordanian legionnaires. It was a long period of recovery. In 1950
he had nothing to do in Israel so he bought a ticket to the U.S.
To San Francisco. Jay followed suit. He joined the foreign service
and was a military attaché in Vienna and Prague where he met his
wife. Her parents were in bad health so they went back to Israel,
but he didn't find his place there. Joe went to college to become
a chemical engineer. One day his whole lab blew up. Jay was an
electronic engineer at McDonnel Douglass. They fired him ten
days before he became eligible for a pension. They sent a guard to
get rid of him. He found a job quickly after with Hughes aircraft
designing guidance missile systems.

"Joe started the restaurant, the Sabra Café, after everything
blew up. He moved around a lot. Finally, the Sabra Café was a
success but he couldn't keep two dollars in his pocket. He'd be in
the restaurant until midnight or one in the morning. Had someone
count his money. Then he'd go dancing at PJs nightclub. Joe put
me up. I worked in Sabra as the chief bottle washer/toilet cleaner/
assistant to the cook. I brought the accordion from Israel. I did
weddings and bar mitzvahs.

"I wanted to study with the best accordionist, instead I was
with an Austrian. Heine Golden. A mean, curmudgeon guy. After
a year-and-a-half with this *kaiker*, I wanted to be with Spivak,
the best player." He reclines right there for a moment, his eyes
out of focus, rubbing his beard. "That was a sin that my father

didn't let me study with him. It's like sending you to study with a street performer versus Edna Dilay. I don't know I could not play melody and rhythm with one hand. I could get used to it, I s'pose.

"My first job I made forty thousand a year in 1976. I had two thousand to buy a home. The other seven thousand was from Esme. I paid her back. The house you grew up in was a good house. I bought it from the Superintendent of Schools, Caldwell. He moved to Santa Monica and took over as Superintendent of Schools there. It was a great house. The floor plan was excellent. The first floor had a huge living room, there was a side room office, the open kitchen, dining room. The bathroom downstairs was a really nice one. There was a bathroom upstairs for the kids, a master bedroom with a marble fireplace. I was thirty-five with a house and two cars."

"What about Atikva?" I ask. "What was his story?"

"Atikva signed with Met Life Insurance and faked like he was selling. He used to show up and leave at noon. Then one thing led to another. His wife was related to Sassoon of the jeans. He learned to manage the thread and buttons. He got fired. He went company to company. He always lied about being a step higher in the business. He'd say 'I can do this job' and once he realized he can't do it, he'd achieved some things. He couldn't fill the order, though…He has three kids and nobody talks to him. I'm very happy. I consider myself a success. I bailed him out of prison once. He tells me, 'You have to come to my house, I'll make you the best coffee ever.'"

"Where'd he get the accent?"

"He made it up. When you don't want to be who you are, you make it up. Now he says he's becoming a farmer. He says he lives with the seasons." Dad makes a stinky face. "Nonsense. *Everybody has a wagon*, he says. You want to fit into the community? You go there and you become something you're not."

I see Dad as being attracted to this character because he's a fascinating case, but maybe I'm wrong. Dad tells me how they used to have guy weekends. He says, "Nobody lived in as many places as Atikva. One time he rented a truck at midnight and had me help him move. I laughed I got hysterical laughing. He didn't make a penny until forty-two."

Dad takes the TV off mute and starts to snooze. Em says to me, "I hope your dad is healthy so we can travel. Nobody asked me if I wanted to do this. Maybe soon he'll lose his appetite. It doesn't mean we make him beef tacos. I feel like they just signed me up for this. He's doing it for you guys. He wants to go to Las Vegas and enjoy it."

I'm confused.

48

Today Dad gives me the hard line: "I want to eat what I want to eat when I want to eat." We have to go to Rio Seco for his scans. He hasn't slept all night. He says, "This headache is bad. I don't know what it is." He begins clearing his throat to sing a classical tune. "What's wrong with my throat?" he says, "You start imagining things. Nodules under the chin pinching."

I talk to Toots for a while. She suggests I take a look at the mitochondria. Dad is a scrolling speech to me right now. "That's what they do in America. They tell you you have six months, you hear four or five days after radiation you're going to regain strength. Did you tell her I'm breaking the diet? Let's not get trapped in numbers. All these things, all these emotions get mixed. We got to stay cool." *Cama tov he-eyeh! Ba shanah haba-ah.*

After that exchange, Em comes in the kitchen crying. "You guys are telling him what to do," she says. I explain I was trying to be political, I explain the need for moderation, I explain that this was poor communication. I'm on the defensive because I'm looking out for his mitochondria; I'm advocating for him because he won't advocate for himself. He won't make preventative choices. Doesn't he just want to eat ten pieces of Pollo Pollo a week with potatoes? Just like that. He won't get what he needs because of laziness and Em will convince herself that these are taste-driven choices. It's eating with color-by-numbers sophistication. Eating out of habit.

On the drive to Rio Seco Dad re-opens the conversation about what he's going to do the weekend that Em heads to Mexico City, when I'll be gone and Toots can't come. He says, "I'm starting to feel real well. I'm feeling well. She doesn't have to stay with me."

"Why you telling me stories?" I say.

"Okay, but by the time she goes, I'll be kicking her out."

49

Tuesday morning, February 7, throughout the house there's an intense ripe warmth, like rotten fruit, because Em is making her cauliflower. We're sitting around listening to the Goldberg Variations by Johan Sebastian Bach. I am very close to asking what does a bird do to entertain itself when Toots writes me about her special pillows at the condo, fearing the maid's arrival. She thought she would make it down to San Diego again before I left, but we tell her not to because it's better she come when I'm not here.

I still wake up in the smaller guest room at the condo and take a few minutes for myself before watching how the clock ticks for you, America. Everything is white in there besides the fake plants and blue china. I sleep on the twin bed nearest the sliding mirror door and use the other for stacking everything but my books. My books are in the middle section of the wall-length wicker bookshelves, where there's a chair and a person can sit and write. That's where I keep the Mordechai Campbell pages I took from the buildup under Yefé Nof.

Em stops reading to share a thought. "Grandparents are usually nice," she says.

"Some molest their grandkids," Dad replies.

"Yeah, but you didn't like your grandma," Em says.

"She was sitting around making big *graipses*, saying, 'I'm dying, I'm dying.' She lived to ninety-three. As tall as she was fat. And from her fourth floor kingdom she criticized everyone. 'Look at this one's hair; look at her, no bra; look at him, he runs, he runs.' *Yeah*, he had Down syndrome. Grandma saw all of it. She criticized for all imperfections. 'Look at that fat one.' Well look in the mirror."

I'm in between organizing the cardboard "office" and putting pills in the small Monday through Friday containers, a.k.a. doing the medication. I let dad know his printer is printing an alignment page again.

"Are you sure?" he asks, "I hated it since day one."

"No."

"No what?"

"It's not functioning for you."

"I'll take a hammer to it."

We have nothing to eat so I ask Dad if he minds that I go to the Natural Foods store. For lunch I make baked falafel from a box. Dad turns his face in disgust and refuses to eat them. I get frustrated with the effort and how very little pleasure there is in the result. I start to insult his cooking. I am flailing.

Em passes by, "I'm so glad that you're feeling good. You're looking good, Biki." That's her pet name for him.

I extend a small plate of leftover barbecue brisket to Dad who tells me, Styrofoam container in his hand, "I cannot eat any more vegetables. I cannot think of eating anymore vegetables. No salad. Meat and potatoes tonight. I am entitled to eat what I want sometimes."

"Anybody forcing you? You eat what you want, when you

want," I say.

"But I'm forcing myself. Tonight is simple."

"I'm going to watch you cook this week. You're going to cook for yourself when I'm gone?"

"Yeah," he says, smacking his lips and humming through the two slices of beef like a little kid.

"That's so frustrating," I say.

"Mmmm, this was so good. This was so good. Mmmm. It was good. With the meat tender."

I have to let it go. I look up at him. That's West Texas brisket smoked to perfection, the fat all melted, full of flavor.

Opening the Jell-O afterwards Dad hedges his nutritional bet. "Thank God I like Jell-O. There's nothing in it."

The Republican Minnesota Caucuses are on. It's really no fun. Dad starts packing when Hannah calls to fill me with some other sound, call it the crack of lightning.

50

In the morning, we're headed to Vegas. Dad's having attacks of the bladder that he hates and doesn't understand. By three in the afternoon we check into the second-tier Orleans and go for the clam chowder he's been talking up. Apparently it doesn't taste like it did eight years ago.

The drive has taken a lot out of him. He says he has no energy, no spring in his step. I'm on the casino floor looking for an anthem, thinking it's all in the delivery.

"Dad are you being discouraged?" I ask.

"No, I'm just hoping tonight's a better night and I'll wake up and see what tomorrow will bring."

"I don't want you to be discouraged. I'll do whatever it takes."

These three days are going to pass us by if I can't just let things be.

As he lowers himself into bed, Dad goes, "Oooh hoo hoo hoo hoo hoo, eyah!" I'm not supposed to wrap my arms around his legs and hold him tight now. You do that when you've given up. I let him know that I'm going to Raku while he sleeps. I promise myself I won't overeat. A little after midnight, I head back to the hotel. I know where I need to be in the morning.

Bellagio breakfast buffet.

"It's not a buffet. You sit at a table."

Dad wakes up with a terrible headache. The trip must have been traumatic. He doesn't feel well but he tells himself, "I gotta get better." He takes acetaminophen and we watch 24/7 News. Possible solutions for Syria, Tyler Clementi committing suicide after being outed by his Rutgers roommate; the debate over whether women soldiers should be in combat, the housing crisis. All these news items make thinking about the issues look ridiculous and predictable. We are in the routine of consuming narratives about things we can do nothing about. It almost makes you give more attention to yourself and the way you fit into everything that's worth talking about. The individual remains anonymous, the citizen aspires to be considered.

Obama says, "We are Americans. We look out for one another, we get each other's backs." He says, "A house is your stake, your claim on the American dream." He requests that "Everybody take part in America's comeback."

Dad says, "Yeah, right."

We get into the car and I crank up the heat. Our plan is to eat now and check out hotels later. If there's a good exhibition then we'll visit it. Then we'll go to the Mirage and pick up our tickets.

At the Bellagio breakfast Dad lets me know, "I'll help you if you can't handle it."

"I'm eating it," I say.

"I wish my taste buds worked better. I don't get to fully appreciate the taste. I don't get the full essence of what I eat."

I tell him, "I've been dealing with that since I broke my nose."

"Ghi, you're not finishing."

"I'm not in a hurry. I'm savoring."

"I don't know if anyone finishes this here. You have to be a serious pig," Dad says with no irony. "Let me take my medication. I don't know if I can get to it."

"Stand up."

"*Eh stand up* and deliver."

"That's right, Jaime."

Some guy approaches us, "Excuse me, did I just hear you say Hymie?"

Both dad and I give a stare of disbelief, not a quick 'it wasn't me' reaction.

We walk around the hotel shops checking out watches. Dad loves that. Cars, watches, houses. He compares his watch to the Omega. "I like mine better," he says. That's good, I say, because it's yours. His hands are a little shaky, his eyes are twitching, he has a tooth-pick in between his teeth, and the hair on his head is spare.

He's got cancer.

51

After we do the Bellagio, Caesar's, Treasure Island, the Mirage and the Cosmopolitan, which neither of us particularly likes, the conversation stays light with an exchange of revelations. "I'm walking so well now. Unbelievable," Dad says in the long hall between slot machine floors. He's equally moved by a Monet lithograph. "I'm telling you. You stand right by them, you think you're in heaven."

The both of us get excited for the night out. My excitement starts shifting into the outcome I anticipate for the show. Things happen so quickly while they're happening we just don't know or don't care. If we could do this again and again, every week, three nights a month—if we moved there and walked every street—maybe we'd start to see all the little things that make the event itself sweet. Those little details make a difference: the sound of a chord on repeat, the familiar tune, the surprise feat, spontaneity within the formal structure. Here we are with all the stimulation of lights and sounds and false atmospheres, trying not to remark too much about the underdressed girls parading around putting on airs, ridiculous. Trying to recharge on the escalators, we are full of the sap of life. Even the velvet ropers can't deny us.

After the show we grab a couple of drinks and I ask dad when's the last time he was in a lounge. I maintain that my party drug of choice is the late afternoon nap and self-confidence. We talk about our relationships. I admit that I better keep my mouth more shut, if at all possible. We get in the car hungry and find a place to binge in Chinatown. Dad's fortune says that 'clearing up the past will always clear up the future.' I say that's poppy-cock. I don't know what poppycock means but the word jumps out of my head. He says, too bad about some of these places in the world where the boys and girls are not above the social order. They want immediate satisfaction. "Look how everybody's dressed in those body socks. I had a patient that was thirty-two, went to Vegas with four guys and they all went out and married girls." I get that story half right. I am passing out on my hotel bed when I try to revise it.

Every day you get up is a small miracle. Every day you eat breakfast together and drive across a state line and know Beethoven well enough to say he "never made anything bad" is something. My flight is in five days. I'm anxious about leaving. I still park so-so in front of the Hacienda and I have to work on that. All these stacks of emotion. I have no time to sit and process them.

52

Dad and I get an early start and unload out of the car at this antique sale along the beachfront in La Jolla. His legs are visibly thinner and he lacks the dexterity of the great walker he has always been as he struggles a little to pull himself out of the car and stand on two feet. He sees something he likes in a store window and says, "Let's check out the prices." The owner is in a chair across the tiny room and Dad doesn't see him, or doesn't care. "Oh, the guy kills you," he says. We walk right out. There's a little kid shaking his head to get the beach blonde hair out of his face. His dad, the high school football coach, is talking to a friend about the team. A girl comes zooming by with wings on her calves. We walk into side streets, away from loud cars. I'm trying to stick to what Dad is telling me about cylinders, displacement, power, and torque, when he switches to watches. "Shitty watches you throw in the river." And then houses. I mention mowing the lawn at the old house on early Saturday mornings. "I know you don't like doing things," he says. "You're not a handyman."

He might be right, but I prefer to think I need proper motivation.

Em opens up the microwave to inspect Dad's lunch. He finds it "pretty disgusting," so she says to me, "make him a bowl of pasta." Well, why doesn't she do it? She doesn't take care of his food and I'm tired of doing it. I can't get thirty minutes to myself without an activity. "We'll try to make a good dinner," Em says. "We're certainly not the best cooks in this house. I'm not. Toots never cooks." If she doesn't cook she doesn't eat, Dad says from the couch in the living room. "But I want you to eat, not to munch. You have to eat well, Biki. You have to eat." Then she leaves to take her dog on a walk.

Maybe I'm relinquishing the role of caretaker and I'm getting taken care of. That's what I want.

Back from rescuing lemons, Em joins me, her boy, his recently re-committed girlfriend, Preta, and Dad around the table to tell us some family stories while we finish lunch.

"Lachacha lost half an arm drinking with her arm out of the car and a bus came by and crushed it. She took everything for pain. Messed her up. But she's still alive. When Carlos' brother had *pancreas* cancer he was in such pain that one day he came over and said, 'Shoot me.' Not me, my friend. Find somebody else. I always said to my kids, if I'm in pain find someone for four hundred dollars to put a pillow on me. The narcos will do it. Instead the business killed his brother. It ruined our lives. It ruined our family. We had thousands of dollars everywhere. Then came the jet skis and discotheques and boats and it wasn't very clear where the vacation ends and the business starts. Everyone was messed up."

The boy says, "No, no one was messed up."

"Not like dramatic. We're not Whitney Houston. But everybody's lives were all messed up."

"I would go to my room and she would trash it and tell me to clean it up because she was having a bad day."

"What if you were disappointed with the relationship?" Dad asks trying to chisel the wall.

"He knows what he wants," Em says. "It kills me to know that he doesn't make it."

The drama of mother and son ensues. Preta asks, "Why are you talking about him in third person? Tell her she's a shitty mother, if you think so."

"Why do I have to talk about myself?"

"You're the only one who can talk about yourself," Preta says. "You can let people tell you about themselves but you don't let them know you and it's bullshit." She turns to Em, "You let him be here. You keep doing this. It's bullshit. You cater to the fact that he can sit there and be present at the table and you allow him to be quiet."

"I don't need to talk about this," the boy grovels.

"Because you don't care," Em says.

"Mom, why don't you talk about yourself? It makes you uncomfortable."

"It's easier to talk to people you know less. I feel like an idiot, I feel like a parrot. I don't need to eat at this table. You don't talk. Like you're a ninety year-old couple that don't like each other."

Preta explodes, "Basically he waited to see that you were upset in order to react."

Em says, "Life is going to force you to do things that you don't want to do. I just wish you would talk a little more. Share your life. It's more interesting to get to know people. Your sister used to say, 'Mom, you don't have friends.' Well, I'm a private person. I have friends. I sometimes think that I make friends too easily, let people in too easily. I need to learn control. You don't want everybody touching your life."

The boy questions Preta about her dad.

"I've never met the man. He's completely fictional to me. A father is a biological factor. I don't call him my father. It was a completely female environment I was raised in."

Dad tells us, "Em's father loves me. Because I'm from Israel, he thinks I can walk on water."

After we say our goodbyes and drive careful—which is Californian for drive carefully—we speak about the little therapeutic moment we just had. Dad says, "I think we can get through to him, but we need long good sessions and he's gonna have to break down a little."

53

A few days later I take Dad to the dentist in La Jolla. My flight leaves in the middle of the night and I have a horrible feeling of loss working its way through me. I don't see palm trees and asphalt,

I feel low reminding myself that this visit is almost over. This is earthquake weather today. While I'm waiting for the dental work to be done I order a Jackie burger with avocado and call an old friend who lives on Whalewatch Way. She doesn't answer. As the burger cooks, I walk along a single lane commercial side-strip, through the beach town liquor store, inhale ketchup, flip flops and lotion, then go back and eat in a room full of fiberglass panels and benches worn out from so many asses.

This is written on the wall before me: There is only one success: To be able to live your life in your own way.

I go to the beach, but I don't have any damn thing to say to myself. I am a social thinker. I connect with references, with people at work carrying out their trade and helping the economy turn. I listen to the heart celebrating its minor victories, the eyes lighting up over indulgences, the sense of suspended imperfections. Nothing starts in a vacuum, no thought originated without some added elements: chance, luck, sun, a way from pain, towards love, a hope that everything will be forever on both sides of the street, day and night, February and June, that everything you ever wanted will come to you as it is needed and as the grand game of mental gymnastics goes on like 80s hits: "4, 3, 2, 1…earth below us."

I call other people. Try to make contact. This girl working at a generic neon-and-speckled counter café is cleaning out her fingernails with a plastic knife when I walk in. I reproduce my dad's way of talking because it comforts me, "I'm gonna take a nonfat latte." The first person who answers my phone is a partner at a law firm that moves faster than money. He says, "This transcends all earthly matters. It hits like a ton of bricks." I hang up with him and write a ditty while I finish my latte.

The next person to answer is my mom. I tell her I'm not excited that I have to leave.

"Yeah, what can you do?" she says. "I have a feeling that the treatment works. Oh, I'm praying for him every day."

Dad is nearly out the door with the dentist when I arrive. "I hope to see you again," he tells him. The dentist puts his palm out to shake and slaps down his free hand on top, "You will, you will."

We shuffle through La Jolla on foot a little more. There's a Ferrari commercial being filmed. Dad says, "In a minute you'll see the house of your dreams."

"I don't dream of houses," I say.

We observe children out after school and surfers. Dad starts telling me, "For dinner I hope you make something I like. I'm tired of not liking what I eat." And then he gets an attack of the bladder, "I'm dying with my peepee today. I don't know what, every twenty minutes, all day. Wait. I need to get rid of these sunglasses. Ooh, ooh, ooh, what am I gonna do?"

He goes between two cars.

"I didn't go much, I just gotta go when I gotta go."

54

I spend the night at the Hacienda so we can leave for the airport early. When I wake up I'm at the edge of my bed in the dark trying to find whatever the hell it is that you try to find when you can't find it at four in the morning.

"Get some light, Ghi-Gee. I'm okay," Dad says.

"Well if it makes you happy," I say not wanting him to wake up before he has to.

"It makes me very happy," he answers getting out of bed in the room across the hallway.

My fists hang by my side so I can still myself. I begin to feel my made-up face cracking. At the end of the short lawn between us I'm an empty pedestal revealing some sad unsculpted image of 'I am really leaving this man' with every step he makes towards me in his mint green underwear.

Dad eyes me where I am. "I'll see you soon," he tells me, straight from the throat.

This is our first goodbye. He sees that I have it in me but I don't. The sight of those skinny legs in the morning. Skinnier than ever. Sticks.

55

Just when the plane lands at JFK, I turn on my phone and it vibrates. It's Em crying hysterically. "He's in an ambulance. He started getting sweaty and he fell and they said it wasn't sugar."

My ears plug up and start throbbing like a knotted hose. I'm stopping myself from the spins. I can't hear anything else Em's saying for exactly forty-seven seconds.

"I know this was going to happen at some point. I know this was going to happen. I can't believe it's on the day you left."

We hang up. I deplane and get to the international flight gate, clammy and nervous. I call Em back. She is more calm. "He's okay," she says. "He's on the hospital bed after some traumatic episode in the brain, about to get a CT scan."

PART FOUR

FEBRUARY–MARCH 2012

56

Dad's eating cereal when I call him. He says, "I'm very sick. Paris is a pipe dream."

I ask him about the concert. He says, "It was elephant shit. Mahler's later works, after he converted and became a devout Christian."

He confirms our fear about his living situation. "Em would like Toots to come as often as she can and stay as long as she can. She feels she cannot assume all the responsibility." What? "Cooking and all. She says she doesn't cook, she eats her food and she doesn't want to cook." What? Laurel said she would come over and bring you food. "No. This is Em's house." So you're going to starve in Em's house? "No. Nobody is starving." Well, what'd you eat for dinner last night? "I can't think of it. Chicken soup." So she can cook.

Hannah and I go to Nissim de Camondo's house. It's one way to reconnect and focus on our feeling for each other. We have a picnic in Parc Monceau, both distracted by the need to reconfigure our priorities. We love each other very much, but the wedding is going to stretch our resources. I already hold in mind that I have to go back to the U.S. and Hannah needs me to be more than a place marker. I need to be involved in the joy of life planning. It's hard to hide my worries so I try to cancel them out completely. I think about ladies with deep voices, or our perfectly random rabbi, or how to sing traditional songs when we know the words and they change the tune on us. I dream I am playing with a diamond ring.

The next day I try to speak about identity, but this is fast and the night doesn't want to be brought out like an organ grinder turning a sad song. My pillar holds a pot of flowers, the ceramic shines, but there is no decoration. I would rather not feel the way I feel. I prefer what happens in inexactitude, three meters below the surface, when we are not overly excited about leaving and we are already receiving a parting gift.

57

Thursday night, Hannah and I are once again in the audience at the rue Copernic synagogue learning from the British rabbi who will marry us: "Anuk! Anuk! Fucking hell. You've never read the book of Estelle? There are two mitzvahs. An order by the Torah and connection. How do you make a law? By a public stick you measure criminals, crimes, victims, and you arrive at a law for all humanity. The law of protection is, protect the poor and strangers because you know their hearts. You were strangers in Egypt. *Saying you're a human rabbi is like saying you are the most elegant prostitute.* The humanity concept comes after tribe and family. An altruist is someone other. When the texts change there were not orphans but poor. The stranger becomes the convert. Protect the convert. An eye for an eye, tooth for a tooth, hand for a hand, foot for a foot. *I'd like to change my foot. It's been giving me pain three days now.*"

On the metro home there's a kid smoking a cigarette. He's watching his buddy pop out advertisement panels and tag them with a weak ink marker. Both these fools are thinking, what's the worst that can happen to me? Nobody calls them out on their shit.

Of course the night isn't over without an evening phone call and some notation. Em tells me, "I don't know what's happening to your dad. He sleeps all day and doesn't have any appetite." You really don't know what's happening? "I thought we were going to have years," she says. When she passes me over to Dad he tells me, "She maybe wants to get rid of me. Get on with it."

I have to think, it's not what's crazy about someone else, it's the points of connection. It's the little bit of light.

58

Talk of tablecloths and place settings and chair covers makes it obvious that people will pay different amounts for the same item depending on who is providing it. Hannah is trying to get through to me about my feelings but I am not responding. I'm out in the boulevards trying to decide what I should wear and what color suits the groomsmen should wear. This local cult newspaper man in Saint Germain who sells *Le Monde* in the evening from his bicycle calls out a headline that immediately draws a Euro and change out of my pocket. He takes it, hands me the paper, and responds to my bitter expression, explaining his spin on: *Assad was assassinated.* Politically not physically, he says.

59

Good news, Dad's latest PET scan shows a necrotic center of the larger region on the golf ball-sized tumor. I imagine it as a giant blackhead.

I get Dad on the phone a minute after he hangs up with Atikva. First I do a quick check in for a small hook into the life he's living, because I need to hook in a little. He tells me the news. My heart goes boom.

He says, "Now it's a matter of who will prevail, me or the tumors."

We continue a comprehensive check-in with Hannah by my side, listening, reaching for my hand. I burrow my head in the small of her neck and she caresses me. "That's France," Dad says about a strike I mention. "The unicorns are strong in France." He tells me

Laurel visited and they had a picnic in Pioneer Park. She brought chicken cutlets. "We can make chicken Parmesan now," he says. "If the doctor can give me seven more months, that would be great. Every day is different hour-to-hour, minute-to-minute. In the morning I feel strong and I don't shuffle. At the end of the day, when I'm tired, I shuffle. Altogether, if it's as good as it gets, I'll be happy."

I hold onto my hope for a full cure.

"Kimbo left on Thursday. She was going to a very good home. You got nothing to worry about. They will walk her and they will let her sleep in the house." I'm not really concerned, still I act the part. Do you miss her? I ask. "Truly not." But you know she misses you. "I'm a little relieved I don't have to walk her, feed her. I always said that when I can't take care of her she has to go. Did I like her? Yeah, she was a good dog. I would be sad if I had to put her down."

He tells me that they went to Lake Murray and it was nice and warm. They sat a little, walked a little. There were lots of ducks, geese, and other water fowl. I smile and mention that I forgot my PIN number in the time I had been away from France so my card was invalidated and it takes such a long time to get a new card that I'm considering a new bank. I only chose mine because they sponsor the French Open.

He asks me, "Are you yawning? I imagine you with a mouth like a baboon."

This is the beginning of the many nights I pass out on Hannah with every repressed thought blocking my awareness all the way to sleep.

60

We're looking for wine and cider and other dinner drinks. I also need to purchase a tallit and kippas. In my brain I'm daydreaming to New Order's "Ceremony" — "*I'll break them down no mercy shown, heaven knows it's got to be this time…*" In the street I overhear a couple arguing. She says, "If you push me too far away you're gonna get fucked. You see what I'm saying? Say yes." The guy is quiet.

Back home we brainstorm songs for the wedding. I'm responsible for music and the bar. One of my greatest pleasures is building the six a.m. list. At the same time I start thinking of Streetrunner games for the guests, Dad is on the line with Em by his side giving Toots and me an update about his necrotic tumor.

I ask, "Did he give you any details, like what are the side effects from a tumor dying there? Worse vision or headaches?"

"We can't worry because he can do nothing about it," Dad says.

"He has to do something about it, no?" I respond.

"It's harder to take out than they thought because anytime you go into the brain it's dangerous."

"What will you do? Take steroids?"

"Well, we got to do it or I die. He was nice, he called me."

"Yeah, very nice," Em says. "So we're waiting for someone from his office to schedule."

"Should we still call the neurologist?"

"If he has anything to contribute to the team. When we talk to the Morph we'll know. Don't get upset. Nothing is happening. I'll do the risky surgery if they say I'm dead in a month. Hell, I'm dead anyway."

"Do it! Plan out your treatment," Toots says.

"Well, enough of that. How's work?" Dad asks.

Toots tells him how she's getting back into it.

"Well, you just do your work. Em will take me. Because we've got to kill this tumor. It's complicated, but the neurosurgeon said we'd do it if it's the last resort. I can say hospice but I'd rather fight."

"I can help you with it. I can come down again soon," Toots says.

"If we need you we'll call you."

Dad has to go to the bathroom, so he holds the line and Toots has me all to herself now.

"He's not going to get better," she says to me. "This is going to kill him. He's very limited. He can't take walks."

Every little cut she makes isn't to my hope or my flesh, it's breaking the boy in me to pieces: my hero, my half-light, I'm growing out of an address, I can't even contain dreams.

"It's not awesome. He's not gonna get better. I don't think you're gonna miss one week that you're supposed to work. But you might miss one week that you're gonna spend with him more. He's not functioning the same. I didn't let him go down to the underside of the house without me. His legs are shaky and like Jell-O all of the time. He couldn't unscrew a few screws and a light bulb. I had to help him. He's in good spirits. He gets very confused and overwhelmed. He's declining. He reduced the symptoms on the brain tissue swelling and he lost muscle. I just felt like I was just trying to keep him alive. The medical solutions are not promising. They're dangerous, if necessary. It didn't shrink. Maybe it will with radio surgery."

I say nothing. I push my pen back and forth across the page like a mine sweeper, brushing all the pain of loss and impotence away. All I can do is listen to my big sister break me up inside.

"You need to get over the hump of coming back and forth. Dad is dying. Dad is declining. He's not getting better. He's gonna get worse. He has a pointed feeling. He told Em. They're going to install a handrail in the shower. You put a stinky cheese on the table and walk away. I'm not Nostradamus, but I know where he's gonna be next week. The doctor is very worried. If they leave the tumor there will be gradual symptoms, sight, functioning. If they remove the tumor there could be acute symptoms. Dad gave you money to do it. I'm in the same position. I have to work. I can't go back and forth."

61

March 20 at 9p.m., Toots calls to tell me "The shit is hitting the fan."

I call my dad and he lets me know he has more strength and that his treatments are going to be on the more aggressive side and the effects are slightly more pronounced. He says Toots wants to come for his first treatment, and she wants to bring Furstman.

In the middle of the day the next day Toots calls back and we talk for six minutes. She's crying.

"I think you have to come now. Dad's beginning to get paralyzed. He got up and fell on his knees. He's not been getting out of bed to pee and he peed on the bed."

I'm walking in Saint Germain after giving a tour, knee-shaking like Elvis because I have to urinate. I tell her I love her and I understand what's happening, I just need a few days. There should be some protections through the contract I signed for work except I didn't sign a contract. I push my way inside a bar, still on the phone, and from across the room the proprietor hollers a drinking motion, rocking his extended thumb and little finger toward and away from his mouth. Pay to pee.

I come out of the toilet stall and stop crying, mid-sentiment. The rush of feeling-inspired days where you wouldn't have known a thing—not a thing—before becoming, I still remember those days for their imprecision: a world of unfinished feelings, the last trappings of distraught boys.

What a bunch of words.

Ten thousand daydreamed memories later I come back to earth reliving our experience in Jackson Square, New Orleans, with nothing on my mind, jazz in the air, my dad full of life, himself.

62

Dad explains, "I wasn't in the bathtub, I was in front of the bathtub. The screen kind of caught me like a net."

"You didn't tell me you fell."

"I don't brag about that."

He tells me, "I fired twenty-one shots yesterday."

"Who did you shoot?"

"A skunk in a cage. The departed is still in his cage."

"Did it stink?"

"He didn't get a chance to spray a full load. Big skunk. Probably killed him with the first shot, but then it kept moving. It took
twenty-one shots with a pellet gun."

"I talked with Atikva. He's saying we're going to build his house
together and I put up with it. He tells me, 'I put him in touch with
his mortality.'" He laughs at that.

I call up sister Toots after a while and she tells me, "This shit is
bad. This shit is real. This shit is bad. This is it. This is the decline.
We are at the crux of it. This radiation is going to keep him alive.
It's not going to help him survive. Last night was really scary.
Really scary. I'm not leaving here until you get here. I have a little
back pack. Last night it took him forever to change. Not good.
This is not good. Ain't good. He tries to get up on his own, he's
trembling. It's like his brain is telling him. It's the worst. I mean,
I'm here. He really needs help. Em needs help. Really bad. It's really
bad times. Really bad times. Oh, I'm sorry, this is the hardest shit
ever I'm just telling you. Anyway, I'm trying to figure out when
Furstman can come because he's stronger."

I think it's awful that Dad has to go through this, so when Toots
cries I ask her, why are *you* sad? And she says, "Don't ask me what
I'm sad for, I'm sad"

Meanwhile, I need the Secretary of State of California to apos-
tille my birth certificate so that I can get married. Funny, all these

tactics and tic-tacs at play here. Each day you should set aside thirty minutes for talking to the shotgun.

63

I call Toots the next day. She doesn't immediately hand the phone over to Dad. "How you *doon?*" I say, anticipating that this is actually what he's going to be saying to me.

"Totally overwhelmed and want to die. I'm running a business from 5775. It's totally fucking hard. He does not remember anything from the middle of the night. His brain doesn't work right. The walker and toilet thing are helpful so he's better. The pull-up thing is helpful. I'm trying to get work done and keep it together. I haven't showered in two days. Hold on, Ghi, I'm supposed to be in a meeting and I'm just telling them to hold on. Em's daughter talked to me yesterday. She said, 'I'm very worried about my mom. She's at a breaking point. She loves your dad and you but she's at a breaking point.' I asked her, what does she want to do?"

When Dad gets on the phone he says in Hebrew, "*Yom echad dvash, yom echad batzal.*" One day honey, one day onion. "You never know. Today I'm walking like a champion. Yesterday I was losing balance, wobbly feet. Toots's calm, running a company, no big deal. That's why TV's so great. No need to concentrate. You can watch whatever you get. Whatever you don't get you don't get. I have three treatments next week. Monday, Tuesday, Wednesday. I hope to be very well in April and we'll see. I really want to be at both weddings. It all depends on how fast I will deteriorate. That's shit. The situation is very fluid." He laughs. "Let's hope for the best. I would love to see you here and I would love to be there. You know it may well be WWW."

I don't recognize this word. It starts with a W and then there's a W and another W that's not creased. In the middle of trying to figure it out I get a manuscript rejection in the mail. I think everybody is looking for polish. That word is whatever I want it to be.

I talk to my mom and she says, "It's hard for him. When you get radiation right in the spot it's hard. So hopefully he'll be alright and he'll get better. It's day-by-day. Day-by-day. Well, I decided to make a wedding cake and that's it. I'm leaving for France the fifth of June and I'm returning the eighteenth of July."

64

We are looking for wine and beer and a suit, but we really have crazy details to work out between invites, budgets and organizing everything for Normandy. I'm letting Hannah do it all. I'm convinced that my French isn't good enough to get what I need on the telephone. It doesn't suit me to try. Everything is really serious. I'm elsewhere. I imagine writing a letter from a son to his father. I've got this impression of the way I love, but it's really the way I'm capable of loving, like a bullet in the chamber is capable of killing. When it's just there people pay attention to the casing on the hip. Dad says they are in the midst of problem solving logistics. "We have to procure a wheelchair," he says, the force of his voice compromised with a slight rasp that shows his wear. "I don't know what to expect with the dexameth and radio surgery," he continues. "No telling the effects. I'm very unsteady. My left foot is moving like I have a stroke. The tumor is shrinking, changing. It's working, I'm sure. I sense changes."

"What kind of changes?" I ask.

"Right now for the worse."

"How's your eyesight?"

"A *leeeetle* bit blurry. It's nice to be able to watch TV and understand. Stupid Lakers lost yesterday against Memphis. The Kid is not the same guy. He misses shots, dribbles the ball off his feet. My head is clear, my spirit is good, definitely good. My foot is dragging. Three more surgeries should make a difference. Big difference."

I get off the phone and scream, *face value, bitch!*

Toots is still on about how "It's really bad," but the doctors say he could have two months or a year. "It's just a matter of time before his body will develop more tumors," she says.

Wait. I have tours to give and I have to get a bartender.

The next time I talk to Dad I can't get the telephone cord to untwist so I draw my head to the receiver and smash it on our seventeenth-century fireplace. Casual. Hannah comes back from an errand just in time to wipe the blood from my eyes.

"We don't have too much experience with this sort of thing. There's a doctor backing up the decisions. So I feel good about that. Today he zapped me a very long time. It didn't do anything yet, but maybe in the long term. In the meantime, I've lost a lot of strength in my lower extremities so I'm not doing so well. Hospice is all for free. Medicare pays for everything. The wheelchair, everything. I'm gonna get stuff. I don't know what for. So… yeah…I get very tired. All these things happening is emotional."

"Hang in there," I tell him.

"That's all I can do…And eat. When you're on dexameth, everything tastes good."

65

Barbecue charcoal grill. Heated up grass and soil. The sky in late day. Coconut lotion. Clouds passing, shade to sun, sun to shade. Walking through dry air to the front yard hose, flowers, hibiscus. Headphones sounding out, "*Life I've always wanted…Mountains o' things.*"

Drawn into my fantasy, I can hear Dad with his old work on the line, saying, "I'd like you to know that I'm still on this side."

Days go by with the same conversations. Dad is stable, but he's finished his treatment so he's in hospice. Em would like less congestion at her place. I left six weeks ago and now she complains that her house is hijacked and she doesn't feel like she has any privacy. Dad drops the most mundane acorns of thought and then a forest grows out of them. "When you get up here we'll go to the house and check it out," he says. "The address light went caca so I put a new neon fixture. We'll take some things to the house. Take some things away."

"We'll have a nice time."

"I don't have a nice time anymore. I have time. I'm not suffering. My life as I know it changed completely. I'm an invalid. I pee in a urinal. I can't get around. I'm in hospice. That doesn't mean I'm dying immediately. It means that I need help."

"What's the conclusion to the story of the catheter?"

"*Go a-way,*" he says, stressing every syllable. "I'm not interested. It goes into your pishy and it has a condom."

"It's a catheter."

"It's a catheter in the rye."

Toots tells me, "I don't have a life. No life. Not me. Nothing. Now we have to buy diapers for Dad. This is just really hard. I feel like I flew to Israel and I just can't get past the jetlag. It's hard. It's really hard. I'm up at six and it's go time. Em says, 'Here, help him brush his teeth, I'm going to walk the dog.' I have to be the strong one for everything, everything. He can't stand salty food. I'm losing it. I'm sure you know. But it's easier when he can move. I'm just a wreck. There's nothing else I can say. Hurry up and get your fuckin' ticket is all."

Toots checks in with Dad. He hasn't moved from his sliver of the couch. She offers him my mom's oatmeal cranberry cookies. Sugar free!

I'm still wondering, "It can't go in the other direction?"

"No Ghi, no," Toots tells me, "and Em is saying, 'I'm not his maid, not his doctor, not his housekeeper. I am his partner and I want him to enjoy his time.'"

Meanwhile, by the looks of the nearly empty box in the fridge, she likes the cookies just as much as him.

"You've all decided there's no way he's going to improve?" I ask.

"No. Maybe he'll be able to get into his walker."

I prefer to speak to my Dad. He reports that the weather is very nice and the flowers smell good. Apparently it'll take six weeks for the radiation to respond on a cellular level, so we'll have to wait. But Dad believes he's been lucky so far. "No bleeding or nausea."

My scooter crashed into a garbage truck. A plate fell to the kitchen floor while I was drying it. A woman tripped over a suitcase in the metro and landed on her wrists. The metro wobbled on its rails. I want to believe I have been lucky, too.

66

My aunt in L.A. gives me a pep talk: It reminds me what happened to my mom before she died, but this is life and this is what happens and we have to do what we can. You know it's really tough to be a daughter or to be a son, but this is what it is. It's all up to God now. It's in His hands. I have a feeling the radiation made him worse and that when the effects go away he'll be better. That's just speculation. Life is beautiful. Take care of each other…Do you know tonight that the lottery is more than a half billion? Six hundred and fifty million. You get three hundred million clear after taxes. They tell you what to do with the winning ticket. You don't let anybody sign it. Anyway. Maybe tonight. Maybe tonight.

67

Hannah and I bring a bottle of Pierre Perpignan to our friend Eva's housewarming party. I hope that it's decent. There are a few things that I want to be able to do better at a party and one of them is have fun. I stand in the kitchen and zone out with a sedated kind of munch-and-sip attitude. I am not smooth in French, but I give it a go. Preparing things to say is not my thing. In English

I don't use premeditated openers; the words usually pass my lips before I can catch up to my voice. So I tell myself when I see someone I'll just ask them if they're having a good time. Is that a distinctly American question? It's just that I'm far too invested in life to back away from conversations. All I can think when I'm trying to think of something of a French equivalent is *"C'est bon pour toi?"* or *"Est-ce que tu passes un bon moment?"* Both questions are weird. Actually, "how's it going?" or *"ca va?"* is the best I can do for now. But I'd rather shoot myself in the face than relent to the basic. I make some technical effort instead. (I tell you we have only so long, I want to say something that cuts and blends.)

The question I ask anyone within striking distance is 'How's it going? How do you know Eva?' but I'm already getting bored with myself and I really resent that I can't bring any life into this party. My first conversation doesn't do it. So there's someone else in the tiny kitchen, leaning against the same counter—a tall brunette who is part of Eva's political party ensemble, who overhears me telling a woman about my dad and then laboring twice as hard over lines about how I'm getting married soon. I barely make out her pupils for all the mascara around her eyes, but I'm looking. When I'm back to standing on my own, searching the narrow hall before me as if to convince myself there is something interesting about it, the brunette interrupts my stretch to tell me, *"Tu n'est pas coupable."* You are not guilty. She looks me right in the eyes and she says, "We all have our original frustration." And then she walks away.

APRIL

68

One day we're sitting in the sun working on the wedding menu—duck and ground veal with a Sancerre—I'm sneaking away to look for a ring and listening to my dad swallow saliva late night over the telephone, then, before I can point my pinkie, I'm at Charles de Gaulle airport distracted from the anxious wait by the shrill laughter of a Spanish woman with severe blonde coils in her hair. She boasts of having met a French man while she was on holiday with her boyfriend. Apparently, she wore her sheer top out with him to Paul Bert last night, which is right around the corner from where I live, and they actually sat to dinner with five other French men, all of them sure that their first bottle of wine was too young, but the second was "like sex," and then in the middle of dinner she felt like having a cigarette so she left them with their steak frites to buy a pack in the Bastille and never went back. "Was it worth losing my relationship? You have to ask my boyriend about that," she says.

My flights to LAX are last minute standby, thanks to a friend. Dad wants me to make it for the first seder, but I am going to be delayed because the connection in Minneapolis is way overbooked.

I called him this morning and he says he's keeping his fingers crossed for Hannah's exam, he'll even say a prayer although he doesn't believe in it. I tell him that Mom flew in from New York and she and my aunt want to visit him and help however they can. He reacts saying, "This is the end of my life and they have to understand that I want to live it the way that I want to live. I don't want this happy get together because it's not. I don't want to get calls from her because it upsets me. You work it out with your mother's sister the way that you want it to while you're with her. A guy comes to take me on a walk. A Mexicano, a friend of Lachacha's. Fifteen dollars an hour. He'll help me, if all works out well. I have somebody from hospice come bathe me."

"How do you do it? With your bathing suit on?"

"Naked like a chicken. She's a caregiver, so what do I care. The guy who walks me is worth it. Toots needs to work so she sits at Buckbucks."

Before boarding my flight I talk to Mom in L.A. and she says, "The funny thing is that he did to me more than I did to him. I'm sorry for this hard time. It was thirty years ago. I really came for him and for Toots. I wanted to see him and make him feel better. If he doesn't want to see me I don't want to push it. When your father dies in front of you it's difficult. I wish you guys have good times with your father. I take things as I see them. I don't want to make any show. He's the right to live his life the way he wants to. Another thing—are you getting used to the idea that you're going to be a married man? You're not excited?"

69

What I can't do is let go of the tension in my chest. It comes from thinking too much and not feeling enough. All the world comes in through the senses, so when your senses start to fail you, you live in a smog conjuring what made you feel intensely alive once. Well, slow death must do something like that. We're living on the clock. We're all our own clockmaker setting the gears to stay ahead of our fate. I'm trying to keep my spirit raised on high. Everything is dulled by time even as I believe I can live time again. I seek insight. I walk miles just to get somewhere closer to this life I'm living. I know I'm all out there where everything has come from. Like searching for a lemon tree on a glacier, I'm interested in the unattainable. It's the only thing that makes sense to me. Everything else is too soon an exit, too serious, or too far removed.

70

Back in the USA with Dad we eat the second Seder and make plans before I'll head to the small bed at the condominium that night and fall asleep singing to myself.

Dad does not want his usual after-dinner tea. "How do you explain that I don't like tea? I don't tolerate any tea."

"We have all the day tomorrow," says Em.

"I don't have anything," Dad answers. "You always have your thing."

Em takes me aside. "Hospice says this is what happens. He's just gonna get weaker and weaker and then he's just gonna stay in bed. They're gonna be here again. I guess this is the point. I just can't do this again."

"Why does this happen more at night than during the day?" I ask and never get an answer.

When Em leaves to her bedroom, Dad says, "It hurts me that she doesn't feel like she has her life."

On TV there's a special memorial for Mike Wallace who just died. Dad's watching closely. "How sad," he says. "He had all the money in the world and he had to die at the care center. You want to die with your family around you."

Dad tells me a random story about how his motorcycle ran out of gas in the 70s. "It was that time. A guy with a truck stopped and helped me. I thanked him. People want to do nice things for each other, mostly. Em's so regimented. She says she has all day, but it's bullshit. Every time she makes a plan I kind of laugh at it."

Em comes back, "Hello Biki. What are you doing, Bika?" She walks through the living room to the front yard.

"This is not an effective way to communicate," Dad says. "She's not an effective communicator."

Together she and Dad walked all over the place for two or three years. Now this is it. She shows signs of her own discomfort.

"I don't know how long I'm gonna last here. She's losing her patience," Dad says.

We talk about Dad's brothers coming to San Diego to see him for what may be their last time together. Em starts in, "Do I want all these people coming into my house? No I do not. But this is what it is. I had a terrible day today. I can't do it. I want to be there for you and cook for you, but I cannot. I'm constantly worried. I don't want to be in the shower and worry about you every time. I can't do it alone."

I confirm that I understand she wants either Toots or me to be here at all times.

"I cannot. I have to live my life. I love you but it's too much for one person to cook, to order medicine, walking, pushing him in the street. I cannot take care of Moli." That's her name for Housedog.

71

I'm watching Dad go after his pills, the smaller one first ('this one tastes shit'), all seven, in size order, telling him details about the wedding. He just gets done explaining "You don't have time for friends when you're older." I say, I wish you could have met my friends. You would have been proud of me. He has his eyes closed and is pointing at the stereo speaker, "Bolero by Ravel."

"Peer Gynt Suite," I say, just because.

"Bolero by Ravel. This is a very important piece. Listen for the addition of new instruments with each verse. The piece starts with one instrument on stage and each enters. At the end you have a cacophony. I should say polyphony because a cacophony is discordant. It's also a good way to learn the instruments. You can recognize them. This is a tremendous effect. They'll change from minor key to major."

"When?"

"You'll notice."

72

An act of the imagination should not be entirely isolated from what is possible, though the farther one moves from the logical expectation the less the expectation rules him. The guts shift about, fear takes to the back of the mind, the clever choreography offers reason for continued faith. A thrill- or pleasure-seeker creates conditions by which he guarantees the unexpected and feels himself moving back and forth in time until time disappears altogether in the fit. He lives in his imagination and manages to rule over time, making time relative to shifts in body chemistry. We want more time, but what we have we need to qualify. Imagination is a source of delaying gratification. It's a way to slow down time. Each of us already expresses to some degree the unformed ideas that grow inside of us. He who is ruled by logic is moved by straight lines and right angles; he can turn corners in a system that was established before him with only a vague notion of him. Those who build their own roads imagine and redesign from what exists. When you want to head out in new directions from the one-horse town you created, you have to offer something up; not something you can live without, but something that lives within.

73

Em is breaking down. We are in crisis over these absorbent briefs and when the hospice nurse arrives we turn to the homecare conversation. Both ideas disturb Dad. He wants to wear his *calzonis*. Em gets a chance to reveal her state of mind to Dad's nurse and the nurse validates her feelings about interrupted sleep. Dad feels as healthy as last time. Stronger even. His mood is good. The Nurse says, "No telling how it's going. Sometimes people turn a corner. I don't think it takes ten years but it takes more than two weeks. It's good that you have care coming to you. What brings you joy will also determine your course."

"I'm going to my mountain home soon," Dad says.

In her talk about being prepared she mentions "dignity therapy, looking over your life, seeing moments you are most proud of," and Dad starts making faces, saying, yeah, yeah, "I don't need anybody holding my hand. I've reviewed my life. I've got no misgivings or regrets."

Em leaves to her music class and we discuss her adjustment.

"Is she afraid of you passing in her presence?" the nurse asks. We don't respond. "You need to have a plan in place if the dynamics start to change."

This is just all feeling, feeling, feeling. The last thing they always ask is about pain and bowel movements. You turn feeling into emotion and emotion into the sounds animals make, the raw and natural, and you get music. It doesn't say everything, but it's about everything.

74

Dad gives me his marriage speech: Marriage is like a house. It takes dedication. Then his computer starts singing and on video chat he tells his brother Ronen that he wants to be cremated. Ronen mentions Dad's connection to Israel and starts in about bringing his body back. Their eyes are watering. "I thought you could have a little thing whoever comes to spread the ashes. It's not happening tomorrow or two days from now." If you promise, Ronen says. They laugh. "But it's happening. Don't let me talk about it more." Let's talk about something nice, Ronen says, and goes on about the things they accomplished in the old days. Dad says, "There's no limit to what we could do to raise the standard of living and education. No country hates war more." He says, "That's something I chose to leave early and I can't regret it. That spirit of the fifties is gone."

I know I need to book rooms and plan his brothers' visit pronto.

In Pioneer Park there are lots of smells, mostly you smell the seeds, everything blooming. I'm pushing Dad around in the chair and I ask him if the fifties were innocent.

"Not so much in Israel. It was after the forty-eight war, the refugees already came. In fifty-six there was the Sinai Campaign that closed the Suez Canal, so the British and French were involved. Together we kicked their butts. We attacked them from the desert. They threw off their shoes and ran backwards. You should see how many shoes were left in the desert."

I mention what Assad is doing in Syria.

"Sometimes it takes a killer for a society to confront its ills. What do they teach in school? 'An eye for an eye, a tooth for a tooth.' They don't teach you to respect life. The only thing that is sacred is you don't touch a human life. Revenge is pointless. The objective of every war is peace. He can rehearse whatever he has in his head, but nobody is born a killer. This evil has to be stopped. I was raised in Israel. Every one of our parents were survivors of the Holocaust. We were not taught to kill Germans. No, we were taught to defend yourself when you need to. There's this guy who wants to start a hwolocaust, how long will we wait until he does it? Who starts these things, these chaos, this war? In some way it's already inside of us. We just need to hear the right thing to get it out. Oye, oye, oye, people have such ugly mouths. There is no need to recapture the pride. No need to own the earth. I like that song by the Beatles, you know, *Imagine there's no countries.* But everyone wants to be the new pioneers."

"Now it's about making it big on the Internet."

"The day I retired I had about XXX dollars. I wish I could've done better."

"What?" I ask.

"More money! More money! Oww," he squeals.

"What happened?"

"Something gave me a *schtoch.*" He points his finger at his ribs.

Every time we hit a patch of sun he enjoys it. "It's delightful. We're gonna do some sun worshipping today. They said that people who have more than fifty beauty marks on their back are much more prone to melanoma. I have hundreds."

"I always thought you were much more beautiful."

"Yeah, lucky me."

This is the guy in the window who schoolkids see peeing into a bottle when they're on their way home from school coaxing young love, caressing a Pee-Chee folder, slap boxing their best friend. They stop to see the man in the window. Awkward kisses, hand candy, superficial blabbblab and the man.

75

While prepping breakfast I consider the kibbutz life that my parents had and the fact that a horse is dirtier than a cow because it only has one stomach. Dad's flipping through a camping catalogue. He doesn't want anything on his matzo brie because he still maintains the Eastern European dream of bland food. He wants to know what's happening in the kitchen and I have to be calm. I quote him that the food's gonna be ready in approximately three minutes. "It's a very quiet cooking. I hear no sizzle," he says. Listen closely. It sounds like birds chirping.

After breakfast he says, "I've got a solution for when the kids are in France for the wedding."

"Ok, what's the solution?" Em asks.

"We can invite Atikva here."

"Aye, Atikva, You should've asked me. It's not only you and Atikva. It's you, me and Ativka for ten days."

"Let's talk about it. We didn't finalize it." Em takes a reflective pause. Dad has his toothpick going strong. "I was thinking ahead."

"The other day he was driving you crazy."

"Don't worry about me."

"We'll see when the time comes. I don't think it's very exciting."

"I didn't say exciting."

"Once Ghi leaves, who's gonna be here all the time. Who? Caretakers? I'm gonna live with strangers, with caretakers coming and going from my home?"

"Strangers or Atikva for ten days. They'll cook, clean, go to the market. You'll only need to order medication."

"But it's a lot. I love you dearly, but it's not the way that it was before. I don't want to feel people coming and going. T. doesn't sleep here—"

"Tell me what you would like to see, ideally. What if I go to the mountain with Atikva?"

"I'm not gonna let you go to the mountain. It's not a hospital. It's not a convalescent home. No, no, no. I'm not gonna leave you. I'm not abandoning you. You need me."

"But you say you need someone around the house."

"So Atikva?"

"But he's strong."

"I don't know him. I've met him four times in my life. You said your brother Yaniv. No, Yaniv is coming now. I don't want T. not to go to a wedding, I don't want Yaniv not to visit you now."

"He would do that. He would come from Israel."

"No, we'll do it together. We'll think of it later. We'll think of it on our own. I don't go to friends, I don't go anywhere. I stay here."

Later when Em comes out of her room her eyes are red. "Oh, I was just overtaken with emotion." She pauses. "We're going to do so many fun things in this room. This room will do a lot of good for a lot of people."

We rent a series Dad will like that we sit and watch together. It's about a paratroopers unit in the First World War. "Does this remind you of how you jumped?" I ask him.

He says, "I didn't forget."

"How many times did you jump?"

"Seven in the day, eight at night."

"You hated it?"

"I didn't."

No matter how many times I ask these kinds of questions they never really force their way into my identity.

The men in the series are up in the air not saying a word before they get dropped. No dialogue. Dad says, "I was weighed down more than this. The bazooka was an encumbrance, hardly fit through the door. You had to tilt it. Nowadays the weapons are different. These guys have no bazookas, no assault rifles."

"In war it's better to wound your enemy than to kill him? Really?"

"Yeah," Dad says, nodding his head. "It creates a burden."

There's a scene where a soldier witnesses someone close to him in his division get killed by a bomb. Dad tells me, "You can have an acute anxiety reaction that lasts minutes, hours, or days. This guy snapped out of it. Yeah, if your best friend is blown to bits it affects you immensely."

"How do you survive if you're the last one standing of your battalion?" This is a question I've thought about forever.

"You hide in a ditch."

"Do you think you can recover from that?"

"Yeah. It takes a long time, but you can recover."

It must be frightening to be in a ditch for a long time.

"They're that close you could hear them singing. We used to get so close in the Golan we could hear them talking."

"Didn't they act?" I ask.

"No because we didn't want to start a war. We were just lying in ambush, securing the kibbutz." Dad takes a look at Em asleep on the couch next to him. "Too bad we waited for her to watch. She has no interest in it."

You hide in a ditch because you have hope.

76

With no specific place to go and Mordechai Campbell on my mind, we've got time to head to Lake Murray. The wheelchair is a little heavy but I'll handle it. At Lake Murray the motion does us better. Em and I are taking turns pushing the chair and we get to talking about her father's homecare. She says that she fought with him for fifty years and he never accepted her, but being with Dad was the one thing she did right and it wiped the slate. Dad says he's glad that Toots turned out much more loving, tolerant and devoted. I tell him that she always had it in her. Em asks me why I want Hannah to convert? I tell her, Judaism is a source of my strength and I want to pass that down to my kids. I want to shape that with her. Somehow we mention my asshole ex-stepfather.

"Falling in love is a psychosis," Dad says. "With butterflies and bullshit."

I added that.

For dinner we pick up the boy and wheel Dad into what some food show called the best barbecue joint in California only to feast on some soulless tri-tip. I should have known better. Before we leave, I take a second look at our paper towel mess that covers the entire surface of a four-top table. At this point you can hardly squeeze enough out of the time you need. You can only be thrilled at what you have and what you do. You throw everything out there and let it stick. Don't try to leave with any of it.

When we get back home Em suggests the boy and I go out and have a drink instead of watching more TV with them.

"Why are you pushing drinks?" Dad says.

"Then go out and have a popsicle, have a glass of milk."

Em has her book club early tomorrow, but she stays up late to meet me at the door and tell me that Dad's down emotionally. "He said he's tired of it. This thing is getting to him. You saw that he was angry when you went to the bar. He hates that other people

around him can't have a life. It's getting to him that he can't do
what he wants on his own."

In my sleep that night I dream my bachelor party is disappointing. I'm the disappointing party.

77

Pepperdine calls and Dad tells them, "This isn't a good time. I have
two months to live." He takes exception to their call. "We were
the unrecognized bastards. We were the Watts campus. Behind
the fence." This was when my dad fell in love with my mom. I ask
him when was the last time he supported a cause.

"The Medrano circus in Tel Aviv came for six months. I knew
all the clowns and animals in the artistic community. They were
long on talent and short on cash. My parents looked down on it.
They were laborers and the artists were elite." He turns the subject
to the Ballet Russe and how Stravinsky tried to shock the audience
with *The Rite of Spring*: "They had a sophisticated audience and
wealthy patrons. It was so dissonant to the ears that they tried to
get us to listen to it and play it in school."

This is refreshing because we talk about caregivers nearly fifty
percent of the time we open our mouths now. Em has a morbid
fear of being left alone. Dad tells me, "The oncologist already said
goodbye. He has no other drugs for me. It will be good. Sometimes Em cries and sometimes she laughs. She can't cancel out her
life all day, all day." Dad looks back at me to see what I'm doing.
"What's sure is that I have a house on the mountain and there
I am the commander. They have everything on the mountain."

The boy joins us for lunch at Dizzy's Deli because we don't
insist that we need the time alone. Dad's going heavy on the gefilte
fish and I'm cringing. He tells us, "In the old days people didn't
have money. I guess you look at me the way we looked at our
parents. They would boil chicken legs and eggs, put it in gelatin,

throw away the legs, keep the meat and the yellow stuff on the legs, put it in a mold and eat it. When there isn't much food you do what you have to do. Your children eat the chicken, you eat the gelatin. And you eat the head of the carp, the whole thing, the brain."

At the next table this old guy tells his granddaughter, "When you're quiet, frogs can't hear you."

"What about God?" she asks.

"He can hear everything. He can hear you breathing."

"Wow," says the little girl.

I ask Dad how his brother Yaniv is doing. "Ah, Yaniv, Yaniv is in the nineteenth century with his one telephone and no other devices. Everybody's doing okay. Everybody with their own problems, of course. Yaniv conveys emotions. I don't need emotions."

We take the remainder of Dad's chopped liver to go and use some of it to catch another skunk.

Dad brings it out again for his dinner. I make faces I almost never make anymore. "You don't know how good it is," he says. That's the refrain I've heard all my life.

"You ever have chicken livers, Dad?"

"A-ha," he says, mouth full about to swallow.

"You like it?"

"Hate it. It's an acquired taste." He's licking his knife clean. "Mmm, it's good," he says. "Mmmm, good." He asks Em, "Do you like chopped liver? You sure you don't want any?"

"No. Yuck. Do you spread it on bread like butter?"

"No."

"It smells very bad, like a very dark secret that a homeless man is carrying with him."

"The sky is opening," Dad says.

I'm thinking about Uncle Danny who climbed into his sleeping bag with all those baby frogs and never knew it that summer up at camp.

"You're all smiles today," Em says to Dad. "I like the mood you're in."

"It's the chopped liver," he says.

78

My mom and aunt call me from a hundred and twenty miles away.

"We don't think the suit you chose will be good for the wedding. This suit looks like you're going out to a party. Dark blue can benefit you better. This one is not for a wedding. I would like to see you in a more elegant, more classic suit. Sometimes plain looks better in pictures…One color will never clash with a dress…Oh, no, no, no, it has nothing to do with the Plaza Hotel…I don't see it on you at a wedding…No, no, no, no, as I see it, it's not good for a wedding. Dark blue or black."

"Dark blue is an upgrade from jeans," I say.

"You don't have to buy it. I'm coming two weeks in advance and we can go together…I have a really fancy dress. I might change it. I don't want to be more classy than the groom…It's boring if you don't wear a good suit…You're getting married, you're not going to a party…The white stitching, I don't like it at all. It makes it look sporty. Well, whatever."

My aunt gets on the phone, "You can wear a part of the blue suit in combination with other things. Wear whatever looks comfy and good…This suit looks a little outdated. The fifties stitching is not classy. Wear one with a collar that looks more classy. The stripes look Hicksville, hickey." She's laughing at the sound of the word. "A navy jacket goes with jeans. I like it with khaki. That's elegant and classic. You can wear a tie with it that brings everything out…This suits strikes me like someone from the Midwest. Like a leisure suit. You need elegant. Stripes is too common. I love navy blue because you can wear it much more…So this is my opinion. Pick up a nice shirt, pink or grey, a nice tie. Stripes are too simple."

"I think the other way around."

"You're the one who has to decide."

Dad says, "You know what your mother did to me for the wedding forty-some years ago? Dark blue. That's what she wanted me to buy and the rest is history. Dark blue makes you look like an Ambassador. They have their taste from fifty-years-ago Israelis."

It's this ballast you know you're going to miss in your life. And you know no matter what comes into your life, you'll have to find your own, even when you have kids.

79

Em tells me, "You can start interviewing on Monday. I'm not gonna be here alone overnight." Dad cycles back to, "What're we gonna do when you're gone, Ghi? We have to find out her needs." We make a list of what we want a caretaker to do: light cleaning, shopping, cooking, general care.

In a watch store at the mall that afternoon, Dad's struggling a little in the heavier wheelchair making obscure faces, non-verbal gestures, questioning, discerning what he could get if he were to trade up for his watch. "Which would you want?" he asks me. "I'm just toying with them. If you want a watch."

"I'm not interested," I say.

"No, huh?"

"I'm not interested in time. I have to be though."

The counter rep is talking to her colleague. She has pink painted collagen lips and false eyelashes. "You'll see," Dad tells me, "she'll come out with a ridiculous price. You'll see, they'll run the serial number and know exactly where I bought it. Oh, they've got Ekors."

"I like that black one," I say.

"When I was young a watch was something that was very—"

"Vanguard?"

"Holy."

"Why?"

"They were in high regard. People were very proud. That's what you got for your Bar Mitzvah. Oh, I hate these colors. It looks cheap. Look at me, I'm done wearing fancy stuff. I'm just checking out the fashions. Think we should go check out the fashions at home first."

On the way out of the mall I stop in a Department Store to look at shoes for my suit. Dad says, "I don't know who's your consultant, I really don't like the shoes in tan. This is the right color for your suit. For me, if I were buying it." He's on the black shoes.

We get to his car. He licks his finger to check a scratch on the driver side door. The method of getting into the car is still fairly basic. He holds onto me and the safety handle and I lever him in there. Dad says, "With my soul I feel I can get up and go but my body tells me, uh uh."

At home, Dad wants me to try on some of his clothes and I oblige him. We start with a navy suit jacket that he got from G&R Clothiers. His immediate reaction is, "It's a nice one. It's an immaculate one. Beautiful. It's really exquisite." He sees me hesitate and I'm not sure if that modifies his position or makes him more objective. "It looks pretty good on you. You have to bring out the sleeve." I ask him why he doesn't plan on wearing it at all. "I'm done with it," he says, "Don't argue with me."

It was a fashion show and then it became slightly morbid.

I try on a few shirts, parading around the bedroom with the checked Bill Bila, saying the collared short sleeve shirt is very California dude ("Well, that's who you are"), questioning if the blue Monte Napa was twenty bucks ("No, that one's at least fifty. I bought it on Dizingoff. Laurel said *you got to buy it*. It's made in Italy. Looks good on you).

Dad gets upset. "Stop making fun. I'm in a serious mood and

you're in a silly mood. I want to give you some good shirts and you're making fun of them." I remind him how this morning he told me that I have a big nose. Anyhow, I calmed down just in time for the Tommy Bahamas knockoff.

"You know how much I paid for this?" Twenty dollars. "No, fifteen. It was on sale. This was the last one, so they sold it for fifteen to get it out. It probably was thirty-five because Bendelton aren't cheap shirts. I said, for fifteen dollars I'm buying it right now. In Lake Arrowhead."

I let out a whistle like one of those stick whistles.

"Wear it on your honeymoon."

"We don't have a honeymoon."

"You will."

"Where should we go?"

"Follow your heart. Follow your sweetheart." He proceeds to give me a short list before showing me the rest of the clothes. After the Guayvera from San Miguel de Allende and the Swiss Army shirt from Livingston, New Jersey, he hands me a belt. "This belt is from Guadalajara. Give it to your first born son."

He wheels himself back to the closet.

"And lastly, here's my Russian mafia leather jacket. You got to lose weight. There's no room for the gun."

"What?"

"Yeah, that's what all the Russian mafia wear. It's not a prophecy, it's a promise. You got to strengthen your stomach muscles and lose fat. This is the time when I gained all the fat in the belly. And I recognize it. But if you want the coat it's yours. It's made in Jerusalem. When Atikva gave it to me I had it reconditioned, painted and squared. As far as length, it's your size. You have to lose the stomach because you're getting the famous 𝒪𝓂𝓂𝓂, stomach. You can't afford it. It's for your health and for your looks. If you don't take care of yourself your wife is going to leave you."

80

We're in code orange. Dad's got to use the toilet. He's blowing the pressure on his bladder out of his mouth in a huge gust—"Shew-wwww"—but it's not working. "Aye, aye, aye." Code Red. He makes it to the small toilet then comes out handing me his wet shirt to put in the wash. Just then Hannah calls me upset after another late night out. Seven a.m. late. She says, "Just two minutes of *me*," just that, and this is ten minutes to noon and it's food time and shower time and pee time and the news that V's got degenerate friends time. I tell her, "One thing is, you've got to own your experiences so that the day can't shift and take them away. You've got to own them with your imagination and through your soul. You can't allow things to diminish what we have. In every part of me there are all my parts." Then we hang up.

Dad continues telling me about V and about his first bicycle ride on Asher Gelmer's full-size girl's bicycle.

"When I learned how to ride better, we went on big streets and the rest is history. He was a good friend."

"But you lost touch with him?"

"Oh yeah. I'm not really good at keeping in touch."

"What does that mean?"

"Oh, I never really kept in touch with old friends. Look at Bobby and Udi, I haven't seen them for ten years."

When I get the shirt in the wash, Em catches me and says, "You see, it's hard. A lot of work. Nobody's complaining, but we're not caretakers."

After that we decide that it's probably better if Dad always goes to the bathroom in his chair.

Dad tells me, "You're gonna be a better, more stable person when you're married." He says he would've like to be a physician. I ask why and he says, "It's not a job. It's a calling. It's a real career. If I had money, I wouldn't have gone to L.A. City College, I would have gone to UCLA. They accepted me. Pre-med, pre-dentistry. I thought it would be a good thing because of my weakness in math. You do what you do because of the way it makes you feel about yourself. But you got to have accolades if your career is in entertainment. Otherwise you're delusional."

I help dad get on two feet for a little after that bit of motivation. "Look at this shit," he says. "I'm walking. I'm walking!"

On our afternoon walk, Em takes the chair more than half of the way up and down sidewalks and past the manicured front yards, and mentions no less than five times that it's a good idea to have help. I ask Dad if he wants a man or a woman. He says someone who's compassionate because everything like that is hard.

"It's hard emotionally as well as physically. But we have to take things as they come and enjoy things. You know what I mean?"

The heaviness descends that evening when we find out that the United States is out of the space flying business. I get a feeling like the one I used to get at Dad's old apartment with the black and white Zenith. I want to stop about caretakers. I can't hear any more talk about dying. I finally understand Hannah's belief in science. It takes dreamers who want to go to Mars and meet Martians.

81

Dad says Jews don't believe in talking about dying. They're praying for good things. He tells me, it's the Jewish way of deflecting, but you have to get into the real meat. I'm in the Natural Foods Store buying groceries, maybe taking a little more time than it should to get what I need, arresting my thought process. When I get home I catch Dad peeing in the living room.

"You're standing up by yourself. What if you'd fallen and you couldn't get up?"

"It would be sad," he says, adding an audible "*hee, hee,*" with his eyes all lit up and sparkling like sunshine on the lake.

The situation here needs fixing. I take a few seconds to make sure that we are all alone so I can talk about Em's fears.

"What do you want us to talk about there? I'm eventually going to deteriorate and die."

"But she can relate her own feelings about that."

"I don't know what she's saying. She never finishes a sentence."

Em appears out of nowhere and gets me in the small room to say, "I know I'm gonna be here like a soldier if nobody else wants to be here like a soldier."

I tell her we have homecare for when she's in Mexico.

She doesn't relent.

"I'm not impressed with T. placing limits on what she can do. When the uncles come, tell her that she's responsible for the lunches, outings, and dinners. Suddenly she says, 'I'm sleeping in the condo. I need four hours a day.' No, I'm not working for you. I didn't know that we're interviewing to use homecare. But the last two years, I'm not impressed. This started in January 2009. Where were you? The boy is all kissy kissy with T. and I'm telling him you got to support me."

"It's not us versus them," I offer.

I have reason to think we are through, but we are not. This continues for some more torturous moments and then I go back to talking to Dad in a hushed tone. He says, "She can't leave anything undone. She's compulsive about the loose ends."

"Aren't we doing all we can do?"

"By me yes, by her no. Basically she wants you around twenty-four seven. She has a limited ability or willingness to give any more than she wants to give. Not many girlfriends would have stuck with the situation. She's vowing to stay with me to the last and she's not going to do it alone."

"But the caretaker doesn't fit in?"

"No, Toots or you, that's her sincere wish. Because with a caretaker it's not so simple to say, 'tell me that I'm right, even when I'm wrong."'

Depression hits in minimal waves as Em begins to show signs of turning. She talks about doing what she's done because that's what she's supposed to do. I think it's only a matter of time before she deviates completely.

Dad says, "Tell me when I have to pack my bags and go to the mountain."

I'm on it now. I go to the small room and let Toots know Em's pissed off at her. Em comes back in without warning.

"He's not going up to Lake Arrowhead. If that's okay with T., that's not okay with me." Then she walks her dog, comes back to run the dryer, gets onto the computer, and leaves again without a word.

I've experienced this kind of inconsistent hostility between two individuals in my childhood. This is partly my memory: You slow play it, get on your bike, go over to somebody's house, jump in the pool if you can, listen to the stereo. Every song is two-and-a-half minutes. Then you get back to your room and worry about how it will proceed; figure out how to leave that room and make things okay again. What happens is that you have to put yourself on the side.

Em doesn't want productive interviews with the care providers (she's already said she doesn't want a stranger in her house) and Dad isn't really interested, either. She's all over the place cleaning the house, dropping comments, and he's on the phone telling someone, "Nothing is forever. I'm stable in my condition. No change in it. I'm pretty happy in it. I'm in hospice. It's the final station. It could last months or it could last forever." Truth be told, I'm thinking about the wedding: the rabbi showing up, but me not being able to get there.

"No, Ghi. We have to be really careful. What, let's just to give you an example, what if someone comes here, leaves the door open and Moli runs out of the house. I'll kill them. You know what I mean? I'll kill them."

But what was my dream last night? I was going to be married to the wrong Hannah or all the décor was wrong. The rabbi was looking around for me and I wasn't there. I wasn't there because I couldn't be. I couldn't show up. And there's the matter, there's the matter entirely. Am I going to —

"It would be nice to go for a walk. It would be nice to go for a walk. To get out of the house." Em wants to get out of the house but she's already been out of the house. I'm a grown man with grown man problems and the calculated obsessiveness is killing me.

Dad needs his urinal. "Quickly quickly, before I pee in my hands."

I'll be damned if I don't keep a dose of something or other around for self-medicating. I find a place to stand and close my eyes.

"We want to go on a walk," Dad says, handing me his half-inch of light colored urine in a plastic bottle, adding, "And I could have some ice cream."

I need perspective. If I were the Congressman from Michigan I could conduct this very differently. Everyone would be less critical about my process.

Tomorrow will be different. The trees will fidget in a different direction.

Well, we have the weekend ahead of us.

Dad won't let me pack his stuff for the mountain in my bag. He's got to pack his. He's disgusted with his condition. He says he can't take disability too well. It gets to him. So after a day like this, when I'm cutting pills around midnight, thinking how Hannah feels "like a beached whale" because we really don't have conversations of substance anymore, and Em's idea of saying goodnight is telling me, "I still don't know how we're going to do this," I've got to get out and run.

I leave through the front door and drive the freeway and main streets to the condo taking time to watch the lights around me, wanting to do something different to break the routine.

82

I don't pass the teeth-brushing mark before I hear Dick Clark dies. What I need is to be a man, smoke some cigarettes, have that late night stop. I could go to a bar. I want to be recognized, self-affirm. I think about calling Hannah instead. That's what I do.

We almost have the worst conversation ever because I'm nervous we'll have the worst conversation ever.

"What is it," she says. I imagine her in our apartment looking into the distant window light. "Is everything okay?"

I start saying some things in French.

"Oh mon amour, je t'aime tellement forte," she strings together. It's a wonder she still talks to me at all. "Why don't you tell me what's happening?" she asks.

I don't because I don't want to talk about it. I don't know how to talk about it. Dad's ways are running me ragged. I want to be deranged and speak in tongues, risk everything and not face any consequences. I can't tell her why. I don't know myself. How do I tell her about my dad pissing in the living room today shouting, *I shpritzed on the couch, demmit!* when I don't have the energy or vocabulary to turn the tragic into comedic. So I'm laughing hysterically deep inside myself and I go in the kitchen to wet a paper towel with soap, but I don't hand it to him, I lob it across the room and it hits him on the bill of his hat and falls to the floor. He yells. Then I see him wiping where he peed, with his nose in the cushion, and he gets excited, *Okay. It doesn't stink, doesn't nothin'. It will dry. There'll be no smell!* How's that my telephonic transmission?

I need to reflect and package my emotions, otherwise I start saying things I don't mean.

"We're just going on the same rotation. No taste for settling in," I tell Hannah. "Every day we're going to the mountain and we're leaving the mountain. We never relax." I need to give her exact words because the reason I'm losing it is in the details. "My dad says, 'Things used to be so much easier.' Processing information and problem solving is different for him now. Then Em comes to me again, and this is what control is really all about, she tells me that she feels like she needs someone in the house from seven-thirty a.m. to six-thirty p.m. I wish I were President of something, so she'd just tell me once and it would be taken care of. This is not the one-way train to Helsinki here."

"So you know, everything you're doing is the total opposite of what you're saying right now."

This is where I start arguing because I've used up all her time talking to discover what I really mean and I'm aware she has to start her morning so she can get to work on time. After our conversation, when I get out my notebook and take a moment to think, I write: *I can't, we're not living. I don't want to live this way. I don't want you to die this way.*

"Don't forget J.D. Salinger," Dad says when we're packed and ready the next afternoon. I'm thinking, life by template, that's not the way I live, but here he reminds me that it is. Toots pushes the wheelchair outside on the porch. He asks, what's the plan?

Everybody has a different need so we arrive on the mountain at five and we're leaving tomorrow at two.

"The daffodils came out and got zapped by the snow," Dad notices.

Em says, "I'm not coming to live up here."

"It's a nice house," I say.

"Yeah, too bad we can't take it to San Diego," Dad says.

83

When Laurel and Dad were together they thought about building a cottage and after looking at empty lots came up with idea of redesigning the cabin. Dad actually found a mug with a picture that resembled what they were going for and he doodled a rough draft while at a continuing education class. But the contractor estimates far exceeded what he had in mind, so Laurel sat down with graph paper and she drew the dimensions of the existing cabin on one sheet and the addition of a master bedroom and office on another sheet and then slid the two pieces of graph paper together so that the space between the new entry and the addition matched up perfectly. It took engineers and contractors about nine months, with the usual amount of aggravation, delays in the actual construction, and compromises, but overall Dad was very, very happy with the results.

84

Dad is like, Oh please, I don't want to listen to a story right now. I don't want to listen to a story. I want to sit on the couch and hear classical music and have you sitting beside me waiting on my every whim. I'm trying to read through *Nine Stories*. Everybody else is wherever they are with their career and that's pissing me off now because I've managed this massive grey area in my earning potential for years and the logic of living without serious work is starting to come apart. I want to stop and focus on how lucky I am to spend time with my dad, but Toots is responding to me with 'you're too heavy, it's too heavy,' and I'm thinking to myself, with strain in my chest, you know why I can't be your friend right now? I'm a stiff, a walking stiff. I can't look you in the eyes. Please, please, please, give me a way to look. Help me see past our gripes and pains. You think I came all the way from France to clean out the fridge, hear about the stock market, empty a urinal. I've got no tolerance for this.

We're only on "Down at the Dinghy," and it takes a lot to listen to a story. Most people can't.

Dad picks up a call. He asks me to write some numbers down and dictates them. "My uncle Jay is *desperate* to talk to me. My secretary Deb called. He called the office. Didn't know any other number. I really don't want to talk to him."

"So don't call him," I say.

"He's my uncle. Never did anything bad to me."

"You didn't want to see my mom."

He picks up the phone, calls the first number, and gets Jay, aka Yakov, from the living room of his sunny L.A. home.

Listening to the small talk is like getting over rug burns. "No good, no good," Dad says. Em is just back from a trip to the shoe store. The sound of the front door makes me yield to a more neutral manner. "I went into pension last July. I paid into it all these years. They'll get away with murder." The conversation comes to a close with false notes.

Dad hangs up. "They're *desperate* to talk to me! Idiots."

"Did he have anything to say?" I ask.

"Doesn't matter. Really doesn't matter. Upsetting."

Dad calls to Em. "I talked to Yakov this second."

"What happened?" she asks.

"He says, 'I don't reach you anywhere.' He says, 'there's no communication.' He had surgery on his back, pains in his chest."

"What I'm interested in is not Yakov. It's how you're doing."

"You know what would make me happy?" Dad asks me reading a card Em brought from the mail. "Shaving. I don't want anybody to shave me. Nobody shaves me. I shave myself. Ghi, I need you to do a few things for me. I need you to help me. Get the razor from the bathroom. Okay, you can throw this card away."

"You didn't like it?"

"No, I liked it. I just don't keep them."

"Atikva! My idiot uncle called me today after years of being out of touch."

Dad's on the phone again because he has to call. He used to spend hours along the canals in the orange groves, with the magnolias and sunshine, but he can't go places. Plus, we're waiting on the nurse.

"I talked to Ronen today. They're all excited about coming. Odalie only cares about shopping. That's what she wants to do."

Moments later Dad tells me, "I start thinking he's not coming and this is not cool. So the question is, do I take a shower without him? You put me in, you take me out."

"No, this is his job."

"But he ain't here." He picks up his daily planner, lifts up his glasses and strains to make out the writing, mouthing, "I'll be damned. It's unbelievable that the nurse wouldn't show."

I pick up the planner to double check, deciding to tell him no matter we probably don't have enough time before the caretaker agency appointment. I ask him if he knows how to interview people.

He says, "I'm a psychologist."

I never made the association.

After choosing this caretaker by virtue of him being more actively engaged and an ex-marine, Dad gets on the phone with his cousin Howie whom I've never met, but have heard about; especially around the time that he worked at the White House. For all the talk of blood feuds on my mother's side of the family, I cannot forget how this family works: I met my dad's uncles once apiece and I've never met his cousins. I met Yakov in Los Angeles when we were still kids. Sam came to visit when he was on his last legs. He smelled like formaldehyde. He never went anywhere with his wife Jean. Not anywhere. Not even to a restaurant. Dad says, maybe that's why she's still alive at 102. Howie was an entomologist. He married a rich lady. Her stepson killed her son (in a car accident.) Howie's brother was a religious nut. Hebrew school valedictorian. His mother is skin and bones, 4'11. If she weighed 82 pounds she was lucky. Apparently wherever Howie goes he always stays in military bases, which would account for why he is calling from Ramstein.

"I know what's going to happen," Dad tells him, "I just don't know when. So slowly but surely. They told me I'll be confused, which is fine. Like Woody Allen said, 'I'm not afraid of dying but I don't want to be there when it happens.' I'll still be around when you come back from Europe. Aye, you know, life is a disease, age is a disease, you know…" The conversation continues with Howie saying, "whatever you guys need, no discussion…" Dad finally hangs up.

"I thought he would never let me off the hook. I'm not good at that, getting off line."

85

Six-thirty the next morning I journey from the condo to be told, "Yeah, this bagel tastes like shit because you didn't do it the way I like it. You take a bagel, put it in the microwave for fifteen seconds, cut it in half and put it in the toaster." I'm using worn-out words like *journey* because I'm starting to feel sorry for myself. That's my cue to shut up. Dad grumbles and grunts in the other room while I force myself to stay patient in the kitchen. "*Got demmit!*" Something fell, he says. He is constantly focused on controlling the damage, crumbs in his lap or otherwise. Dad would rather me shove an orange slice in his mouth than get his hands sticky.

I give him another bagel, "Is that good?"

"It's okay."

"Are you sure?"

"It's better than the other one."

"Is there something I can do better?"

"Well," he puts the bagel to his nose to smell it, "No, this is fine…Ah, this is good. The bagel is soft and edible."

I can already imagine the phone calls today, "*I had a bagel this morning. What a piece of shit. A brick.*"

Dad is chewing faster than a nutria rat and he starts talking in between heaves to catch his breath. "We have one little problem. May not be so little. No big deal. Em wants to visit her daughter next Friday and stay the night. I have to find a place for Housedog. Let's talk about that over lunch."

Em begins to turn the conversation into a question about where we can physically go in a crisis. Dad tells her we'll have a place to go if needed. She mentions that her mother went into the hospital to get stable. Dad says, "But I don't want to go to the hospital, remember?"

"What if you have bleeding in the brain or you go into seizure? They told us in December that you could have pills for that, but it never happened."

"The nurse told us if he hasn't yet had a seizure then he probably won't," I answer. He also told Em that she's reacting because she's a mom and this is a nurturing role. But I disagree. I think she has always taken the oxygen first.

Em gets up. "I need to plan things that physically work. Not talk of things that work. It's my house. I need things to work. If there's nothing that works then no way mister."

86

It's been five weeks. The Morph's nurse asks Dad to undo his shirt a little so she can listen to his heart. He tells her, "The doctors say below the neck I'm perfectly healthy."

Birds, the gurgling sink, my clicking pen.

She asks how he is feeling and he is eager to describe his loss of balance and weakness, especially in the left leg. "Right now I'm standing and I can take a few steps."

The nurse tells him he's doing very well.

"For what I have," he says. "Meanwhile, Dr. Chow cancelled my appointment. He didn't want me to come back."

"Oh, he's a great doctor. At least he was great for my mom."

"The other thing is that they should have given me an MRI when I had a severe headache. They said I had non-viral meningitis. They didn't do anything. Didn't send me for any MRI and maybe if they had, they would have detected it. So I don't know if my tumors shrunk or what. I declined neurosurgery. It's dangerous. I'm going to die anyway."

"Aw, well you look wonderful."

"I'm really strong. I don't know what happened. I'm really strong. True story. If I feel like this, I don't mind that I don't walk. I do mind. That'll be nice. To have six more years like this."

I suggest that we sit outside at the Iranian place in La Jolla for lunch so that we can talk about the two of us going to the mountain alone next week. Halfway through our dried out kebabs and plain pilaf rice, I manage to transition the discussion to neurosis versus psychosis. A light affair.

Dad says neurosis is distortion of reality. He says everybody has a prism on which they interpret their reality based on their experiences. "Some are oblivious. Psychosis is a loss of touch with reality. You start having delusions, hallucinations, paranoia. Bipolar is a particular form of neurosis. It's nobody's fault, nothing. It's who you are, how you are."

Three weeks of problem solving is a lot of problem solving, but I have tried to take each moment on its own and remind myself how a person can get a phone call and find out about someone they love suddenly dying. Still, these situations are stacking up and I need to avoid the all-out crash.

87

The word on Dick Clark living to 82 is that he believed "the moment you mentally atrophy, you get old." Everybody has their own recipe to survival. Dad says, "I was aiming for eighty." My desire has been for 120.

Apparently Dad has a headache under the right eye where one of the two tumors is positioned. We continue watching *Face the Nation* with steroid dosage on our minds. I complain a bit about losing touch with Hannah. "You still have a cordial relationship with her?" Dad asks. Yeah, without much context, I say, kidding. "Well, you have the rest of your lives together," he says. Em was here hovering over me a tick tock ago. She's like a ghost, coming in and going out, in and out. Dad keeps standing up to check his balance. She's around. She left eggs, potatoes and oil on the countertop so I can cook. It's Dad's fourth time peeing before nine a.m. and he's going crazy. He tries to regain patience humming Terry Jack's "Seasons in the Sun," mumbling the words he sort of knows in the chorus.

"I feel a change coming on," he says. "You know, a little less balance. Here and there headaches. It's been a month since my treatment and it could be that the honeymoon is over. It could be."

We have joy we have fun we have seasons in the sun. Tee tee tee, ta ta tum.

88

Preta shows up in 1980 secretary chic, wearing pumps, fully motivated since her break from the boy. Dad gets angry because all that's innocent is the perfume of the geraniums and the poor man's bile. Under the good-girl varnish, there's an alcoholic and he doesn't want her running out to the bar with his son.

We go to a bar that rotates Whitney Houston's "How Will I Know" with some well-worn sappy songs. She's telling me about some dude from Maine she's been dating who's half-retarded. I don't even know what that means.

"Look at this bite on my arm."

Shit, I'm looking for the scratch-n-sniff option.

Camisole, V-neck, boat neck, wide neck, layered tank tops.

A quick chomp.

"Trippy, tho, right? They don't listen to you until you flirt with them. Maybe I don't remember."

"Maybe you gave it to yourself."

"That's really creepy. That...who does that? Who doesn't remember? I never want to drink again." She makes an exhaling 'as if' sound effect: *chhhh*. "I collapsed on the floor in the club and he was so scared, like, are you breathing? He was freaking out and I started laughing. He goes, 'are you seriously laughing right now, I think you're dying.'"

"We're talking about love you think is going to last?"

"I prefer a type of mess-you-up rough love. One-foot-in, one-foot-out opportunities that never go anywhere."

"How do you want to be loved? You want a lot of attention, appreciation, feel special?"

"Guys always want a parking spot. When you gain your independence they put their foot down. That's when they step in. They sense that. '*No, I care, I care, I care.*' Love is the addiction. It's the fun part. I don't think of it anymore."

Polo shirt, Oxford button at the collar, rugby.

"Just because I kill it doesn't mean it's not gunna bite me. I knew I wanted to marry seven years ago. Two-and-a-half years into our relationship. He moved in but he had personal struggles. He projected his stuff into our relationship. You have to be happy with who you are and your partner adds to that."

Maxi dress, spaghetti dress, mini-skirt, bandage dress. Nobody's knocking the pencil skirt.

"Do people say what they mean?" I ask.

"People don't."

Tunic, shift dress, boxy dress, Jackie O.

"I want him to come to me."

"He never will."

"Maybe I'm not for him."

I hear, maybe I'm too much for him.

"He has to be strong enough to let me go."

"You want to be let go?"

"I want to be where it's not being forced. He's closed-minded to being with somebody else."

"Somebody as good."

"He sits in front of me flaccid. Who does that? *I can do these things. I promise. Don't leave me.* I would love him to say, I can't. It would make it so much easier."

"You're getting what you asked for. He's not driven enough, he doesn't have enough gusto."

"It's not like he cares to harbor good relationships."

"Maybe you're a guy's fantasy and not a real person."

89

The brothers are coming. Dad could barely stand when he shaved. His forehead was hitting the mirror. Em starts the vacuum and cuts it when she needs more cord. "It's a nice day. Beautiful day," she says. "Don't be inside today. Take them out, you know." She knows what she's doing. Too many machinations and permutations. I'm in the supermarket holding a tray of sandwiches she ordered—the kind of pink matter between white bread that ends up in the office lounge—saying *what the fuck* to myself. What a hunk of shit. This is my dad. My dad, who we have been talking about like, 'It is what it is, it's going to be okay.' I imagine the brothers' reactions to him when we're wheeling him around in the neighborhood.

First the nurse arrives while Dad's pissing in the living room, so I walk out and intercept her and talk shop in the driveway. Then minutes later the brothers drive up with Laurel behind the wheel. She picked them up from the airport and is lending them her car.

Both brothers are tall with contemplative faces; Ronen is bald and overweight and Yaniv is skin and bones. When they come all the way from Israel to represent themselves and the family spirit, we feed them this "lunch" and reinforce the welcome with sugary pastries that will reappear the next three mornings before a houseful of diabetics, including Ronen, who has lost toes to the disease. Each has something to say before settling in the living room and nobody has anything to say after. Yaniv passes out on the couch, mouth open wide. Ronen plays with his e-gadget. His wife, Odalie, checks her phone. Dad breaks the silence.

"Nobody's eating?"

After the early lunch we get them situated at the hotel, and then I give Laurel a ride back up the coast to Orange County. We talk at length about everything and no minor thing. She tells me, "Of all the men I've known in my life, your dad would have been the perfect family man." I take that as I can, knowing he wants grandchildren. "You oughta hear something he told me when we started," she continues. My inclination is to fight feeling even as I seek comfort. "Dad accepts people for what they are, and I'll never forget how he meant this. He told me, 'Say anything you want about me or anybody, but don't ever criticize my kids.'"

When I get back they suggest we go to a huge warehouse store for toiletries. Dad wants to stay home. A couple hours of shopping later we eat Chinese. I bring Dad home his order of sesame chicken, and it's like crickets all over again until Yaniv finally wakes up from a nap and here come the stories. How Saba hit him and broke his hand because he was running with the *shebob* and all the other people he used to run with when they were kids. I ask him about his work in the lighting department of the Cameri Theater, my head in the catwalks, but he continues to tell us stories of sweet nostalgia in his excited squeaky voice — and he needs complete attention or else he pinches your arm, as if there's more in the eye than in the heart.

"Do you remember Estelle Bleiman used to play with sugar, taking sugar out and in, all the time playing with sugar?"

This is all in Hebrew.

"Arlan Schriener whose mom's legs were never fixed. They said today they'll fix them and in ten years they would go bad."

He says how strong his hands are thanks to the kibbutz.

"You remember Kedma? So if you saw three donkeys you were passing her house? She went and got pregnant."

That's when his twin brother Ronen finally gets involved. "What is this stupidity? Come on, seriously."

"*No*, I didn't know why she was a bad student."

"And it's not your business."

Later on in the evening, they call me the conversationalist. They ask why I'm not running for government. People are making such a mess of our governments and what am I doing?

I say, "I'm getting married."

Standing over the sink next to my chicken soup, the pleasant perfume of ripe cantaloupe rind coming from the garbage disposal, I'm reminded of the madness of a large family on Friday night; adults with such particularities compelled to say what they like and how they like it.

90

Before anybody arrives this morning, Dad and I talk. I wanted to know what he felt like being on his own for so long. "We are not lonely people," he says to me. Then we have a brief moment of silent reflection on the couch together and out of nowhere he tells me, "You're a good boy."

I want to just take it, but I say, "I'm a good boy because you're a good man." By verbalizing that to him I have already deflected my emotion so I am compelled to add, "And in a moment Toots will be here."

"Only if you go get her," he says.

Yeah, I go get her from the airport.

My synapses are firing. I'm remembering the whole point of loneliness on the drive, or at least understanding how when I was eighteen and leaving home I managed to break down in front of my dad. We were in Rio Seco, the city he moved to a year after the divorce, where I first experienced that funny feeling for which I had no accurate name. He actually came to the surprise college send-off my sister hosted at her apartment and he spent a little time meeting my friends. Then something happened to me when he was leaving and I found myself reacting, like a timer set off inside of me. I never knew how to show him my deep feelings. I loved my dad as a boy should, with pride and respect and fierce loyalty.

Here he was the one bowing out early so that we could literally start the party, and I thought I was following after him to fulfill some routine act of closure, but the truth was that I was about to be emancipated from some of my complicated emotions. I was saying goodbye to him. I couldn't have known that I was also saying goodbye to my childhood identity. Even if Dad was a part of the stress and conflict, all of that was crumbling with my unconscious realization that this was final: I would never live with him and I had to move on with my life. I was saying goodbye to everything, everything, especially the notion that those eighteen years were all the time we had and a lot of it was wasted.

I never saw it coming. The apartment door was nearly closed behind me and it was the two of us alone outside on the welcome mat. I think I nearly threw up it came out so hard. It was confusing at the time. You know that you're sometimes a monster and you know how to make yourself kind, but you don't really ever know how you love until you have to let go of what you love. Dad was saying, "You take care of yourself. Watch your back. Keep in touch," and I was nodding, nodding, nodding, until I went to open my mouth. Then it was pure catharsis. Those tears, that closed up throat, my dad's arms around me; I was crushed, totally crushed, devastated to my center.

I pick Toots up curbside and she tells me something like, "I don't know because I gotta work," and I say, "Don't start with that bullshit."

I'm anxious because I have to leave tomorrow for my bachelor party and in the back of my mind I also have to say goodbye to Dad. Toots tells me that she's an insomniac because of anxiety. She takes what she calls insomnia sandwiches. I have to accept her for who she is. I have to accept people for who they are. She's telling me why she won't be able to stay in the small room at the Hacienda when I'm gone. *I can't. I need to sleep. I need quiet and I need dark.* I look for some answers in my notebooks. Anxiety is a state of mind. It's the projection of unpleasant situations. You are alarmed and worried usually about something not there. Fear of an elephant charging, for example. It can cause major sleeping problems.

I would love to go to sleep and wake up in the morning and realize that this was all a dream. In between dreams and waking there are miracles.

Toots is not the only one doing business in the after-noon — *Well, actually I want five hundred units shipped to Mars for Saturday* — Dad continues to hold the schedule and watch the stock ticker.

"What is a week from yesterday?" he asks me, rubbing his mous-tache, searching for something. "I'm trying to make you some money," he says. Well I didn't ask you to make me money. Just make yourself happy, I say, repeating to myself that I will leave this notebook unread, leave all the pages closed, let Toots focus on her computer, ignore the crisis of priority.

"Making money makes me happy."

The crisis? My sister who can't sleep, who still bites her cuticles, whose dad is sitting in a wheelchair, spared from the war, made for the war, the result of it, checking his wristwatch, not ready for "For Esme with Love and Squalor," the one story I've been waiting to read to him, the one story that says everything? He looks at his wristwatch again.

I go pack for my flight and listen to Toots carry on and on about visions and brands. I ask if she knows what time Em needs to be at her opera class tomorrow. *I don't know anything about her life*, is her answer. I say, I don't want you all to turn against her.

She says, "No, we're just having fun with her." Well embrace the quirks, I say. "I can't break up with her," she says. Dad would say it takes discipline and compassion to see the best in everyone, to work with their healthy parts, but Toots is traumatized from the way Em yelled at her, and the worst is yet to come, I'm sure.

That night I spend all night stuck in the dark on top of the covers with a sock still on one foot and all the lights on overhead.

91

Anyone reading at the airport is reading a bullshit supermarket novel. I find my departure gate and I call my dad. He peed all over himself. He says, "Everybody's gone and I'm with Ronen. Yaniv tied a knot in the bag at the back of my wheelchair where I keep my urinal and Ronen is very lame on his feet." I transport myself back a few chambers of experience to a time when all I really wanted was to make the most out of a minute. I realize now that the difficulty is not being present in time, it's in being everything that we are at once. We never get to live every part of us at the same time. We mentally prepare for the next step and then something else arrives. The only way to avoid inevitable calamity is to expose your vulnerabilities and continue failing in small ways. It makes sense not to fight too hard against the inevitable, but when you let life impose its limits on you it's like sanctioning a neighbor's hedges in an open yard. You shouldn't have to trespass on your ambition.

92

Days go by. Sometimes I don't even realize it. Sometimes I don't even participate in them. And then April 27 comes along and I'm in New Jersey for my bachelor party. I'm nervous. My only expectation is to spend two nights and one day in the company of these great men I love, but I have to rise to the occasion no matter what. to make this weekend legendary even if I don't have the gusto.

My friend Frank Worzel is in the laundry picking up his dry cleaning. I'm in the front seat of his car wrapping my head around the fact that this debauchery is going to be for me. The heat is on full blast and I'm melting. Worzel comes back saying, "I gotta go pick up a box. This is my life, picking up stuff." I'm still giddy about this new alias he earns from the mistaken identity on his dry cleaning ticket. He has a wife and kids and a job he does very well, that pays as much as it strips away his free time, and this weekend is his creation. I'm overwhelmed with emotion yet fairly sure that nothing going on with my dad will translate into this event past the moment we all embrace. Once we're on the casino floor it'll be a bloodbath.

We're in the office for the van rental and the space shuttle Enterprise passes overhead in the sky on top of a plane. History in the making. Not a bad start. Heading into Manhattan, Worzel pulls out some of the finest bourbon that's ever been made. I wish we had hours and hours, but we have three hours and the possibility of traffic and a duffel bag full of fantastic liquor, all to be taken neat. He says, "Baby, if you got the sense that this is some half show, we're drinking like men. We're not boys no more."

I fear I can't make anything happen because of the depression I feel underneath my laid-back exterior.

We park on Third Avenue and like East 80th street, beside a building with a ton of scaffolding, jackhammer blasting, orange cone steam vents coming out of the asphalt, the weather just above cold. The boys show up with their bags one after another and with each I'm moved and re-moved because they come from the heart, from only the heart. The way it hits me is like lounging on a warm night after a day of sun: the afterlight.

By the time we get to Providence, Rhode Island—our destination—we are fully wasted. Dinner is going to have to be amid the rise of adrenalin at the gambling establishment. Some guys are meeting us there, sober.

Our server is either a gypsy or her name is Gypsy. She is the final stranger that I don't offend. There is far more wit and charm among the table degeneratti than the hammered bachelor wearing a sleeveless shirt that says, *Fuck Sleeves*, could ever hope to harbor, so what else can I do but watch as the boys take turns being gentlemen. I am too little of a presence to occupy the center of attention. One guy says to Gypsy, "Look deep in my eyes and tell me you're gonna quit and come with us." She smiles and lets the involuntary laugh of us hungry ogres confirm that we eat babies. The guy sitting next to him says, "Sixteen dollar burger! That thing better jack me off."

That is the last note I take.

Sunday night back at my mom's apartment, half dead, half down because of this all-too-quick experience, I have Hannah on the phone, her long aristocratic neck pulsing for a few wild seconds, "I need to get your birth certificate notarized? You know how much time it's going to take?" I try to zone out but I can't. All I'm doing is undermining her when I listen. It's like I'm on asshole autopilot. But who gets to see that?

Later in the night my mom tries to help me salvage my relationship and we have a video chat conversation with Hannah about elitism in music schools where I open my mouth and say something about love that I don't really mean. Hannah hasn't been influenced by all the commercial nonsense Americans are exposed to, so she's fresh and it always seems fresh with her, like I may not ever know her and I know it. She usually doesn't have patience for these kinds of pseudo-intellectual conversations, and here she bravely revisits my summary of the bachelor weekend, "Did Frank mean to drive your van over a flock of ducks? He had to get people to the airport on time. You can't accurately judge someone on their passionate performance." I like that I have to start thinking before I speak.

93

I was able to rehearse saying goodbye by not saying goodbye. On Tuesday morning I'm back in the San Diego airport getting in the car with Dad, Toots, and Furstman, hearing stories about Odalie being great, Yaniv getting locked out and having to take a crap in the bushes in the back yard, the new Mexicana, Olivia, letting Dad fall from his wheelchair, and all that Em and her daughter did which takes almost forty-five minutes to tell.

Dad is now wearing the NASA briefs at all time. Odalie convinced him. "I am peeing right now," he says at the Hacienda table. Em went to work out. I have so much food in front of me and we're supposed to go to the Fish Market for Toots' birthday. Dad gripes about the people around us, namely the boy and Preta—"He's an idiot" and "She's juvenile"—and he says taking a walk has become "too hard and it's no fun." Hannah is coming Sunday to spend a short time here before the wedding. It's supposed to make up for the fact that Dad won't see her any other way. I hope we have good days.

Down at the wharf, Em says, "You're gonna have so much company."

"It'll be your company, too," Dad responds, Olivia sitting quietly beside him. Em hasn't modified her stance. She still calls it, *this thing,* and it's now she starts to resent the changes. Dad takes a deep breath before he restates his case. "I'm tired of this phase," he says.

MAY

94

Dad and I are alone. We're going to the mountain and stopping by our famous burrito stand to takeout two extra-large meat and rice for lunch. Before we leave my mom gets me on the phone and starts asking me question after question, "How do I get to the Moulin? What are the dates? What about June fourteenth? What's the civil ceremony?" Dad checks his watch. He's sitting right at the door, not saying a word. When I'm off the phone he says, "This kid has the patience of a saint. So help me, the patience of a saint. I don't know how he doesn't scream or anything."

It's about ninety degrees in San Bernal today and people are going for their pools and water slides already. When we get up to the house, I rush Dad to the toilet and then we eat. The way he grips a 7Up can, he crushes it. His burrito is disappointing, though. "Some of it is lost on me, except the salt. I don't get the full taste that I'm used to." The chewing sounds and humming that accompany the meal are very familiar.

Dad stands up on his own. I ask him what he's doing. He says, "Trying not to poop." He asks me, "Can I gain access?" To what? "To the chocolates." He eats some of that and some pineapple chunks while we watch the Lakers game. I'm passing out. "You're taking a nap. Aye. I want the blood to come back to my feet."

Instead of going through lazy and cranky phases, I get up fully and prepare us for a restorative sleep. It's the first time I'm helping him by myself. I ask him what he wears to bed and he tells me, "I wear my t-shirt, that's all." Me, I'd rather wear shorts.

After settling him into bed and being told, "I handle my own glasses, everybody else scratches them," I shut the light on the cockadoodle collection like he asks and I think about a line he said earlier: "I don't look back, I just look forward."

That night I hear a whistle and I launch out of bed because I think I may be needed. My feet fall loudly on the wood floor as I round the corner to his room. It's just my dad as I know him, but he's lost his bowels in the worst way. He's incapacitated, sore, and drowsy and we have to deal with the accident. I quickly decide a strategy before struggling to get him out of bed and into his chair with the least mess possible. It's a world of skill and every boy wants to impress his father. I can't lift him into the shower so my best option is to lower him to the bathroom floor and drag him in there on a towel. Then he's just lying on the floor unable to move with the door rails of the shower cutting into the back of his head. He cries out a little because it hurts. My chest bursts with stress, the sinews in my arms tightening. I rush to grab another towel and get it under his head and make this cold hard failure tolerable. We get the NASA briefs off and clean up as much possible and I attempt to dead lift Dad off the floor, but I'm not strong enough. With the help of his arms we manage to get back in the chair, across the house and into the bathtub. He bathes himself. I help him dry, then change him, put the antifungal lotion on under his genitals, treat the rug, and get him back into bed. At that point, it's about five in the morning. He says to me, I've got to go to the bathroom again. This time I sit him up on his toilet and leave him to do his business.

Ah, peace and quiet. One of the best things. Two of them.

95

Dad feels like he's sinking a little. The mountain air makes me tired and I don't want to do anything, but everything has to be done. I see Dad staring outside and I ask him, You like observing animal behavior? He says, "Any behavior. People, animals."

When we went to Kings Canyon for the fourth time and he broke this squirrel's pelvis with a stone, other campers were screaming at him, but my dad never explains himself. The rodents were climbing in the wheel well and eating at his car hoses so he was in a chair by the campfire trying to scare them, except his throws were pretty accurate and he hit one. That animal lay on its back and revved its left leg like it would never move again so he decided to take it out of its misery. I was in the tent and I heard the pounding and the loud grunting and I got curious. To my horror there was my Dad under the tall pines on one knee, head down, the sweat soaking his baseball cap dripping from his temples, tears in his eyes, the branch in his hands and the bloody squirrel on the ground. I stared at him as the deed was almost done and I asked him what he was doing. He shifted his attention to me and told me not to watch. I wanted to know more, but I listened to him and turned away.

We leave the mountain at five sharp, driving back through bumper sticker land. Sometimes I try and speak Hebrew around Dad to get that familiar feeling, but he usually corrects me. Recently it's been with a simper. Bad grammar is a pet peeve of his. He doesn't mean to make me feel flat. It's just I do, professor. Dad tells Em what happened last night while she was in L.A. with her daughter. She admits she is not the bravest person and wouldn't be able to do it herself. I like to question motivations to get a little below the surface, but it's easier to fly the holding pattern than to engage.

Em says she's anxious and nervous and doesn't sleep enough.

She says she needs to exercise to stay in shape (for the war with the Chinese). Their conversations remain circuitous. *Feeling good?* she asks. Not too good. *Why? What not too good?* Tired and down. It gets to me not being able to get around. *Take anti-depression meds to help you.* I'm not depressed. The answer is not medication.

96

Toots and Furstman get back from their weekend getaway in time to accompany me to the airport. Hannah should be met with cute lip-smacks, flutes and handclaps, but instead we could be breaking the sound barrier with our individual tensions. I am emotional about seeing her and the only thing I talk about is what can we do today?

All the kids go to a decoration store to see if we can find fake flowers to use as centerpieces for the wedding dinner which has been elaborately planned in my absence. I wander off to the unseen aisles hoping to land a treasure. The overhead speakers are playing *"If you happen to see the most beautiful girl in the world."* I'm telling you, she's in the leather department sniffing purses.

Dad says, "Okay, move." He wants to make a move. He wants to shave. He wants to be ready for his shower. There's cabbage with turmeric and chia seeds on the stove top. I'm in the back yard scribbling out lines that make no sense, forcing creativity. Hannah is beside me reading in the serious sunlight. Is my long term goal to leave Dad's legacy to the world? I really don't have any single goal. The body has evolved, the brain continues to grow. I'm doing the best I can.

Dad encourages Hannah and me to try our own resources. He says, "Ever since my grandmother was fifty she took a half a valium to weather the afternoon. Ten miligrams. She was anxious. From age fifty to eighty-three she never left home except for a couple of weddings. She looked down from the balcony, "This is the Creeper, this is the Loafer, this is the guy who runs all the time. She named them by their disabilities. Basically, your sister got my stuff. Resist the anxiety pill. Don't worry about me. I worry about me. I worry what's gonna happen in the morning. Is Em gonna get up or just leave it to me? If she doesn't want to get up, I'm going to go to sleep as late as I can and wake up at six a.m. I can go a long time in that space age technology. I can do anything if it comes to it. If you're worried about me, don't worry. I can handle it."

Hannah's thinking ahead about making it back to Paris for her surprise bachelorette party, but she's really not saying anything. I know where she's going and as much as it's possible to transfer my feelings about everything to the tension around her standby flight, I'm unable to deal with the fact that this may be the last time she spends with Dad, and the fact that he's not going to be at my wedding the way he was at Toots', and the reality that Em and this household are crippling our flow, so I explode at the wrong person.

Em is in her workout clothes when she walks up to me on the patio and hands me a check. She says, "Ghi, you go to the bank when you get a chance. He was in a good mood with me. Whenever someone new comes he—" she starts to cry. I try to maintain my distance not wanting to ruin the moment with bathos, but I can't help myself. I say, "Cause you wouldn't fucking listen to me. You treat him like shit." I head inside where Dad is looking at his pawn shop show. He is by himself on the couch sitting on a bath towel and two blue absorbent underpads with a glass of water in front of him.

"You still watching these?" Em jokes with him. "How many of them do you have?"

Dad's response is, "Whatever I watch, you'll criticize me."

Em heads back out the door. Dad has me wheel him to the

other room where he starts looking at bills. He has no idea what just transpired. I turn off the television. Em comes back. She tells Dad, "Every time someone in your family comes to visit, you turn against me."

Maybe I didn't say what I think I said.

Dad grimaces. "My feet are kind of frozen, paralyzed. I have no control over my body. I don't know why it does it. Only today. I kind of feel weak in the midsection of my body. Yeah, I hope it goes away. Hard to say. After the massage I felt like a tiger, now I don't."

The boy passes from the kitchen to the living room to check out the Lakers game. "So where's our next lunch adventure?" he asks. We're finishing eating desert in front of the television watching the team who taught me about never giving up, who now make me nothing but tired.

"Ghi! You're falling asleep on me," Dad says.

"You do it to me, what's the difference?"

"The difference is that you have to get up and drive across town and you can't do it."

"You want me to put you in the bathroom?"

Dad sighs. "Yes, put me in the bathroom and tell Em so she can come out and get me. Now that I have Olivia, you don't have to come at seven thirty, so take your time."

This breaks my heart. All of it.

97

One month before the wedding my restored communication with Paris is still trial and error:

"The bride's not the first place, maybe she's the tenth place."

"I told you I understand."

"I'm taking this on the fifth."

"I understand. I'm not going to tell you I don't understand."

I don't understand.

"I'm going to be honest with you. I asked you to be honest with me about what's going on. We had a fight. Now we've got to digest it."

I'm not going to say I understand.

"The rabbi said, 'If he dies within thirty days of your marriage I can't marry you.'"

I disagree.

"You don't want to understand where I'm coming from and my plate is full."

"This situation does not exist."

"You can't say that because you're not a doctor."

"Then there's nothing I can say. What if I say that I'm ninety-nine percent sure that it's not going to happen?"

"But it could."

"I have to be honest, I can't say."

"I've been practicing for this conversion for a year."

"Can you forget about this stupid rule?"

"What I know about this rule is that nobody, nobody told me that this was going to happen. I've been spending years hearing your parents pronounce things, teaching me how to put things on the table. I've been going to synagogue every Thursday and when this came up he said it's risky. But we have to go through with it."

"You are not available to be positive?"

"Put yourself in my shoes. I am not perfect with it. It's not going to happen the way I wanted it to happen and this fucking solution is horrible. That's why it's so dramatic because I can't talk about it. I'm hurt because everybody says it is what it is, it's not a big deal."

Two minutes gone by, maybe, two hours.

"Nobody told me about it. I'm pretty sure nobody told me about it if he says I'm not going to do it because it's too risky. I feel retarded because I don't know these rules. I'm pretty sure everybody actually knows this rule and I'm very upset. It's not going to change. That's what happens. I'm upset."

What do you want?

"I'm upset. I'm very worried. I didn't like what you said at all. Honestly, it's like I'm doing everything. I'm starting to have a real problem with the way you think about me. I don't believe the way you think about me. No, I'm not upset, I'm just having a problem with the way you talk to me. You judge me, criticize me, in a way I don't feel good. Me myself I want to feel good, patient, understanding. When I tell you about my feelings, it is just kind of surprising. The first time that someone tells me that my marriage is not going to happen, I get upset. I just need you to say that this sucks for the both of us. There are things that are going to come up in the next four weeks. We don't need to get in these fights when I come very calmly. We need to be careful because we are sliding on things we shouldn't be. You should know where I'm coming from."

You should know that I'm not on a stage.

"I'm in pain. I'm not doubting that this is the right relationship. (*Crying, crying*). I wish there was no ceremony. It makes me so sad. So sad. I just feel it's a waste of energy and money and beyond. I just can't hear I'm selfish and thinking about me. (*Crying, crying*). I can't feel that you're against me. The way you're looking at me. I want to talk about a painful situation. We need to be together. It's a process that's tough for me to go through and it won't be the same for me and it's really painful for a million things beside Beth Din shit. And I don't like people telling me that I'm not going to have my wedding. I want things to happen the way you want them to happen. If I had known then it would have been a different decision because I don't think it's fair to either of us, but that's my feeling. It's not ever fair that we have to deal with it while you have to deal with the stress with your dad. I fucking hate the process. It's one in the morning. It's one. Ghi, the intellectual

American. You've got to hear this. I fucking hate this. It fucking sucks. You're putting it on me. I'm very upset."

98

Dad says, "So these are random notes you're gonna put together and publish someday. Send me one."

"What?"

"Send me one. A published book, short story, whatever."

We're preparing burgers for an early dinner and he is in a funk, talking to the nurse about what's the point? At some moment he corrects her grammar and says, "It's not rude. I'm helping you for life." I tell him to take lithium, to which he replies, "Suicide isn't an option." Then we have a light conversation about that, and alongside his insertion of the fact that "Lithium is a salt," which I have yet to confirm, he mentions my note taking.

Can I say something? I interrupt. "You can say whatever you want," he says. This is your shit but we are all with you in our own way. I recognize my deficiencies. The fact that we aren't afraid to be part of your hope is what matters.

The nurse reiterates that in hospice everything takes place around the patient. When she leaves we try watching some Westminster Dog Show videos online and Dad says, "I don't give a shit. I can't get into anything these days."

Then Em leaves us and it is just the both of us and Dad says to me, "For some reason you and Toots got this idea that it's endless."

"What?"

"*What*. My money. Look at the bottom line. Look at what I had when I retired, look at what I have now. I spent twenty percent of it. Well, what did we do from December to now? Thirty-three thousand."

I'm forced to talk about finance. "You have social security and dividends," I say.

"No dividends!"

"You made money in January and February and it was reinvested and lost. It's only on paper."

"Do I think I have enough to last me?" That's the question that Em asks. "Olivia sits down all day by me, she does nothing. If Em was more strong and able."

"If a flock of chickens was a pack of monkeys."

"Don't be smart. So, I make sandwiches. It's not a problem."

"It's not for you that it's a problem."

"One day. Why can't she do it? One day."

"It's psychological. She's with it all day and night."

"I'm going to run out of money."

Next thing we're checking in with Toots and Dad's back at it.

"Em starts asking if I'm gonna run out of money. She's worried that I won't be able to afford the services and —" he exhales heavy here.

"Why do you let her talk about that? Just kill the subject by telling her it's not gonna happen."

For some reason here I wonder how my dad would have dealt with my mom if they had stayed together. I never have this thought.

Changing tack, Dad's looking at the back yard and mentions the wild tulips in Tel Aviv. He says, "I used to get a bunch and give them."

"To whom?" I ask, relatively surprised at this act of tenderness.

"My mom, dad, grandma."

"You don't talk about your grandma much," I say.

"There's not much to talk about."

Tonight the Lakers play in game three of the second round of the playoffs. They crumbled in the first two games already. They aren't what they used to be. Some people still admit how depressed they've been since Chick Hearn died ten years ago. People connect him with their childhood. With their spirit.

99

Tomorrow I leave for Paris and Em is heading to Mexico. In the car to the San Diego Amtrak station we're listening to a Schubert overture: the Trout Quintet. Toots is driving. Dad's in the front seat breathily half-singing, "*Here comes the sun*. Fan-tastic." I'm thinking *disconnect*. Em can get on the train to L.A. and disconnect. What am I going to do?

Dad carries on as if he has read my thoughts, giving me rare words to contemplate: "You know what they say? Happy wife, happy life."

This is it. I'm going to get married. Leaving on a jet plane. I hope he doesn't decline in my absence but I know that he will.

"We shall overcome," he says to me when I get out of the car. I'm leaning into the passenger-side window searching his face for the source of this platitude. These words he never spoke to me, that must have spoken to him the year he arrived in America and then buried quickly and deeply, only to surface four decades later in an ironic gesture. I believe he has always empowered me to heal myself. He does not go on to tell me, "I may not get to the mountaintop with you." But I do. I say that. I say that in words that I bring down my esophagus, like comfort food. Will this be *the* speech, I wonder. I'll give that speech to you instead, dear reader. I'll be thinking of you and the light will go on in your heart, even if nobody will be able to see it or hear it.

I hear that the pain you cause yourself fuels you in some way, but I am a façade. I wanted to be this perfect boy for everyone. I'm passionate and I'm reeling, a dull knife in the kitchen that couldn't cut the frost off a whore's lip.

On the train I spend some time thinking out the month of June: Hannah's birthday, the Town Hall reception, the wedding. Tomorrow I'll be back with the most generous human being in the world who knows how to love me and smells good, but right now I feel that, by and large, everything is mental.

After a hectic day of wedding shopping on Abbot-Kinney in Venice, Blake and I *intox* at the Patio and run the streets from bar to gallery to club to house party. At three-in-the-morning we're at a bungalow surrounded by gorgeous transvestites and casual Hollywood anti-Christs when I overhear this conversation.

"How do you feel about the theory of marriage?"

"I think it's nonsense. Partnerships I've had are far stronger than those tainted by exploitation. I also think nothing is better than new sex. The first time you've held someone and talked—if you're lucky that will last nine months. Then familiarity breeds contempt."

"When it was my turn I didn't go for laughs or sex, I went for it all. Straight to the heart. It gets harder to get carried away, to lose your mind, to let go, but when the heart moves, we're happy."

100

In the air I'm thinking about my wedding speech.

Hannah once told me that I get a lot of attention and that coming over to France I would have to deal with getting less. Something like that. I don't need to tell you that I'm just glad to be alive, but to be here with everyone I love, giving attention to each other, taking on causes in our individual lives, loving our families, our countries, our traditions, the question I have is do we have to question everything, and if the answer is yes, I have to tell you why I didn't write this out before I let the thoughts work over me. Sure, it's just the stories you know that don't need much rehearsing. Only sometimes they need translating.

Five years ago I met the girl who asked me, do you believe in what you say you believe? Do you know what love is? Do you know how to love?

At separate times I've known how to fit in and how to do whatever I felt was right. I don't know if my marriage to Hannah is either of those things. Maybe my legs grew tired. That sounds terrible. Considering that at some point I thought there was no way I would ever be able to decide who to love, I have to admit that I just didn't know how to think big. I used to want a fireman's pole in my house. That's all what I wanted. Not the house. I wanted what a lot of us want—to stay away from complication forever. The more things got complicated, it seemed, the worse they became.

If love is everything, I guess I need to stop speaking. Love grows out of whatever we have right here and now. You guys are my beating heart.

If I could wish one thing—especially on this occasion of celebrating the beginning of our life together—it's that we give up all of the ideas we have, all the things we think about how things should be, about marriage, and about our experiences. Maybe I'm an asshole. I would just rather get to the meat. I have to tell you, I almost lost Hannah because I couldn't choose this. I was trying to let the love in. I wanted it in pure form. Maybe that takes a lifetime. Like we go outward to go inward. I don't know. All I know is I nearly lost myself.

There are a lot of people here who don't doubt that this is what we start out like, that people change and other things take over and all that. Hannah made me promise to love her forever. Okay, I promised her. Have you ever heard of something like that? Stick around. This is only the beginning.

JUNE

101

Back in Paris I sneak away to deliver the balance on the ring and they tell me there is no ring. I'm on Faubourg Saint Honore. There has to be a ring. A white gloved woman asks me to sit and has a sparkling water brought over to me while she calls over to Nice to where the ring seems to have been shipped.

Tonight the rabbi has something new to say. He says he's sorry. He will marry us anyway because my dad is an Ashkenazi. He thought he was Sephardic.

I call Dad at a normal hour, his time. He says, "I fell off Mt. Olympus. I'm not the apple of her eye anymore." He's been moved to the small room to sleep nights. "We need to talk about Mordechai Campbell," he says.

102

Two weeks to the wedding, all I'm dealing with besides work is my suit, the bar and the religious ceremony. I have to get serious about finding a shirt to go with my suit. I spoiled myself with an haute couture suit and if I don't get that shirt it's going to spoil the suit. Rabbi Williams' very next move after apologizing to us is attempting to ditch us for a Rothschild and giving us instead some Argentinian of the cloth who speaks no English or French. I convince him that it can't happen because we need him and we're the ones who reserved his services far in advance. He calls to tell me how much he's losing in that transaction, "I'm making a big effort for you—You should know that. I'm sending this other guy to the other wedding. I bar mitzvahed this boy and I know him twenty years longer than you."

Family craziness is inevitably on the rise now: in the atheist corner there is some opposition to wearing a kippa; my mom wants to know when I'm going to take her to the wedding site; and, Loic expects to bring his kids to the rehearsal dinner along with his Thai girlfriend who was a prostitute back in April when he left their mother.

In between giving tours, I make every effort to stay positive while my somewhat laughable personal dramas seem to mount. On the hunt for a suitable shirt, nothing I try works and I'm told

I'm too late for a custom made one. I also can't find agave syrup anywhere.

Then my telephone rings and it's serious news.

Less than twelve hours after Em agreed to have a special bed brought into the Hacienda living room, the empire falls. She wants Dad to go to hospice emergency care.

"We've got everything in place and now she wants to take it all apart. I'm kind of surprised and now I have to talk to her. Sounds like she wants me out. I have no idea what happened at night. I have to talk to her and see if I can get some meaning out of this. She was happy, happy, happy yesterday and now she's freaking out."

Toots is also on the line and she tells me, "Ghi, she doesn't want me to come tomorrow, she wants me to come *to-day*. We're going to take him back to the mountain and get him twenty-four hour care. What are your thoughts?"

"Can Em get more extreme?"

"I was asleep and she called at three in the morning. I called back at seven. She starts screaming at me, *Why didn't you call back in the middle of the night?* I said, I take sleeping pills. *I don't care if you're sleeping or you took the pill, you answer the phone when I call you.* She says, *I'm very sorry to tell you, your dad has to leave to-day.* I was in a T-shirt and underwear shaking all over, saying, okay, I'll figure it out. *No, I'm tired of this. You need to come today, to-day. You are a bad daughter. Shame on you. You always come when you want to.*"

At this point I'm in a passive distress, guilty of being useless, miles away from the action. Dad hangs up and Toots continues to tell me she's going today. She just got off the phone with Laurel who was already planning to visit him.

"She's been going every Sunday. I told her, the day has come. She says, 'What day?' I told her, Em is kicking him out of the house. She says, 'Get the fuck out of here.' I'm going to call Ronen and Yaniv. I already packed a bag. The airline wouldn't change my flight so I bought another ticket for six hundred dollars. We're gonna move him to his house, he loves it there. I already called hospice. Dad keeps saying, 'No, she'll change her mind.' I told him, you have to trust me that I'm an adult and you raised me right. It's gone too far. We're going to move you."

In the morning Dad calls to tell me, "Em feels my family isn't doing enough and that she can't be responsible for me. I had to cancel my Uncle Jay's visit. Everything will be alright. I'm going up to my house in the mountain. Nobody can bullshit me. They have hospice in the mountain. I have to cancel my massages. I have five left. It's lots of money. Too bad I have to give up Olivia. She's magnificent. It's absolutely the right decision. I've had it with Em. Now she'll have Moli. We'll get a handyman on the mountain. Anything can be done for money. The only good thing is that I can invite everyone from work. Today is the third, two weeks from now you'll be married and I'm determined to make it. Gives me motivation to keep going. I don't feel I'm dying. Em gave me too much Ambien in the night. Too much of this shit medication."

This all happened because Toots told Dad to take a whole sleeping pill and he started losing his mind, trying to take off his underwear in his sleep after Em gave him more.

When Toots' arrived at the front door of the Hacienda yesterday, Em and her daughter were icy cold to her, but they let Dad stay one more night. There was supposed to be a hospice meeting in the morning, so Toots left Laurel at the condo and she went back to the house, took her pants off, swallowed a sleeping pill, and went to sleep for four hours. Dad was in the living room on a hospital bed. In the middle of the night he rang his bell to be changed. Toots asked if Em wanted her to do it and she said she would. Apparently, she was yelling at him, *Bridge! Bridge!*

This morning at seven, when Em and her daughter left on a walk, Toots looked outside and Laurel was coming up the driveway.

"I said, What are you doing here? and she says, 'I woke up and

I asked myself what the fuck *am I* doing here? Why do I need to stay here 'til nine? Why can't I just go now?' So we wake up Dad and tell him we're going to take you to your own home and it's going to be great. You're going to be in the woods again. Laurel, Olivia, and I rush to pack the cars and we're almost done when Em comes back and we remember we're supposed to be meeting with hospice. But what for? I say. This part of his life is over and he needs to have a good end of his life. Laurel asks Dad if he wanted to meet with hospice and he said, 'No, what for?' Then he went on for the last time about how he wanted to give Em money to have the walls painted.

She was sitting on her stool in the kitchen. Dad was on his wheelchair at the door. Her daughter was sitting at the kitchen table. I didn't want to bring it up, it was awkward. I say, Em, my dad wants to give you money for the paint. She says, *You don't owe me anything. What you do owe me is an explanation. You're just going to move him like that? No explanation. What about the hospice meeting?*

I was thinking to myself, you picked the wrong daughter to eff with. I said, You told me to move him today. 'Come move him *to-day.*' I had to open her email because she was denying that she said it. So then I read it out loud and her daughter says, *Really, really?* Yes, really, I said. I... You think I'm going to let him stay in this dysfunctional house? The moment you said so it was over. *Really, really? You've been cold to my mother for four years.* I don't think so, I say. And you know what, shut up, you haven't even been involved.

You're going to do twenty-four-hour care in his home? Why didn't you do it here?

I say, Em, you told me to move him out. This isn't a conspiracy to move him out of here. This is an end-of-life plan. There's like a compassion chip missing in this situation. This is my dad. He's dying. This isn't a conspiracy to take him out of here. I wouldn't have even thought of it.

Then we were outside and I said, Em, you've done a really

good job, you're invited whenever you want to come. I mean, why was I even telling her that, she said for me to move him? I gave her a hug. I begged her, please come. It's not for me, it's for him. Then we drove off and we were heading to the mountain and Laurel was following us and I asked Dad how he felt and he said, 'Relieved. *Re-lieved.*'

So it was a good decision?

'*Fantastic.*'"

It's Hannah's thirtieth birthday today and we do our best to enjoy the beginning of her surprise getaway in the wake of this short-order horror.

103

Hannah is studying when I get home from the specialty olive shop. She is pissed off that a week before our wedding the owner of the Moulin decides that two double rooms we've reserved in our contract need to be vacated for her people. This is just contributing to the many microscopic issues she has had to manage for a weekend with one hundred and forty invites. There are ways to console her but I am not very authentic with my approach or delivery because I'm in a rush to dinner at my mom's rented apartment and I'm thinking about my dad on the mountain, singing "We feel free. Em is not bugging me. She slowly worked me out of the house. She's full of contradictions. Anyway, I ain't comin' back."

My mom wants to know how I feel about getting married. I don't commit to any specific feeling. It's one of those questions that doesn't demand more than standard lip service, so I'm bummed. How do I feel? Hannah has done it all without a planner and my petty to-do list is barely coming together, which is to say I'm consumed with self-interest and unable to project myself into any future without being overwhelmed. I'm hoping that Dad focuses on himself and not Em's guilty feelings. He's not relaxed. He tells me, "Relaxing is when you're in good shape and you enjoy snoozes. I get tired." Of what? I ask automatically. He says, "Of living."

104

After dealing with an Egyptian anesthesiologist drilling me about the 1789 revolution in Paris, I finally find a shirt at Charvet in Place Vendome and it fits like body armor. I have notes to write on the bus to the eleventh arrondissement Town Hall where I'm meeting Nordic to check the Internet connection so my dad can see the civil ceremony en live.

My first friend to arrive signals the stress of a DIY wedding. I barely have done anything but somehow between programming the music for walking down the aisle and pulling together the many elements of style which are missing from my suit, people come from everywhere and I am choking on the love. I quickly become more groomzilla than I ever imagined I would be. Simple things threaten to pull me apart: still not finding agave syrup for our cocktails, sitting far off center at the Friday night dinner table, fighting for silent sleep when staying up is all the rage.

Eventually I put my notebook and pen away so that I can be fully in the moment, and instead of developing sober portrayals of the British rabbi, Irish barman, French photographer, or deejay Woody, I head to a lumber yard with an architect friend and spend two days in the country building the wedding bar.

105

June 14, 12:40pm, just before being married in the Town Hall, I'm eating lunch below our rented rue de Charonne apartment where these two Demoiselles who do healthy home cooking have never seen my face and smile uncomfortably when I try to explain the stakes of this meal. *They said to take a moment and this is my moment.* People from all over the world are making their way to Place Leon Blum and I am savoring every bite of my smoked salmon sandwich to tell myself that this is all going to be a very short dance so let's make it happen.

If there ever was a concrete notion of before and after an exchange of vows, a man has orchestrated it. While I was considering everything that was about to change, I realized I had to abandon my personal myth narrative and just breathe.

You look out and see all the people in the crowd that have been with you for most of your life and it's hard to access all that's happening through the exhaustion of stress and blaming and working over the minutiae of days past, days coming to you. The shocks of beauty never fully fading away couldn't even take you out of the cloud of one week spent running around. It was that way. Each of us with his own capacity to love, to relate, to force the fuse and drive the flower through the stem. Each of us with his own particular set of malaise and happiness, the well of tragic, the peak of comic, the will to be carried with the moment, to go with the flow. The little moments made up for it. The I love yous, the wild strawberry you found and put on my plate, the bold hugs, the bises. For stepping into it, for all you said—if only I could remember it word-by-word. Well, we'll have to do it again. Again and again until the ink runs off the paper.

106

The day of the ceremony Dad is in his suit on the couch with Laurel, dressed for the occasion and watching by way of Toots' video chat as the guests assemble on the lawn past the river mill. The best men are circled up inside by the grinding wheel with a bottle of exquisite bourbon, saying wonderful things to me when the rabbi comes to ask about the bride. We hand him an envelope with thousands of Euros in cash and he says, "You already fucked up my day, but I'm leaving if she's not here in another half hour." I scramble to reconcile the problem which is not in the least diminished by the sight of Dad. When my mind is gravitating to the center of the earth with the alcohol and all the rest obscuring my clarity, the thought of my dad wishing me the world does not compete for my terrible half-attention, as I need Hannah, my belle, to appear. It looks like I am here, but I am also not here. Dad is in the same boat. I have to keep moving.

Of course, everything works out. I am escorted by my mom down the aisle, the bride comes into my view with her dad. We're smiling like two people who haven't seen each other since the great floods. Sometimes she's a composite of after-images to me, but here in her long white vintage dress, she is the love of my life, the one I'll always bring to the dance, a completely real person.

We are finally crossing into new territory. The rabbi barely keeps it together as he proceeds to insult and praise this matrimony. My family sings louder than he ever expected and they bring me to my spiritual feet. I can only cling to reality for so long before we are supposed to walk away as the couple and take some minutes to ourselves. We are already exhausted, but our friends and family lift us up and we manage to stay up until eight in the morning, dancing and drinking and eating and dreaming. Hannah has more heart and soul than the City of New Orleans.

These are my two favorite moments: When I see that *everyone* is wearing a kippa and when they get me on that chair.

107

Fine grey stone plates, Japanese silver candlestick holders, half-empty green bottles of Burgundy wine, Domaine Hertz, vielles vignes, 2007. White folded napkins, half-setup bar, bottle caps intact, pour spouts, spent tea lights everywhere, around six tables, pillars from ceiling to floor in equal distance. Stopping at the entrance to the ballroom, a locked door, the wind picking up outside after the rain. One hour of darkness and clear morning light would return. The carpet wasn't littered, the tablecloths were ruffled, though, strewn with debris of a night. No jewels in clear sight, no jackets, some small couture handbags. A stale, sweet, lingering scent, the cheese left on the tables, decanted wine. A sign of blood on one chair. A single bullet shot by the imagination. Water spilled on that table top. Happiness was here. Did it leave in a hurry? Will it be gone long?

108

Dad is confused between day and night. Infants have the same issue, but they get better. My ticket back to California is for July 3rd through August 8th and we have family and friends in town so instead of the big newlywed blowout, we're going to Brussels for what I call our "moneyhoon." Adding a little to *Document 120* helps me deal with the emotional fact that we don't always know how to live. The body's coming undone, the boy's coming undone. Pain-free time must be given more meaning. In between the dark days there shouldn't be any dark days. The light has to come back to me. Hannah is here willing it.

PART FIVE

JULY

109

Now to the end of the story: the last-second chance clutch of the hand, a teenage boy armed with carpe diem, a sixth-grader at the talent show; the constructed versions of life and death that go backwards and shape the way we think and see man, woman, and child — all that pop and circumstance — forever.

So it's like I never left. I am feeling circus blue at the airport sitting next to 63 pounds of buck teeth sucking her pantyhose covered thumb, pimples all over, talking about, 'I don't like getting in trouble or breaking rules.' This is it. Toots is driving. Curves and rocks along the mountain highway, dust and bushes on the hillside. Heat. Sun glaring off the road guard. We're all going to a slumber party up in this house. Like old times 1981. Dad sleeps in the living room again.

110

The question this morning is "Do you want socks today?"

Dad hesitates, "I don't know. Haven't decided."

He is in bed more and more. He knows what's happening. He tells me, "I'm gonna wake up and ask if it's night or if it's day. Because I sleep so much I lose the date, become disoriented." His complexion is whitening. He can't move his legs, but he can still control his feet, and he still has cravings. He makes his own odd conversation, starting and stopping with new irregularity, making gestures I haven't quite become accustomed to, but he also continues to remain the same, shouting his familiar call for "Pea-*nuts*!" like a vendor at a ball game. What else can I bring besides nourishment?

We go on a walk to the Ice Castle International Training Center. Inside the skaters twirl and twirl.

"Leo," Caretaker no. 1, says, calling him by his chosen middle name, "You want to go to the rink? There's an exhibition."

This is Kay, a tall brunette valley girl, mama bird four times over and born again grammarian; long polished nails, once of smokey eyes, hair still in a ponytail. When she speaks she presses her lips together and leaves a small corner for the words to escape. She's always standing and bending her knees. She can't stop moving. She has "bink" and other sound effect words in her vocabulary: "The squirrel gets that cone and eats the seeds and then — 'bink!' — the core comes out." We would have something in common if we talked long enough.

Dad says no, so we continue downhill in the heat.

I'm not surprised that it's harder to get him in and out of the car. I'm surprised that he remembers every house in the neighborhood around the lake and that every time we pass one that he knows really well, he tells its story.

"That's one we could've bought. It has no hallway so you couldn't get from one room to the other."

Kay is tender and selects her words with aplomb. She doesn't have any bitter, mean, or controlling attributes. I'm a little shaken by how this compares to the former setup at Em's. It's like coming back home. I begin to make odd references and use humor to stunt my remorse.

"Aye, aye, aye, life is getting harder," Dad says.

"How so?" I want to know.

"Every bowel movement is an adventure. The toilet is so small."

Laurel suggests we get a portable potty and Dad agrees. I think they are kidding until Laurel announces, "The decision has been made," and delegates Kay to call hospice.

111

This is the Laurel you've heard of and don't know much about. She's from Brooklyn. She grew up going to Coney Island and the Catskills. Dad met her at Atikva's wedding when I was sixteen. I was there. Atikva's third wife had been Laurel's sorority sister "a million years ago" and Laurel was having a good time when Dad came around obsessing that I was late because I got a ticket on the freeway. I'll never forget that ticket for crossing multiple lanes. So Laurel arrives in our life by way of news about my failing. You know what she said?

"Have him pay for it."

She's a very blunt person. I believe her involvement in Dad's life resurrected his sense of liveliness, which made me feel like everything was going to be all right with him. She was the one who got him to go places. She was the one who encouraged him to invest in making a small cabin in the woods into a mountain home. She promised that she would be willing and able to help with Dad whenever it was necessary and here she is out of love, loyalty and respect, not out of a sense of obligation.

You never know what's going to be your history and you go and go, swimming through time, but it still isn't history until you settle back into it and you're floating in your house with your hands behind your neck, laughing, making jokes and all that, and you don't have to try so hard to recreate the feeling. That's your history.

112

We have the Tour de France on. "You wanta watch something else?" I ask Dad.

"I don't care," he says. "When you get to France, no more Jelly Belly. Go to the gym every day. Do runs, do gymnastics. Otherwise, in four years you'll have the belly of a leviathan. You're genetically correct."

I don't know what that means.

Later that day we go to the Village. Dad is pissed at himself for not wearing his sandals because it's hot outside. We take some pictures in spots we've visited since we were little kids. Toots complains that it's hot as hell and I tell her hell is actually cold. She says, oh really? I tell her to ask dad and then I do so myself.

"Is hell cold or warm?"

"Right now?" he asks.

"Yeah."

"Warm."

I sneeze and dad reacts, "*Aye*. Can you ever finish this? Take some allergy medicine."

I have a sore throat I'm not talking about.

The four of us, Kay included, head to the dock that goes out pretty good into the lake. It's like local parking up here. You put on your bathing suit and drive your boat from your place on the other side of the lake. We're looking at ducks and people and generally taking in the beautiful sunny day. Other people are hanging out in the village, shopping, walking around. I want to know what's fun about paddle boarding because there's a guy out on the lake doing it and it just doesn't seem interesting to me.

Dad says, "It's freedom."

Toots asks in her muted Zen chopping broccoli tone, "What's fun about anything?"

Kay says, "You're walking on water."

Dad's birthday is in five days so I ask him, "What do you want for your birthday?"

He pauses. "I want cake and ice cream and chocolate."

Every day is pretty much the same thing up here, but here we

are. He's worried about the big stuff we left at Em's. We assure
him that we are going to get all of it. When he wakes up from a
nap he asks, "What's the date and the time?" and I tell him. Then
he asks, "You sleep well?" and I tell him, "It's the afternoon."
So he asks, "What did you do today?" We're fluid like this most
of the time. Some things require emotion. After dinner there's a
moment where he asks me to sit by him on the bed. But even that
ends when he finds out the time. "Oh, boy. Midnight."

113

Somebody's always eating around here. Now there is an overbear-
ing and pervasive smell of canned tuna in the kitchen. The nurse
comes for a checkup, takes Dad's blood pressure, and gives him
a wow. He has perfect blood pressure.

"It still doesn't change my diagnosis," Dad says.

"No sir. Everybody pushes you around?"

"Yes. Just in the chair."

"As long as you get out."

"I make a good passenger."

There are seven of us in the living room: Kay, Laurel, Dad, the
nurse, me, the director/owner of homecare provision, and Toots.
We're having a conversation about end of life. He really doesn't
need to have it in his face so we whisper.

He's got shortness of breath when he wakes up and at night
he starts to feel congested.

The nurse advises us to keep oxygen at home because it'll help
him get back to sleep and he won't have that extra anxiety. "How's
your appetite doing?" he asks.

"Like a pig."

"Your abdomen's a little hard."

"All the food. I eat it all."

"You said that with great satisfaction."

"Is that good or bad?" the rest of us want to know.

"Nutrition is good, but it's inconvenient."

The nurse gets a little personal and tells us about himself. He says he used to be an electrician and a contractor. He starts to talk about narcotic pain medications. Dad doesn't want any of them.

An eighth person knocks at the door. It's Gordon, the guy who owns the land next to us. Very nice man. Rides his motorcycle up in good weather from time-to-time to dream about building something. We tell him to come back in the evening when it's not so busy.

Director/owner says, "If you get a headache, you have pain medication."

"You have morphine right now," Kay adds.

Toots says, "He's not ready for morphine."

"Take acetaminophen for pain relief," the nurse advises.

There's a little elbow ribbing and director/owner implies that she has access to marijuana. "We've established that there's a wellness center up here and all he has to do is show up to get a prescription, but I can do something so long as we don't talk about it." I imagine her searching for the pot brownie connect at a rebar topping off party.

"If there's swelling, elevate the legs. It works faster than medication," the nurse says. "We're at the end of life and medications aren't absorbed by the body so well."

Dad tells the nurse that hospice has been by to bathe him regularly. "I'm stinky today because we sat in the sunshine. The more sun the better. It's nice in the sun. Man, it's nice."

"Do you like Eric?"

"He's okay. I can't get a better looking person?"

"You're stuck with him."

"He'll do."

After the nurse leaves, Laurel sits with a glass of milk and reminisces.

"This house is beautiful. My parents went to a bungalow colony for fifty years. It started out as a farm. A woman from Poland, not Jewish. It's called Cachaling. You cook yourself. Really low budget. You slept in one building. Each room had a family, two double beds and cots. No privacy. You shared a bathroom. The whole summer. The second building was the community dining room. The shared refrigerator was in there. You marked your stuff with initials."

Dad's in the kitchen where he brushes his teeth and makes his coffee. He manages to pop the top off of a new jar of coffee. Pretty strong from what you usually do, Kay says.

"Fifty years in a row. Down the hill there was Kutchers. They sold tickets to the Borscht Belt comedians and musicians. Ex was a waiter in the Catskills from the time he was fifteen. You got opportunities among the community. What we got wasn't anything like we would get on the Pacific Ocean. No exposure to lifestyles."

114

I suggest to Dad, "Let's take a walk down the hill after."

"Boring," he says.

"Ready?" I ask.

"It's not up to me. I'm a prisoner."

"The question is do you *need* to shave?"

"I don't need to shave. You want me to shave."

"You'll look better."

At the Post Office we park the SUV between a 70s puce green Mustang and a monster truck with a U.S. flag propped up in back, the driver inside gripping his steering wheel and a metal coffee mug. Kay is telling us about her husband's car and the subject of their relationship triggers cascading psycho-luminescence. She tells us, he still looks at beautiful women and I'm okay with that.

Dad says, "As long as he still looks at you."

Afterwards, Caretaker no. 2 switches out Caretaker no. 1. This is the first time I'm meeting Kay's daughter. Her name is Titian. She seems to have a big-boned, inelegant figure, brilliant aquamarine eyes, skin that tans easily, and a massive set of breasts. She says her best friends are children and dogs. The rest of her is a confused adolescent composed for cameras. Kay asks her something about the neighbor and the way she answers — "I seen her this morning" — I know I'm in trouble.

Dad's outside on the phone with Em, telling her, "In the meantime, you need to get out. You need to eat...The city has to come and condemn it. Eventually it'll fall." He starts laughing about the house across from the Hacienda. I think he's happy having this conversation. I think so. The man's got his own porch and a deck.

Titian is on the couch describing how she actually wanted to live with her husband before she got married but her dad *was like, no.* Kay admits she said, okay, and asked God to bring people around her that were gunna give her good advice. *I'm just afraid now he's put her down so much she's not gunna come back. She was some pistol. She started out so young. The difference between the boys and the girls. My God. I think only the good Lord understands.*

When Kay leaves we head to another part of the mountain, near the golf course, and walk and push the chair a good distance until everyone is exhausted and hungry. I ask Dad, *You want raw meat?* So he tells me, "You have a decidedly awkward sense of humor. Well, I guess everyone has their way of coping." I'm on the verge of arguing when a young guy emerges from the woods covered in a head-to-foot sheen of dirt with a beard that begins at his eyes, like a B-film wolf man. He's heading right into us, but takes an angle before we cross paths. The looks on our faces must have given him reason to laugh. I focus on the plastic bag of groceries he has in his hand.

Dinner bugs me. Dad's holding the table with his left hand and I'm watching him fold onto his side. He cleans his lips after each bite of fettuccine, picking up whatever falls on the table. He finishes fallen over with his head below his plate. "Ghi, help me stand up," he says. I embrace him and sit him upright with difficulty.

I'm talking about the fires up north and I tell him I talked to Hannah and she says hi. He says, "Next time you talk to her, tell her I said hi back. And when you get a chance, I'll take some ice cream. It'll cool me off." What kind? I ask after a short hesitation. "Black and white. What else is there?" Well, we have all that money to buy ice cream, what flavors do you want? "Black and white." I go scoop out the ice cream, recalling to mind Mom saying she'll have to be here to sit shiva with us when Dad dies because she never had an official Jewish divorce. I feel bad for telling her no she doesn't and I don't want to talk about it, and I serve the bowl of ice cream by pulling the over bed table too far into Dad's stomach. "What are you doing?" he says. "What's the idea?"

In the evenings we've been watching the Tour de France recap and his pawn shop show. I get excited about showing him France and he's seriously awake in his reclining chair at about a quarter to nine tonight, telling me aphorisms like, "You lose by a nose, not by a longshot" and "Sometimes you're a seller, sometimes you're a buyer." We ask dad if he's ready for bedtime. He says, "Wait, I have to think. We have a lot of windows open. I'm not gonna sleep here am I?"

"This is where you sleep," we say.

Titian and I start talking after the entire household has gone to bed. I overhear her on the back porch getting angry with her ex-husband over child support and I steer her into a conversation I want to have. She tells me about how her family kept moving every six months and how she has dyslexia and left high school at fourteen and emancipated from her parents before meeting a twenty-three year-old guy with a kid. *I was legal under eighteen. I told him I was eighteen. One year later he was abusing me. At twenty-eight years of age he gave me a kick in the face in front of my two kids…He's an alcoholic. I say, if you can't beat 'em, join 'em.*

115

Hummingbirds visit the garden, July tenth. "We're going to have coffee and cake and the first surprise of the day," Laurel says. (A cure for you!) "Okay, let's see what we need to get organized here."

"Do you feel like it's your birthday?" I ask Dad.

"In the course of the day I might start feeling like it."

I'm acting out on some unknown issue that coincides with talk of today's plan. Something about the nature of celebration. Or the news that a homeless guy broke into a place in the foothills and raped a terminally ill hospice patient. My sister asks me questions: Ghi, why are you being so weird? Why are you being so complicated? It's just not what you feel like doing, right?

We try to come up with a movie we can go see. Most of the options get the pained "*aye*" from Dad. We end up going to one about male strippers. Kay looks pretty uncomfortable during the screening. After the show she admits with some red splotching and lip smacking, "My thing is, my ultimate goal, is to keep him out of bed."

Back home, Toots is hot and complaining and Dad's capital U — uncomfortable. He's trying to open a package of chocolates and he can't do it. What would be more comfortable? We ask. "Who knows," he says. "You do this, you do that." Have you always loved chickens? I ask, pressing him about his collection, thinking about how I want to go to the land where popcorn doesn't get eaten to show around a prose experiment I finished and dedicated to him for his birthday. There is a chance I'll get to have Henry Rollins' unguarded opinion of it at my friend's literary event. Dad's fixed on the package of chocolates. It's your manual dexterity, I tell him. He says, "It has nothing to do with Manuel. I don't know Manuel."

He's devouring cake and looks up, "A nice day like this makes ugly houses look good."

Then, he points at the checked red flannel shirt on the armrest of the sofa. "How did this start looking like a *shmate*?" I stand there. It's not your shirt, if that's what you think. It's my shirt. He pauses. "That's some good cake. I don't ever complain about lack of cake." He begins humming *Yerushalayim shel zahav* and I whistle along with him until he tells me, "You're ruining it."

Dad has the television on mute and tells me to put on Vivaldi's concerto in D minor, rv 242, because it reminds him of his father.

"Reuven couldn't sit down on the plane. He tried to walk off. *Doesn't matter that we're right now thirty-three thousand feet in the air, I'm getting off*, he tells me. I was very upset. I couldn't control him. He won't sit down. He's standing by the door. That was my father. He didn't care that was how it's supposed to be. *What do I need to eat in a restaurant?* he'd say, *Chaya's food is better*. At Shuk Hacarmel he would negotiate over a cucumber. *Six shekels, for a cucumber?* He finally got it down to two. He was going to give it to you for one. *No, I don't want it anymore*. The merchant asks, 'Where'd you find that guy? On the road?' I wanted to say, Dad, you're driving me crazy." (I've never heard you say that.) "It wouldn't have helped."

"Your father wouldn't have whipped you?" I ask. "He used to smash tomatoes and make you drink it."

"No. I was Saba's favorite. He has good insides."

"That's because you lived in the U.S.," I say.

Dad says, "We're having really good days aren't we? Really good food, good company, good conversations."

I go down to the basement with a flashlight, unlock the lock, come back out and the lock is gone.

116

I climb the back stairs in the dark of a moonless night expecting the wolf man to attack me. I can hear Titian in the light defending herself for what she calls an oversight. Maybe she didn't forget to give Dad his pills. Maybe it's the ghost of Mordechai Campbell. I want to go back and search for the lock, but I keep still. The dark woods have always frightened me. I think about how Dad felt about being alone up here. Why is he not afraid? I'm preoccupied with human nature, not the woods themselves. Maybe doing what he did to make people better, he could smell a killer.

Meanwhile, Titian is going on about family, how she used to call her grandpa, Sir. *You never talked back to your elders in my house. One time my mom and I got into it, I told her, 'Go ahead, hit me. Hit me 'til you kill me.' My dad said what he meant and meant what he said. His dad took his life. He had depression. Things affect you when you are young, and they change you to the core. I just thought life was too difficult and I didn't want to do it. I was done. I didn't want to stick around anymore. At fifteen years old I took pills. It's hard when you don't have a great relationship with your mom when you're young. Every girl wants to have something different about them. My mom was always a loose cannon. I always thought they would miss you when you left.*

Dad says, "I think the only thing harder than marriage is—"

"*Children,*" I say to myself.

"Divorce," he says.

Suddenly my phone rings. I pick it up, heading back below to the buildup for some privacy. It's Hannah. I immediately begin asking her the caring questions, not telling her about my nerves. Her voice emboldens me to revise theories about the dark and search for that lock, but I'm still expecting someone to grab my wrist and take me. When I was a boy I used to get chased by older kids with cobalt eyes and switchblades and I've always had this nightmare that one catches up to me in the dark. Hannah irritably brings up her reason for calling after I keep restating what she's said to prove to her that I'm listening and I don't make sense.

"There's a moment that we didn't get. Time ending something and starting something new. We were taking care of people, attending to new relationships. We didn't get a trip where it's about us. It hasn't been and it won't be. We won't get that moment of feeling like newlyweds. Not Disneyland, take off your dress and go on something crazy. It was take off your dress, put it in the closet and go back to eating cheese and salad. How many times I've been here on my own. I feel like a bachelorette. I feel like we're dating. I'm watching all the romantic movies."

If somebody asks me, how my wife is, I say, "She's good. She just has some daily stresses." As usual, they say. Two weeks into this hard time, our phone conversations, video conversations, email exchanges, everything plunges me deeper in despair.

"A woman wants to be first priority, but not over the dying dad. Don't even think of me," she says.

Don't even think of me. I will stab you, though. I will stab you in your side with my flesh-eating sword. I'll say, aren't we going to be poor, never own a car, never have a nice apartment, never be near each other for very long because of immigration, writing, and illness. *What kind of torturing shit is this flip side of supportive?*

"There's something called honesty."

There's something called menstruation. Why am I being bashed this way, all my triggers set off? We live in your back yard. You have your whole family here, your fantasy wedding—all the stress, all the joy, just to tell me you feel like it never happened. You *and I* are sick and I am so angry at myself for tumbling so hopelessly at this sickness and the reason why I have to call you names. I should just retreat into something else. Take a deep breath. I am in horror. I'm in shock. I don't want anything but to forget this despairing state of mind you put me in with your way of fast forward and rewinding.

"I just want you to reassure me. Reassure me that I'm going to be alright."

I should just give up is what I'm thinking at the very moment the lock comes under my foot and skids across the stones to the side of the house. I catch my balance and exhale. I don't communicate my delayed response. I swallow it.

"You're going to be alright. We're going to be alright."

117

Afternoon in the southern California mountains, late night in Paris, I'm cooking a compote of prunes, apples, pears, and cherries. "It smells of cinnamon," Dad says, waking up, squinting his eyes and lifting up his glasses to rub around the bridge of his nose. I ask him, What's it feel like inside your body right now? He says, "Nice." He sneezes, uncrosses and re-crosses his legs with some effort. Kay asks, Do you want a regular tissue for that nose? He pauses. "This nose will accept anything." You sure you don't want to git out on the porch? she asks. He says, "No!" and laughs, *hahaha*, satisfied with himself.

This is when Dad starts going out of the house less and less and our walks become infrequent.

I get Hannah on the phone. "How you *doon?*" I ask, like my Dad. Not good. "What's wrong?" So, I got in a fight with my stepmom and I got in a fight with my mom. "Tell me more," I say and the reception cuts out.

Then Dad proceeds to announce, *aye, aye, aye, aye, aye*. I start to massage his head and neck because I want to be right in his face. He says, "I'm in no playing mood."

"They tell me that all illness is self-limiting. What does that mean?" I ask him.

"That it will put an end to itself."

I am quiet.

He continues, "It will heal spontaneously, or not."

I tell my dad a story I just heard about someone who went to Africa and was cured. Dad hears me out and responds, "A believer would say it's God, a non-believer would say it's time."

The minds of the healthy are often concerned with healing. The minds of the sick are probably trying to live. Having a relationship to time takes all our effort. How about let's forgo the moving lips and batting eyelashes and take a bottle of liquor or a box of pills or a movie or a book to slow it all down so that we can see it, feel it, reproduce it in our mind, unto it's innermost parts, until it's the sort of stuff that moves the immobile.

On the classical station I hear this enthusiastic radio voice announcing, 'It's beach time surgery! Beach time tummy tuck, outer labia chop, breast lift, implants, botox."

We need to create and maintain contexts. Things are happening at all times down every exit off the highways of the world and most of these things are never seen or mentioned, like time passing unnoticed.

The current shooting in a Colorado movie theater is an incident that a gives us the chance to talk about gun control again. Dad is saying that he thinks there should be a psychiatric check at the purchase of a gun. This is the world he's leaving. I ask him why we're seeing this happen. He says, "People are angry. But that's an inadequate answer. They have no appetite to put forward specific gun control laws. Money from the gun advocates is ten-to-one in Washington." Then the circuit breaker under the house goes out and we lose our lights.

"Every day brings more disasters," he says.

But why can't every day be magical?

Because if by the calendar July 20 had any substance it would have to be provided to us. The only reliable traditions seem to be the ones provided to us. That's why alcohol is so pleasing. Instead of sitting, we rock steady engaging with the least likely parts of ourselves, and the days of the month, the minutes of the hour, the year itself, multiplies.

July 20 is all a pretense. Today there are no new memorable monuments in the city. I will place one. I'll conceive of a title for it and commercial applications.

"A hundred dollars if you name this," Dad says.

I say, "I don't know this from Strauss."

He winces. "This is by Marais. The Bells of St. Genevieve. Ghi-Gee, do you remember a couple of weeks ago, two big airplanes passing through the night? What was that? What I heard was two giant airplanes that passed clearly over our heads."

"It might have been the space shuttle flying to the east coast. I don't know."

"Are you gonna sleep today?" he continues as Titian moves to change him.

"Where are you from?" she asks as he thrusts his pelvis up.

"I'm Jewish," Dad says.

"I'm German, Scottish, Irish and Czech," she says, like she's been replaying this exact line all her life.

And all those nations have people of distinct civilizations who end up being desert rats.

"That's good," Dad says. "There were twelve Tribes now known as three at the origins of Judaica."

"Everybody comes from somewhere," I say.

"My dad always says we're gypsies," Titian says finishing up the change. "You finally feel like you can cool off, huh? I'm gonna take a nice long bath tonight. I have a jet tub."

"Hmmm?"

"I have a jet tub at home."

"Mmm. I want some orientation," Dad says.

"It's the twentieth of July, quarter to six on Friday," Toots says.

"It's my aunt Estelle's birthday today," he says. "I want to call Em today."

"When you're calling her is it for her or for you?" I ask.

"Aye, leave me alone."

"You've always said that."

I'm onto cooking with garlic. I've got the song, "Stuck on You," in my mind and I'm imagining some nuns living their whole lives in a single house and praying. That's all they do. And work. I'm sure they work.

Would they know what's happening to my dad now? Is God de-creating him?

118

Family puts you to a good start and you make up the story afterwards. Your parents bring you into the world and then one day you leave that world, and in between it's all negotiable. Confused feelings, estimates, abstract desires, and the sometime need to see the truth can kill you if you let it, but every day you are dying anyway, so you need to work that out.

I ask Dad what his Ph.D. dissertation was about because, I explain to him, all these years ago Toots and I used to listen to his recordings. He tells me about how he used actual couples and examined their relationships by comparing their performance on thematic perception tests with their performance in psychodramatic roleplaying situations. He mentions that a rudimentary version of this was the 𝒪𝓃𝓌𝓂 method of reconciling issues of inheritance. Apparently family secrets were once more sacred than material wealth. I was six when I started listening to the recorded sessions, trying to figure out who my dad was. That was the year he moved to an apartment in another canyon and it was difficult to know much about him. I liked hearing his voice. It helped me form a concept of him. I figured he was busy making these recordings every day. Mom stayed home and took care of the kids, smothering us at will, but I had no substantial concept of Dad to accompany my memory of waiting for him to come home from work. When he stopped living with us, those cassettes maintained his presence.

119

The prospect of Dad going outside has become more complicated with the increased loss of mobility. The first decision is always the same: car or no car today. The director/owner of homecare provision is on shift and she's got no muscle so convincing Dad to get into the car is going to be difficult. We're walking on the steep switchback street, pushing and pulling the chair and all these drivers are shaking their heads at us. We go over some of the flora we're seeing: eastern redbud, golden raintree, bleeding heart, strawberry plant, hazelnut. Director/owner asks, How many years you been up here? Dad answers, "Seventeen years up here. Up and down." I sneeze. "Yeah, yeah, yeah, sick like a dog for three weeks. Sneezing left, sneezing right." (I'm not sick.) When we get back to the car it's the morning routine in reverse. Dad smiles to me. "You don't have to question the patient so much," he says.

At this point he doesn't have any control over his legs and his upper body has gone limp. Watching him laid out in the front seat, his head jabbing into the SUV's central console, crying out, *Ouch, ouch!* it is unbearably sad and unbelievable at the same time because the machine is still at work searching for intelligent solutions—Dad is spitting out ideas calmly, floating along, maintaining his humility.

In the car with the engine on and no air, he sits quietly, staring at some people at the gas station charging two dollars to wash a car, sucking at his teeth. Nice churchgoing people is what he calls them. He turns to me and says, "You never washed my car in your life." Now it's my turn to say nothing. I'm trying to take the mailbox key off of the car keychain and I know that I've only got two seconds before he attempts to be critical. Besides, he missed the irregularity of attention I gave to his car once upon a time.

"What's a matter with you?" he says.

"You have a way of saying something two seconds into the time a guy tries to do something differently than you would have done it." I have the same way.

In his mailbox Dad received a free magazine on whose cover a female model poses in a familiar desert to lend credibility to this headline: the outing of the moral majority. Most people need to follow some sort of storyline otherwise they cannot become who they are. If they read this one they might discover that apparently love is not the most sought after and packaged, self-regenerating concept there is.

On the drive home along the rim, looking down as far as I can see into the valley (without running off the road), I contemplate the lush, green, thick-leafed trees, the palms bobbing their heads, and the bald hills.

I ask Dad if he knows the composer Lalo Shiffrin. He says, "He's Jewish. Yeah, I went to his house once to play the accordion. I knew he was a musician." Dad played accordion in places all over the nation. He may have played once or twice for us.

We decide to stop by the lake for some fresh air. "Just for a second I want to see what goes on here," Dad says. "Looking at the birds takes away sadness. Takes you out of self. The natural world puts things in perspective for a while." How much of this he actually says, I don't know but it's fitting to recognize, when a bird just stands in front of you at a not so likely place and time, you forget yourself. You're simply embedded in this deeply human activity.

"This is good," Dad says.

We're all eager to touch something that we feel slipping away.

120

The interminable Stellar's Jay squawk, with notes of rising and falling tenor coinciding, is nature's wall of sound in the morning. I smell the stain of cigarettes on my hands but I haven't smoked. I am deceived by the rush of heat and body functions. Today is the day I begin thinking about lizards and rattlesnakes and twisted spines.

Kay reports, "I had a dream that Leo was walking. We went to the grocery store. Interesting dream, huh, Leo?"

He's slow, tongue slack, body fallen over in the chair. No words. I give him baby kisses when I lean over his head. He asks me, "Where did Toots go?"

I ask him, "Do you agree with the psychologist who said that a nine year-old and a five year-old don't understand permanence?"

He says, "You know, I was nine when my grandma died. I knew she wasn't going to come back."

When he's out of hearing range he disengages, but he's highly engaged in his way.

I give him a back massage. Every day as many as three times a day he gets a back massage or a foot massage.

"You're doing me some good," he says.

Usually I hear I got fingers of bone.

We've been talking about cremation for a while. Dad says he's having lucid thoughts. "My body is telling me to sleep."

Laurel says, "There's no air on him, you realize." She gives him his lunch options while Kay intervenes. "Gefilte fish, blintzes, kashavarnishkes."

Dad stares into space hoping if he closes his eyes the choices will reset.

"You feel social?" we ask. He shakes his head.

"You feel anti-social," I continue. He shakes his head again, makes mouth smacking sounds.

Laurel says, "You're not gonna eat some salad with us?"

He says, "I will."

As he eats a salad, Paris calls.

"The amount of energy I'm spending doing what I'm doing for the rest of my life, it has no purpose. Beyond that we are walking on a thin thin line. I can't explain how much stress I have right now. I know there's more in life. I'm thirty years old and this is literally ridiculous to me. I've never felt so stupid. Everything I do is for a job and I get no job. I work like an asshole and I'm an intern. That's it. This weekend I'm fact checking with a blue book and I'm married and you're not around. Ridiculous. I could do anything else and that's what I'm doing. Nine-thirty at night and I learned that. That's not good news. You're not coming back to a happy Hannah. I'm retiring from the whole thing. I know what you're going through. I have to play with commas and periods. I'm doing whatever it takes, just so you know. Nine-thirty. We hired someone for this. (Just do the best you can.) I think I have bad luck. Meanwhile, the apartment is stuffy. I can't open the windows because I have a cat and my mom is too lazy to get it. So it's thirty-eight degrees Celsius and I can't open the window. If you have something positive to give, I think I can take it."

Dad's watching some 24/7 on Romney, muttering '*sonofabitch.*' He's not in LaLa land. He's listening to our conversations. He switches the channel and starts humming the Olympic song. Tonight is the opening ceremony of the London Olympics.

He wants water with his very early dinner. He says, "Water'd be a good idea because I'm afraid of what they're gonna do to me." Drinking the pink liquid I got to jumpstart his bowels seems awful, but he's also repulsed by water. We spread out the food on the table and ask him if he wants to try and get up. "That's an idea," he says, "but an idea, that's like, what d'ya call it?" He searches for the words. "An idea that's out before it's time. Novel."

Toots asks, "You want your glasses so you can watch TV?"

He says, "No."

I say, "You want to sleep all day?" Toots hits me.

We spend the night talking about all manner of thing and in the back of my mind I'm thinking, I'm probably going to have to say goodbye soon.

121

I head to down the mountain into the smog and heat because I like the motion of the road and there's a Rotary meeting I want to observe. Pineapple teriyaki chicken is on the menu. In the dining room of the Country Club there are lots of blue hairs with their hearing aids and sunspots who have served society in a dignified way. The 93 year-old newlywed in attendance designed the grounds of this eucalyptus-lined golf course with a view of the snow-capped mountains. I've never eaten here before. Not when it was more exclusive, not when the city was still liquid. In the cheap seats today there is a high school freshman from the Canary Islands, just arrived to this part of the world probably thinking Mickey Mouse or Baywatch or something like that. She gets the keyboard pianist jamming a throwback tune over the luncheon.

A teacher blames the state legislature for the thirty-nine kids in her class. She says there is a direct correlation between the way kids are educated and how cities are run. This city operates like a house of worship that wants you to keep coming back. My anti-hero Harry Holmes (of cold storage fame) says that in 1928 his grandfather's factory was producing 300 pound blocks of ice with state of the art equipment, but now because of absentee landlords and shipping people in who are on probation, there are fewer productive citizens. Yeah, it's called brain drain and it happened because nothing happened. No innovation. No interest. No positive development. No particular identity. Someone else says fifty percent of the citizens here are on welfare. It's generational.

You can't control a kid's parents. It seems there is only high end happiness and middle class mediocrity. We have set things up to shun those less financially successful.

AUGUST

122

Wednesday, August 1. Laurel, Toots, Kay, and I hold a morning bathroom conference to remind ourselves that we have to be upbeat. We need to provide gentle reminders of who Dad is. We come out with energy and try to convince him to go bowling because it's very social. "I'm not social," he says.

Laurel jokes about the bagels she got, "You know Dad, you can never please him."

"Oh, you had a glass of milk," Kay says, very positively.

Dad lashes out, "Write it down, write it down. If she doesn't write it, they wake me up at two-thirty in the morning. I got to get up sometime. The liquid doctors are after me."

By dinner he won't be able to get out of bed. He'll be dizzy, but he'll say he's alright.

We watch beach volleyball. During a diaper commercial, I ask him, You ever change diapers? "Yeah," he says. You hate it? "It was your diapers."

Forget about trying to get him to drink a banana date smoothie I made. He tells me, "Tomorrow."

Toots hunts a big mosquito hawk, breaks his leg, and now he's suffering under the fridge when the head nurse arrives for a checkup.

"I have some silly things to ask," he says. "If you know the answer, okay. If not, you'll know why."

Dad nods. Kay's upper lip is folded over her teeth.

"What day is it? What month?"

"I don't know."

"What year is this? Who's the President of the United States?"

"Obama."

"I'm going to listen to your heart and lungs…There's no skin breakdown, no swelling. You're getting good flow in your ankles, so that's good."

We talk a little about cell-to-cell communication and the abnormal growth in his body. Then the head nurse takes the rest of us in the master bedroom and talks to us about the decline plateau. He says be ready for more decline, more confusion. Hospice is comfort, not cure. Nobody on this earth can cure him. He's coming from a far place.

"What stage is he in?" we ask. "Active dying?"

"No. There are no hard and fast rules. I don't know. I can't say… There will come a point where he doesn't want to take medicines."

Laurel launches a counterstroke, "We happen to have a neuroscientist in the family who thinks there's something peculiar about the fact that he has the same diagnosis since December. He says the diagnosis hasn't proceeded 'fast enough.'"

"It's not unusual to go slowly. Some go rapidly, some go slowly. What's important is that you are talking to him and being around, as family, reinforcing what day it is, keeping him as oriented as possible."

"I have to say, I do that," Laurel says.

"You're gonna do the best you can. This is gonna get more difficult. He's gonna need you more."

"Can we still go on trips with him?" I ask.

"If he's not afraid."

123

The morning Foof arrives, Dad's cutting a bagel in four, saying, "Nobody does things totally right anymore," and then he skips lunch and dinner and goes to sleep for the night at seven p.m. Foof is Toots' best old school pal. We spend the evening sitting around Dad talking about how we were the last generation without computers, about first cars and getting on restriction for changing into thigh-high stockings at school, about coming out to the chilly facts of adult life.

Toots tells it the best: "How's it going, Cheepster? He's got a beer in his hand. 'Not great. Sandie's sleeping with another man.' Glug, glug, glug. No, Cheepster. Are you serious? Come on.

"I was a seventeen year-old girl. He used to drive a salami truck. He had nudie mags in the glove compartment that we found once."

We laugh about how the director/owner of homecare provision was massaging and kissing Dad's feet the other day (and how Laurel told her to stop.) We talk about our history of significant others.

I close my eyes and not knowing what time it is, my body says I could sure use the snooze. While I'm drowsing I conjure an image of a man in the room holding a knife ready to attack me. This time instead of fighting myself awake I just admit that it is what it is going to be. Stick the knife in me.

124

One crow screams in the high alpine branches.

It sounds like I have to leave again.

We're in the living room together watching the Olympics contribute to making cancer survivor narratives mundane. We know the arc. The viewer is supposed to get hooked into continuing to watch and even if the survivor athlete loses he is still a hero. I still want to believe Dad has one shot in the dark. In the past he gave an average of ten shots in the dark to ten patients a day who he could help get better. He has no gold medals to speak of and no complete stories that he has the right to tell, but I imagine that sometimes the care he gave worked and sometimes it didn't. If

I understand this now it's not from anything other than the passing of time: we need to learn a new life together without him. My heart expands, inflates at that, I don't know what—and then it comes to pass. You have to have internalized something to relate to when the day arrives.

Marvin Hamlisch died today. On some level we are constantly mourning a loss.

"Feel any better, Dad?" Toots asks after having Titian massage the blood back into his feet.

"I'm not the expert at this one," he says.

Titian's up to sharing how she texts her emotional life in a self-proclaimed "redneck" way. She reads us her latest message, "'I've been chasing after you for a long time. You're pretty fast, girl.' If I haven't answered for a year, you're pretty slow," she laughs, her uvula visible, fluttering.

We all want to occupy space in other peoples' lives. Sometimes the only space to settle is in the imagination where whatever is gained or re-gained is going to be lost. You don't often see people sticking around for the end-of-the-road, mind-numbing parts; they stick around for the contest.

The day I leave Dad decides to take off the beard he's worn his entire adult life and all I can think of is that I've never even seen his face. He lays drowsily with the window behind him open to the roving mountain air. I say, "Dad, I have to go now." He tries to ask me a few questions, but it all comes down to making a move I'm not prepared to make. So I stand still memorizing the position of his hands clasped against his chest and he slowly delivers his parting words.

"You be careful. Take it easy out there."

PART SIX

125

Chorus: Oh, sadness, dreadful, dreadful sorrow.

With ~~death~~ coming closer, Dad has lost his faculties as a man, a universal giver, the leader of a pride. They have been taken from him. Who would continue to tell me, 'Enough now, okay' for all the stupid things I have to obsessively repeat? Playing these emotions out on paper is like falling asleep to the sound of an air duct humming. The alarms go off throughout the house. If he thinks he's dying then I think I'm dying. What we know is that it's entirely up to us. We have to do what we feel. He's in a place where nobody panics, where we're all taking care of him and leaving him to get as sick as he is.

I'm barely a day back in Paris and Toots is already telling me, "I'm gonna be here for two weeks by myself because you're not here…so good luck to me…I don't feel like there's a plateau. I don't know who told us about his. There's no plateau. He's getting worse. I think he's getting less and less able…I don't know what's gonna happen…just stay in touch with me and I'll let you know. I'll talk with Titian. It's gonna be hard for me to do work if I got Dad on my mind. And we won't succeed if I don't work. It's helpful when Laurel is here. I don't know how I'm going to do this for two weeks."

A guitarist in the metro will never know that the song he covers puts me at peace before my conversation with my mom and while my dad and I are on the phone and I hear everybody outside on the mountain.

Mom tells me, I can't wait twenty thousand years, I'm going to sell my apartment myself. Advertise it and sell it. As long as it's money. Money is money. What I'm concerned about is health. Money, you make it and spend it. That's my philosophy of life.

"In your dreams," Dad is saying about getting in the car and going for a drive. Laurel says she just can't, meaning she can't help put him in the car. Kay thinks to use the *towl*. She tells Dad to scoot forward. He has me on hold while they make it work.

Dad asks me, "Did you tell So-and-So to buzz off? I'm going to die…I don't think I'm going to see them again. I'm going to die. A person knows."

I'm fighting down the tears and the desire to tell him: all that's reasonable in us comes from you. You can't die!

"Well, that's not your job," he goes on saying.

"What's my job?" I ask.

"Your job is to finish this two hundred and fifty page novel and publish it."

What? I'm wondering. Where is he getting this from because I don't have a novel, I have him. But then someone turns on *Car Talk* and he's already laughing.

How do you relate to the wild eyes of your bemusing son who can't sit there and pretend to have control of the dangling strings of his heart?

"Try to write something good and work hard," he says.

I send out my own kind of prayer: that our children will continue to realize what is possible, not to fear making their own in the world, not to forget their own way, not to wait to see the life in things. They will see and be proud of what they see because it will be true.

126

Everything I'm doing is at the fastest pace possible with anxiety against the fading light. Cancer has shown me that even with my genetic predispositions, my better habits, and the good part of my desires, there is little that I can do to prevent myself from forty, fifty, sixty, death. I'm stuck in this shit stance, on my own, all day reflecting on how I'm going to function, what I'll do for work, if I'm happy to take a straight line and never turn a corner, never come around the bend with real commitments that stick and have purpose. I need something to prolong the minutes between the church bells of Saint Marguerite ringing. I need time to search for inspiration.

Walking to the metro, I feel like I'm addressed by the empty-faced, no-emotion men whose lives can't be communicated. Their glances remind me that every day you repress your learned responses you take a risk. I reveal my smile, or at least lift my lips into a bright line, and they see my general admission with suspicion. I have no idea what undercurrent must run through them leaving them plain, stressed, competitive, and dull-eyed. All these mugs. Everybody's mugging. Pull up your face, bring us to your pueblo.

I begin to get much deeper into the novel, anything to distract me, to raise my spirit. Distraction helps me accomplish more. It turns out that *Document 120* is based on the youngest ꙮꙮꙮ, story.

> This is a film of the final year of life with my father. I don't really know what to say, but I'm saying it so that's something. When I was thirteen we moved to northern California from Atlantic City. I didn't have anything particularly appropriate to share about myself, but my accent made me stand out from the crowd so I knew the girls were never going to like me when I did speak. I was convinced that I had to do something about that. What I did was I stood in a mirror and practiced talking like a surfer. I over-exaggerated. Then I dyed my hair blond and laid out in the sun even when it was a little too cold. I figured no kid living in Marin County would be able to

forget my face. I was a white boy named Mario, growing tall, playing sports, dedicated to his school work and in love with the world. My dad had to ruin it all.

SEPTEMBER

127

Newsflash: Dad doesn't feel pain. When I get him on the phone he tells me that the sun is shining and the wind is blowing. I ask, Dad, are you relaxed? He says, "Extremely."

I tell him about the dream I had last night where I killed someone who tried to kill me first. I don't describe how the final frame of the guy's eyes were like cartoon objects, two dimensional, blinking under water. I say, I remember his eyes. I explain how it felt to live with the fear of being found out. I don't say caught. It's the public finding out that bothers me. You feel like the world will give you what you deserve. So maybe it all depends on what you think you deserve. I don't want any ill will. I don't want any pain.

Dad probably falls asleep to the sound of my common concern because he doesn't say anything. That's okay, I've been falling asleep with him on the line for the past few days.

128

I'm flipping through television channels, uninhibited, provoked by the joy we get out of famous peoples' secret lives, thinking, we live in the default world. *To the left is a dusty, pale earth spotted with rough clumps of manzanita, white boulders of granite and here and there a vacant house, half hiding in an assembly of pinecones, gates, and tall trees.* Many of us are set on becoming like someone in history. Like Christ, like Buddha, like Elvis, like Jake from *Sixteen Candles.* It depends on where you get your history. And where you grew up. To be sure, growth requires the exploration of boundaries. It requires a range of three word mantras that can be applied as needed, like: service, accomplishment and modesty. Personal growth is tied in with real objects, the thing itself. The story of the thing is pretty ecological, but we want resource acquisition and personal advancement along with our growth, so our society prevails by helping us keep some variables sane and simple—default things, such as a dull curiosity—which allows us to push other needs forward.

Dad, you were born into the horrors of impossible war, battles for individual liberties, and the successful moon landing. If there was anything that they kept from you, it hadn't been the need to dream and not to give up easily.

I've come back to work in Paris some, I've experienced the life and times of our mini-family, and soon I'm heading back to see you, probably for the last time. There is no taste in my mouth for this. This is a low gut-rumbling, a rolling of my deepest abyss. After grinding all the hypotheticals together for some time, I'm sick to go, I'm sick to stay.

I get Dad on video chat and tell him Happy New Year. He goes, "hmmm, hmmm, hmm, hmm, hm, hmm, hm, h." It's been one year since we went to Israel for Rosh Hashanah. I repeat, I'm seeing you at the end of the week. He says, "I guess that means I'm going to see you." I ask him, you alright? He stalls and the air through his teeth forces the first syllable, "*Yee*-ah." Whatchu been up to? I ask. He tells me, "The usual."

129

It's midnight, Friday, back in the Inland Empire, curbside at the airport feeling the cool whoosh of the dry and dusty air. I have time to notice things. This obese boy downwind from his cigarette-smoking grandma is stuck waiting for a ride. A wife welcomed home gets more love from the pet Labrador than her husband.

A pretty teenage girl exiting baggage claim prefers the role of luggage handler over daughter. Flip flops gets a kiss on the cheek as an afterthought. I sneeze. Things could be worse. I could be out of words.

At Dad's place the next morning, I see that autumn has begun. I piss for twenty-six seconds, my stomach grumbles heavy and sounds like a dog abandoned on a broken sheet of lake ice. Toots gives me the update in the car, the old check-in before it fully starts. Dad had a good day yesterday. He goes up and down. He still doesn't drink enough very hydrating liquids. He needs comfort, wants comfort—the video chatting and the back rubs and holding hands during enemas which he resists. Titian's boyfriend punched her in the face. They don't talk 'no more.' She's wrecked her car three times, got into a fight with her best girlfriend who bit her more than once, and she witnessed her ex and a friend beat the shit out of her boyfriend.

Welcome back.

Toots admits to being angry all the time. She says this isn't a job for us. I've been gone a couple of weeks. I hope I can help. She talks about how Dad isn't the same Dad. I guess I want to say that we all aren't the same. I can guarantee my affections, but what will come of my natural inclinations, I do not know. Everything is some form of happiness-seeking. Being in the observing or the cerebral mode, one might gravitate to beauty and good things. Some pleasing harmonies, say. There is life in anticipating highs. I admit I've pursued deadening. I can't say my thrills come each day anymore.

I interrupt the death arrangement conversation father and daughter are having and Toots asks, how long 'til the soup is ready? She says the birds are out of food, goes '*whoof*, we need to water those plants,' and ribs me with, 'we're talking about the markets, genius.'

I see how her book is putting Dad to sleep.

Titian tells me about her troubles trusting people and things.
She lets me know that in twenty-four hours, she'll *be drinkin'*.

That night together as a family we watch one of Dad's favorite
films. I note the Vikki Carr song, "It Must Be Him."

130

The first day is always difficult. On the second day we're listening
to Tchaikovsky: Variations on a Rococo Theme and Dad decides
he wants to go to see the Rio Seco symphony at Our Lady of the
Lake church. I don't hold judgment. At the church these things
come across clearly: The old men, they can listen for a while
longer than their little brothers. They have more vivid pictures
in their heads they play witness to and applaud—variations to
the end of a line. A child with dirt under her nails itches her
inner ear not understanding that the encore composition is off
the program. She would rather have another she recognizes,
or something else. We have to make it a point to feed the ego.
I adopt an orchestra member, second row, platinum bangs, over
fifty, serious, sincere, and bitter. To what end do we *conversate*?
I suggest to her, why don't we cut this short? Everything is a story
about one thing before it becomes something else. Anyway, the
creation doesn't have to be so brilliant. Not from the start. Just
enough to lose yourself, to find a muse, an audience, someone
to speak to, dance a three beat with, someone to accompany in
the old one-two, one-two repeat.

Release comes to those who know restraint.

Simple questions like, wild berry or strawberry? leave Dad staring straight, owl-eyed, no attempt at moving his lips. Why I see
a train pass by and do not step in front of it is all programming
to me. I've been living my life loosening up all that fixes us in the
traditional fabric and now I am losing my father.

Last night I took a knife to my arm and imagined cutting it off at the wrist. It was a bread knife. I carried on after I put the knife down. It had a stain of some sort on it so I left it in the sink. I've reacquainted myself with cold weather and confusion, the outside-only language that accent and perception can maintain. My wife is my entourage. She continues with her days and I live with mine. I might never turn the bend.

131

Wednesday, eleven-something, a.m. It's Yom Kippur. Toots is in L.A., Dad's in the shower with Eric, my left kneecap won't stop clicking, and two kids are losing it somewhere in the desert while the male authority in their lives rants on about how their mom sucks off guys everywhere. There is no escape from this. This is more than a cabin in the woods. I just want to hear the sound of life happening. The voices are proof better than whiskey or Dolomites or trick ponies or crosswords that don't ever come to a conclusion in my town.

I get ninety pages into reading *Madame Bovary* to Dad before my brain muses over how he used to think I would make a great rabbi. If only I wasn't a Hebrew school dropout.

Before sundown the rabbi is under the table; after sundown it's a honky tonk bachelor night. Kay's laboring over Dad and I'm on the phone with my mom, whipping back and forth between ancient and new feelings, head in a dust cloud. My mom asks, "What are you eating to break the fast, by the way?" I tell her, hot dogs. "A man like you eats hot dogs for dinner? Eat better than that, okay?" she says. Yeah, I usually do more than that. "Okay, enjoy it. If you were here you would enjoy a cake I made. Are you reading anything? You said you wanted to read…"

Dad's whistling along to *Live at the Lincoln Center*. The world could fall apart so long as the 6:30 news and classical music kept playing.

I try to give him one of his medications after the phone call and he says, "You made a mistake. You should have given it to me before the end of the piece. I'm not taking it."

"You're not going to take your pill? Sure you are," I say.

"Don't tell me sure," he says, hitting his square fingertip against the bed table, punctuating each of his words, "*Don't—tell—me—that.*"

"Who is this, Leo?" Kay interrupts to help me.

"This is Pinchas Zucker. Tchaikovsky, Souvenir d'un Lieu Cher."

It's Yitzchak Perlman.

The New York Philharmonic makes all that was crystallized in him flow, and there he is on the couch, wide awake, and I'm the one falling asleep now. He says, "Mario, you're tired, go to sleep."

132

Friday, the nurse is here telling us what we need to know exactly.

"You've got to remember that he's still his own person. He's the one going through this. He calls the shots. Days where he becomes lucid will be more spread apart. His body is going to stay going. It stores energy. That way it keeps going. He's doing well. There is a significant amount of inter-cranial pressure, though. The tumor is getting to his motor functions."

We tell the nurse that we have to feed him and it's driving him crazy. He says, "That means he loves you so much he's willing to do things he's not used to. He doesn't want to hurt you. He's willing to let you do things he'd let nobody else do. He's probably getting ready, pleasing you guys."

He lost three centimeters from his waist since July. We're trying to get his brothers to come again.

"It'd be a wonderful thing. We don't know how long he'll be here. When he knows that you guys are okay and he gets to say goodbye, that's the time that he'll go. He'll hold onto something until then. When they're dying, you can't die if you're in turmoil.

Or in pain. You can only pass away when relaxed."

That night I improve dinner. I make grilled steak and chicken, warm shrimp rice, and a double desert of chocolate-peanut-vanilla shake and mint strawberries. Then we watch *The Color of Money* until Titian takes over for her mom and proposes an early bedtime because she is drunk and needs to text and pass out. She does her job, but she doesn't know how to be part of a family. She knows how to fake it so that she can get what she wants from life.

"I haven't seen you," she says to Dad.

"You haven't been looking for me," he says, stumbling with the words and whistling through his teeth. I'm sure he can smell her cheap strawberry shampoo and the liquor on her breath.

"How you doing? I haven't seen you. How you feeling?" she repeats, head lowered, fixing her sheets on the living room couch.

"I'm here."

"How you feelin'? Feeling good? How you feeling?"

"Okay. Good."

I know that I would question this if it weren't already sorry enough.

Out of nowhere, at midnight, Toots texts me this one word: levity.

133

The following morning I let it all out on the front porch. I've used every opportunity to tell Dad what I've wanted to say, even when I didn't have anything in particular to say. Now this is what I have left. This is one of those things I had thought about all my life, but I still don't know how to do it.

And so I start babbling the history of my love for him in anecdotes from my age of awakening all the way to our most recent camping trip, until I'm under his nose showing him a photo of us hiking Angel's Landing in Zion National Park. He's hunched over in his chair with a blanket wrapped around his shoulders, eyeballing every glossy print. At that point I'm not waiting for him to come clear to me because he won't. It's not his way. We're facing each other. He has his back to the house and I'm looking at him on my own chair, glancing up and down from the blue sky, trying to think of something to say that sticks so that it winds up comforting him and with any luck is the one concise thing I've always wanted to tell him.

I want to tell him the truth. He says something about a bird: "That's a big one. It is a Stellar's Jay, I think." He asks me to read and when I read he passes out. The flies are driving me nuts, zapping me in the ears, so the words I read come with swats and flips of the wrist, mostly pathetic, to go with this outpouring of sentiment I put into the words. In between Flaubert's lines there are moments that come and pass when I tell myself this is when I say my last goodbye.

With no small effort to restrain the pain that comes with acknowledging to him that I know he will be gone soon, I finally find my voice and just let fly.

"Can you feel what's happening to you, Dad?"

He brings his shriveled head up very slowly and looks at me. "Yeah."

"Are you scared?"

He shakes his head. Wipes the salt water from his eyes.

I take as deep a breath as I can and I start to say th e last thing I can, given that he is right there and this isn't his final gasp. I say, "You're mellow. I'll try and keep Toots that way. I'll still bug the shit out of her, though."

He laughs.

Whenever I'm not awkward, I know I'm hitting the mark. Here, I'll be trying too hard because selfishly, I want something for me. Dad doesn't have it in him to tell me anything. I know that. He has grasped my hand when I least expected it, he has winked at me, he has greeted me daily and nightly with the kind of joy a person gets from witnessing a bioluminescent sea—and what an honor it has been to be loved that way—and now filled with tears, I can't tell if he needs relief from me, but I know that I need it and I know that it has always been this way. He lets me be who I am. There is really nothing more to say. But as I look inward I see myself there at that moment and I think, all of life is a string of moments that come and pass, some bright and clear, some muddled and pathetic. I have lived long and well and I can start to consider the timely death of the boy in me if Dad can confirm it fits into the stories of Mordechai Campbell and *Omnium*. I don't think I can ever let go of the inventions which have time and again spared my health and sanity, but at least I'll drop Mario.

I see Dad there and I have the memory of this moment right along with the rest of life.

Nature moves and makes a great polyphony.

For some time we exchange glances, then I open my mouth and say one more word: "Gravity. One foot after the other. Like on Angel's Landing. (Scariest thing in our lives.) Well, that was gravity, there."

Dad laughs again.

"But I'm gonna go for levity now," I say. "I have to lighten it up before I leave."

134

Saturday, September 29, the corrupt logic of a waking dream to accompany my dejected body: Trucking up to the house where I was raised, after placing the embryonic form of two highly aggravating psych ward kids in plastic bags and then throwing them in the neighbor's yards, as if they passed out (uh-oh, no oxygen!), the sun was setting and as I left the beautiful houses on the hills, the clean graphics of a particularly attractive elementary school, and our local noodle restaurant, I start to go tense thinking *what if I killed these boys?*

The two of them confronted me in the Paris metro. I took a few punches preaching how you don't hit people and then I pushed my way free of them and I found the pisser and it was a golf hole-sized cup too high to aim for, so I wet myself. That's when they came back and they made me feel bad because they pretended to be of a deeper sensibility, well-behaved and interested in me. But as soon as they had a chance they went after my wallet and at that point the only way was to beat them. Beat them so badly that they became embryonic again. I smashed and smashed their noses. And my fists weren't even connecting.

135

All my relationships with the world become questionable and pivot on this idea of confusion. A deep, dark, cold confusion. Those are Mario's words. You can't speak it because you're not sure, so you put it in a notebook and attribute it to him. Raindrops that keep falling in this dark apartment where the continental cold is ready to sit on our heads, require us to find some thread, some through point for the day that merits life-resuscitation — joys the people who want to see you each day can bring you.

Thinking backwards, because familiarity is more poignant, one has these connection issues and is unwilling to see beyond them. It is not necessary to read full sentences to catch the meaning. One has to fight for one's affections. Just to be alive and in the company of warm, breathing human beings is not enough to establish anything. Your inner nature is under attack from this foreign thing. Being *you* is having character at the airport, is the sound of the six o'clock news in an otherwise empty room, is the hamstring twitching at 35,000 feet above the ocean, is the driver side door sticking out in Left Bank traffic.

Upstairs the rain punishes our rooftop, splattering over the zinc panels, crackling, making it impossible for us to see Paris in this darkness. Who can feel the pull of museums? You needed to escape your own reality.

> Reporting the situation in southern Yemen, the facts as they were studied and nderstood by him, the dandy sailor held his ground as the taller admiral leaned over, visibly bothered: "Whaat?" Face red from drink he feigned poor hearing in an effort to intimidate his underling. Said sailor spoke again, this time from knowledge. The counter-strike was fast and dismissive. He turned to his study of Arabic and threw sane sentences together. Without much to argue the admiral shook his head and walked away gaining the attention of a young lady who smiled oddly not knowing what to do but pretend she had not just seen him naked.

136

Today there are torn messages all over the metro floor. This city hosts the world's largest variety of vacationers to ever laugh up their core dreams and genetic pains. Brahms's second piano concerto plays over the scene. Being overlords of our unique destinies, we want thrills instead of loafing, we want outside affairs to feed our sinews and not inside parties to leave us figuring out how to take oxygen for ourselves.

I've been calling home nightly and now it's somewhat more difficult because Dad doesn't respond. He's always sleeping anyway. I get Toots on a video chat. She says to Dad, Look who's on the phone. Dad says, "Your momma. How are things going in Poland?"

"Where'd you think I was?"

"On a screen. What are you up to, Ghi?"

"Dad, why are you closing your eyes?" I ask.

"Because it's a good thing to do right now," he says.

137

I'm waiting in the living room of this sprawling apartment in the sixteenth arrondissement. There's a series of questions the female gynecologist puts to her patient that I can hear because it's in American English and my ears are sensitive to making meaning. The girl says, "Is it normal?" Doc says, "Show me." The girl replies, "The best of us show and do not tell." I'm just flipping the pages of a magazine I could care less about. The advertisements are easier to read. After a little interlude of non-verbal interaction, this girl says to the doc, "My boyfriend has been beating up my pussy lately."

My wife is kind of wondering where I am in the world. She notices my head being elsewhere and rarely hesitates to comment, but here I am with my eyes all up in my head and I lower them right level with hers, the beautiful round blue discs that make my heart pitter-pat, and I start humming *"all we are saying is give peace a chance,"* thinking, impregnate her with that.

138

Gruesome pigeon, marble-eyed,
You died fat, cross-feathered.
Your lungs don't burn anymore.
If I stare at you long enough, maybe you'll attack me, though.
Straight to the face, soaking wet, your sharp beak parted slightly.
You were made of air, you flew quickly through that same air.
I think I see you moving now.
In Saint-Severin there is a wedding.

All the men and women.
Ladies in their old style hats.
Tourists come by and see the little house.
They don't look for recently dead pigeons.
I heard the boys playing so I watched.
"Il est amoureux," one said to another.
He's in love.
They are barely six, it seems.

Even we used to say things like this.
How do we feel for so much of our lives
and not have any means to touch
what it is that we feel?
A pigeon dies,
a couple gets married in a church,
the falling rain quenches the earth.

139

I drove up to the mountains to where my father lives. I said, Dad what can you tell me about courage. He said son, I can tell you I used to jump out of planes and every time I jumped I was just as afraid. It doesn't take courage to die, it takes courage to live.

OCTOBER

140

Dad's telling me about his beard growing in. I tell him about the general strike on in Paris and I let fly my familiar filterless speech. What's a manifestation? I ask. He says, "It's an expression." Toots is kind of directing the conversation because he can't hold the phone. You have cold hands, she announces as she props the screen up on the over bed table. We're hanging out. That is what this is. She tells him, I should give you a facial. He says, "Are you serious?" (I have the photos.) We talk to him about things. Music. Dancing. Toots asks him, When's the last time you danced? He says, "On your wedding." That was over a decade ago. "Well, we can all dream of the future."

In the future I will be in full health eating sugar and salt as I please, having a strong physique and greater stamina. Maybe I will run with my wife, maybe we will swim. I'd like to have a healthy retreat in the countryside, but I should think of ownership. I want to own a fine apartment in a nice neighborhood, a place where children can play outside, go to good schools with people from various backgrounds. We should increase our wealth by owning an apartment and then invest in a place in another country that we can let our friends use. We could trade. We will travel three months out of the year, embrace world cultures, visit, create, walk, and run.

Dad says, "I'm glad that you're skinny." He says that his intestines are hurting. He looks at the screen of the phone knowing I'm there and that our conversation is casual, and continues pointing to his forehead with his square index finger, "You need to understand here."

Hannah and I argue in the aftermath of my conversation. She thinks I could be a dangerous person because I'm different with her than I am with other family or American friends. But I'm only myself with a few people. There were certain parts of myself I let go of that became dormant and meeting her woke me up to them, so now I'm back to being more free. Instead of letting go I'm losing myself. Hannah tells me that a lot of people think I'm mellow, out of a movie, so cliché. She says, "I hope I'm never going to be a cliché. That's the worst. A divorced woman not able to meet anyone. It's horrible. You are that person. Sometimes you worry me."

NOVEMBER

141

My life remains completely unknown to a stranger from whom I'm requesting a cigarette. She is only too happy to listen to my poorly constructed French (exhausted as I am from being crushed in the striking metro) so that she can put me down. I consider this another indisputable truth about failing to connect with the local population. I write out of anger and discomfort at someone laughing in my face. They think I need a cigarette. They think I'm off, the way I ask for one. There's a box full on their café table. At least I think there is.

The knobby-kneed girls take glory in their full-lipped, youthful rejection. They want to show their male suitors that they don't dance for their rent, they have others dancing for them. I don't yet understand this person who sees me and hears me and is still suspicious about how I want to indulge her and her friend. I let myself go.

You both think you are the highest you can get. Not London, not New York, not Rio, not Moscow, not Buenos Aires, not Melbourne, not Los Angeles. I'd have run you out, you see. I'd have run you out. But you only care for your immediate circle. I care about you all. I'm contented with that. The lean, the flow, the mad dash. I'll love you 'til the morning even if I don't see you 'no more,' and there'll be sweet suds in the washer when I'm gone.

DECEMBER

142

I'm in my apartment, aware of the direction, nord, est, sud, and ouest. The only word on Dad has been that "The man's still eating," and now Toots calls to inform me, "You don't have to tell yourself stories anymore. It sounds like it's happening. They started him on twenty-four hour oxygen. He's having trouble with all his muscle control. They are using a thickening agent so he can swallow."

All the stories that came before my own, including those split-second tragedies, I never imagined an ending like this. I'm hosting an aperitif that night and I shatter a glass. Everyone says it's better that it's not me I shatter. If it's all the same, I'm holding on for the crash. I haven't gone to bed in weeks without a smoke, even though I know I can. Days go by reminding myself that this is no dream. At a certain point I arrest my thoughts. *Dad hollering, Lakers! Dad on oxygen. Dad eating like a pig. Dad unable to swallow. Me, Toots and Dad. Dad, no Dad.* I can't keep on doing this.

The stupid fucking mutation.

Afterwards, walking past our Schezuan dive and the American Lowe House, Why should I give a shit about you? is what she says. I have no answer. Can't you create some reason? I ask. "No, I'm not good at that." Okay. This is on the heels of a poor reaction to the very early end of her own big night and one-and-a-half hours of transit so that she could come meet me. "What is it?" she asks, "You're trying to give a shit about me when you don't, but I have to be happy about it?" I may not be so much more innocent than Hannah. I'm supposed to be decent and I'm not being decent. I get help filing bureaucratic forms and I'm hyper-critical in return. Although tolerance is a matter of conditioning, when I need to make a choice I don't inspire total confidence that I want to change. This is how we do it: faces upon faces. The texts keep coming at her and she's making more faces, loudly exhaling. Her brother's lovesick and her sister hasn't replied. The health office is closed. I'm the consistent stable thing, but my comment about how she busts my balls and seems pessimistic upsets her and all of a sudden it's a terrible walk.

She's supposed to get her exam results in a few days. I ask her about her mood.

"I've been stressed out since Monday last week. I'm not trying to be in a bad mood. I'm purposefully trying not to be in a bad mood, pretending to go around talking about something else. You're basically asking me not to express myself. Obviously I'm selfish. The problem is just me. I'm the one who has a bad attitude. Obviously!" She mocks me and waits for a response.

So now I'm supposed to calm her but I still have a few notes to write and I can just barely formulate an open-ended question to the effect of, what were you doing before you met me? while setting the last words of our dialogue on paper for future reference, insight into speech patterns et cetera, you know.

She reacts. "Stop writing down everything between us because one day I'm going to burn your shit. Stop writing everything down and handle it another way."

Social scenery helps me to ignore my inner world. I start to detach by watching people. Eighty percent of the time the way someone looks is the thing we remember about them.

We get back to our apartment making loving faces at each other, me searching for a sign that she accepts my ways, her mouth still mocking but moving into loving. I push myself to call my dad. This far away there's nothing much else you can do. It's enough to feel obligated. It's the only way.

Dad can't talk. Toots tells me the nurse says maybe he'll be alive for another 72 hours. I have to go.

143

My words are down, the electricity in my brain bee bee buck shot, all thought is threatened with short circuiting. On December 6 at about two a.m. California time, I hear the news from Toots. Dad passed away in his sleep.

The story I tell myself is that I was at a concert the night he died. The shit you tell yourself is the sentimental story of your life. This isn't how it goes. Twelve hours ago I was at a concert taking a film that shows very little of my desperation and some of the joy I get from melancholy songs, and now hiding beneath a blanket on the floor of our bedroom watching Toots stroke Dad's face on video chat looking at the body that was my dad, I don't know what to let in.

The last days of his life still gave him pleasure. He enjoyed food. He had no pressure sores, no respiration problems or pneumonia. His only difficulty was swallowing. In the end his brain couldn't send instructions to his body. It was not pain, it was confusion.

People who say time goes by fast, they're not able to buy time. Somewhere inside of me I am thinking about what our love has been this past year, and all of my life. I can only use relative terms to describe the real pain now. I shed alligator tears. It's similar to a broken heart. When I talk to my mom and she consoles me saying, *I know you have a broken heart*, I tell her, I don't have a broken heart. It broke a long time ago and I put it back together again.

Kids think they can be smarter than their parents. Everybody wants to be so smart, but this is how it works: you listen to your baby cry himself to sleep for the first time and it breaks your heart and then you get used to shit like that and you know how to talk about it and survive. And getting used to anything is the beginning of being wiped off the face of this earth.

In the moments to come I try and find a balance between stating my dad is dead as a fact and forcing my everyday mood.

144

The next day Hannah and I get on a flight to L.A. This is about us now. On the plane I write notes for hours. Notes about anything: hope, exhaustion, bravery, society, identity, morality...until I get to this last note: *gone forever.*

Some people spend every moment of every day considering where they are in life compared to others, trying to make themselves feel better. I'm watching a bullshit movie, telling myself it's okay to be pessimistic. I bark at Hannah, I bark at the TV. I make myself remember that it was all leading up to this. For a time I have the faraway eyes of someone whose thoughts are elsewhere. I keep at making my dad's words come to life: "Whatever you do, don't name your kid ⟨scribble⟩. It's a horrible name. Nobody could say it." Dad never made life more difficult than it had to be. Me with my notebooks, waiting for inspiration, hesitating to write real lines, inking only coded words. Nothing for anybody else to read.

145

Tuesday morning we arrive on the mountain in decent humor. The sign hanging outside still says *Yefé Nof*. One of the first truths that Toots speaks is that the whole death business is bullshit. A neighbor tries to console me by saying, I bet there'll be an impulse to emulate your dad in your lifetime. I consider the way I show Hannah the heat lamp switch in the small bathroom as exactly that. I don't know. The death of a parent is extremely destabilizing. For some time we tell each other stories about him. They are mostly stories about ourselves.

My thoughts adjust to those early voice recordings of my dad when he was working on his doctoral thesis. In my mind I take to the spare room that my sister and I used for our entertainment and the closet space next the garage door where the cassettes lived on the bottom shelf along with the player. He was my dad and I was proud of him. It was his voice in the leading role that I loved. I recognized that even when I listened back then. I try and remember myself listening alone the way I still like to do. There were other voices in the recordings and a lot of empty air. The sound quality wasn't very good. It was the sound of the seventies to me. The sound of our childhood. The crackling and rolling dust on the surface. Each of us is sensitive to different things. I was six and everything was just a little off. It took a lot of time to make my feelings manageable and my dad occasionally helped me get to that place.

146

Laurel, Hannah, Toots, myself and Furstman will be up at the house for two weeks or so. The street is kind of strange now. It's like the place where you come to drop off your husband before you leave him. It snows, it melts, it snows again. We have a lot of thinking to do and I would rather pay one of you to do it. Dad liked to say, *You always have a house.* It might make financial sense to dump this place but then we won't have a where to come back to him. At some point I announce my idea for the locus of something literary to move back to Blue Jay and Lake Arrowhead. First we have to fix the back deck. When Dad did the renovation he kind of skimped on the back deck. People are weird and morbid—they'll want to come up the back deck and take a look around.

Toots feels sentimental and I'm usually up for it so we all talk about how you had to have a strong ego around Dad. There was no praise and not many compliments. We reflect on the probability that he didn't know our childhood. We all continue to wonder why would he never play the accordion. Toots says, "I don't know. He said he wasn't very good. I walked up on him a couple of times and he was pretty good."

I have my mom's words lingering in my head, 'Ghi, we're Jewish. It's only seven days, that's all. It'll go away fast, whatever it is. I would feel very good about that. I raised you as Jews and I want you to be Jewish.'

In the morgue—on 12/12/12—we ask, how do we know he's in there? You have to trust us, they say. They pick you up and bring you back in a box. Super easy. I pass a mirror holding Dad's ashes in a black box. What I'm not supposed to do is look at my reflection.

147

The snow is confining. We are closed in by a frozen white one foot deep in this tiny valley. Where the leaves and stars were visible, now it's gleaming white with shivering pines. The ice storm and blowing fogs rest above like a ceiling on mind space. There is nowhere to go. The roads are closed. We need to stay put and work things out.

I ran into an old friend in my dream and told her about my dad. We had a coffee at our place in Paris. We talked a little about kids. I looked at her. She was wearing green eye shadow that had slipped in between her eyebrows and down the bridge of her nose. It was the luminous zinc oxide lifeguards wear. She was just like I remembered in the face, only without mental energy. The fire in her eyes had gone out. It covered the land with white blankness, a kind that the living have to fill.

148

Hannah holds me during our improvised ceremony. The ritual is what pulls us closer together or closer apart. In many ways we are different people and we would act differently in the same situation, but this is what we have to live with: things going both ways. In with our dangerous actions and out with emotional interaction, the serendipity of our moods, the testing of deeper waters, the seasonal blooms. We both want to make each other happy. Words get in the way. We can all admit to having gotten more raw over the last years. I am often confusing the art of living with the art of doing everyday business. I seem to want the marrow and the mystery more than an association with the self-made kings, but I continue to react to a corner I still have not turned and artistic failure I have never allowed to really rip me apart.

Before the ⟨𝑀𝑀𝑀𝑀⟩ kids are on our way up to San Francisco in Dad's SUV, I put a little more thought into writing *Document 120* under the pseudonym Sidi. I imagine leaving a letter in our car full of stuff: *Dear passerby, should you choose to accept this SUV, you assume the life that comes with it.* SIDI.

The first night in Santa Barbara we offer to pay the check if a group vacates their table and they say no. The second night the distinct heating element smell from the motel in Paso Robles accounts for Toots' parting words as we take the final stretch to the Bay. "I don't monumentally stay at motels like that," she says. When we arrive, we're all completely drained. Hannah and I sleep at a friend's in Oakland and not everything's alright this side of the pillow because despite all the support we get, the heavy stress, lack of exercise and absence of deep breathing leave me sick for a few days. Hannah takes tender care of me. There isn't much to do except lay low and consider all we've been through, all that keeps happening. Love and death.

Dad once told me that his mom stopped hugging him at age five because she thought that's when you don't need it anymore. I repeat to myself that I am my dad, I am my dad, but I'm different.

The day Hannah and I are flying back to France we're at an overstock department store and I see a kid punch his younger brother in the face and deal with the consequences while they wait for their mom to reemerge from the dressing room.

"Is my head really that hard?" the younger boy says, dried tears on his cheeks.

"Yeah, look how red my knuckles are."

"I'm proud of how hard my skull is," the younger continues.

"I'm sorry I punched you. You didn't share. You were being unfair," the older one says.

"Don't punch me in the face anymore," the younger replies. "My head's that hard?" he adds.

"Stop saying that," his older brother says.

I look around racks and racks and asphalt and random uncut threads. I know Hannah is here somewhere. This is it. This is the way it ends. With my life in front of me. I have the sudden urge to kiss her. And what luck, I can. I realize *I can*.

EPILOGUE

The following winter we went to Tel Aviv to commemorate the anniversary of my dad's death. His brothers made a plaque for him and put it between the plots where their parents are buried. Going to a cemetery is not the same as looking out into the forest.

Behind the house on Inspiration Drive there's a huge boulder where we once stood above the treetops and talked about plans for the future. Dad badly wanted grandkids. He told me so. I have it on a film where he shows me how he plans on building a treehouse and a ladder around that boulder for his grandchildren. I always wanted a treehouse. I guess it was only a matter of time. Last July my wife became pregnant and this promonostory was conceived as my son was gestating. He was born on April 15, 2014 and we named him after ⟨signature⟩. So there's a lot more to Mordechai Campbell and the ⟨signature⟩ that may surface someday. The guardians of progress will do best to remain curious.

Acknowledgements

I would like to express my deep gratitude to Annabel for always enduring the mystery.

A very special thanks to early teachers: Mom, Sis, and all the lifelong friends I made before I traded in napkins for notebooks. A special thanks to those who I leaned upon during the year of mutations: Paula, Michelle Jeske, Ohad Cohen, B. Ward, Terence Cullen, Nick Rosenberg, Mason Richards, Gabe Lora, Magali Charmot, Todd Zuniga, Pam Dobie, Adam Gerson, Matt Goodman, Brent Large, Dave Seigal, Mike Pincus, Salky Jon, Adam Winter, Badson Robbins, Nikki Giacobazzi, and Jessica Pressman.

Thank you, Ambarish Manepalli, filmmaker extraordinaire. Robert Rorke, editor haut de gamme.

Thanks to my family by birth and by marriage. The Warren Wilson MFA community. Darren Fancher for 1042. Ed Aguila for shaving my late fees. And to all involved with the Yefe Nof Residency (YNR).

This project would not have been possible without the crucial funding provided by 350 Kickstarter backers. Thanks to Peg Alford Pursell, Phil Aslin, Craig D. Baron, the Benhaim family, Francoise Benhaim, Marion Benhaim, the Blanchetier family, Virginia Borges, Pierre Brousse, Benjamin Chen, Jim Cohen, Mike Craig, Nordic and the Cullen family, Eric Deeds, George Demienne, David DeRosa, Pamela Dobie Key, the Engelberg family, Roee Engelberg, Deva Finger, Andrea Fishman, the Fleischman family, Julie Frimmer-Sauvage, Matthew and Nadia Goodman, Jeremy Hinman, Supriya Kakkar, Adam Kerpelman, Leigh Kimbrough Louis, Jan Klasinski, Leah Klinger and Arman Javid, Geoff Kronik, Paula Kruger, Jenny G. Mason, Rich McCracken, Jerry Morris, Carlos Ortiz, Phillip Pfeffer, Tom Rector, Brian Robbins, Roderic, Taunia and Tom Rogers, David Seigal, the Serpette family, the Sitowitz family, the Sivan family, Liad Sivan, Geula Soltz, Christine Tasker, Erick Van Tuyl, Brett Ward, Tanya B. Williams, Tal Winter, Lincoln Wood and Amy Kermott, and the Yaron family.